*The new Zebra Regency Romance logo that you see on the cover is a photograph of an actual regency "tuzzy-muzzy." The fashionable regency lady often wore a tuzzy-muzzy tied with a satin or velvet riband around her wrist to carry a fragrant nosegay. Usually made of gold or silver, tuzzy-muzzies varied in design from the elegantly simple to the exquisitely ornate. The Zebra Regency Romance tuzzy-muzzy is made of alabaster with a silver filigree edging.*

## HEAVEN IN HER CARE

Bryan Deverell thought he had lost his mind. He opened his clouded eyes to a large cloth pig and a brightly painted wooden dog. His head was throbbing, and the first light of morn, having waked him, did nothing to ease that pain.

"Of all the inf—"

"Hush," warned a soft, feminine voice. One quick look upwards showed that the voice belonged to a young female with high cheekbones and full lips as well as lustrous curls of auburn hair.

"The girl on the beach!" he called out.

"Do speak more quietly, please!" Clarissa Tregallen said softly.

She showed concern, although she couldn't have been a timid priss. It seemed that the two of them were fated to address each other only in whispers.

"I put my arm around your waist and you put yours around mine." The recollection caused him pleasure. "You insisted."

The vision dropped softly into a chair, dipped a cloth into a bottle of water, wrung it out, then eased it onto his forehead . . .

"I never knew that heaven is a small room with wooden dogs and a cloth pig."

# THE BEST OF REGENCY ROMANCES

**AN IMPROPER COMPANION**                    (2691, $3.95)
by Karla Hocker

At the closing of Miss Venable's Seminary for Young Ladies school, mistress Kate Elliott welcomed the invitation to be Liza Ashcroft's chaperone for the Season at Bath. Little did she know that Miss Ashcroft's father, the handsome widower Damien Ashcroft would also enter her life. And not as a passive bystander or dutiful dad.

**WAGER ON LOVE**                    (2693, $2.95)
by Prudence Martin

Only a rogue like Nicholas Ruxart would choose a bride on the basis of a careless wager. And only a rakehell like Nicholas would then fall in love with his betrothed's grey-eyed sister! The cynical viscount had always thought one blushing miss would suit as well as another, but the unattainable Jane Sommers soon proved him wrong.

**LOVE AND FOLLY**                    (2715, $3.95)
by Sheila Simonson

To the dismay of her more sensible twin Margaret, Lady Jean proceeded to fall hopelessly in love with the silver-tongued, seditious poet, Owen Davies—and catapult her entire family into social ruin . . . Margaret was used to gentlemen falling in love with vivacious Jean rather than with her—even the handsome Johnny Dyott whom she secretly adored. And when Jean's foolishness led her into the arms of the notorious Owen Davies, Margaret knew she could count on Dyott to avert scandal. What she didn't know, however was that her sweet sensibility was exerting a charm all its own.

*Available wherever paperbacks are sold, or order direct from the Publisher. Send cover price plus 50¢ per copy for mailing and handling to Zebra Books, Dept. 3130, 475 Park Avenue South, New York, N.Y. 10016. Residents of New York, New Jersey and Pennsylvania must include sales tax. DO NOT SEND CASH.*

# The Heart's Intrigue

## Evelyn Bond

**ZEBRA BOOKS**
**KENSINGTON PUBLISHING CORP.**

ZEBRA BOOKS

are published by

Kensington Publishing Corp.
475 Park Avenue South
New York, NY 10016

First printing: September, 1990

Printed in the United States of America

*For*
*Scott Siegel*

## Chapter One

"Clarissa, my dear, do be reasonable." Aunt Hetty's starched lace cap quivered on her gray curls. "You are a young lady. You are attractive of feature."

Clarissa Tregallen had not denied either point during the course of her aunt's lecture. Nevertheless, it was far better not to say so, not to be pert. She kept her lips pressed together.

"Despite those advantages, as I have previously said, you cannot be forever considered a suitable match," Aunt Hetty continued, shifting on the high-backed chair like a stately galleon in full sail. "You may never again receive so splendid an offer."

Clarissa kept her sea green eyes fixed respectfully upon the tapestry frame in front of her, long slender fingers continuing to push the needle in and out with an unchanging rhythm.

"And you must agree that the Duke of Mainwaring is an admirable catch, is he not?"

"The duke fairly reeks of respectability, Aunt."

Aunt Hetty proceeded in her duty. "I must remind you how difficult it would be to find a better man up and down Cornwall, Clarissa. Further, once you are settled, your new connections from Aubrey's side of the family will make it simpler to find an equally suitable husband for Maude."

Clarissa didn't protest that Maude was four full

years younger than herself. It was bad enough that she, Clarissa, at twenty, was being forced to consider settling for some man who would be as dull as a night's sleep, as placid as some farm animal.

She longed to let this argument pass her lips, and follow it with a series of dazzling epigrams to which even this most selfless of guardians would be unable to make an answer. Instead she concentrated on a violet petal that was part of the tapestry and closed her rebellion-prone lips a little more tightly.

Both females suddenly turned. Squeaky footsteps were proceeding down the passageway with unusual slowness toward the parlor of Narborne House.

It seemed like a caricature of Maude that appeared within moments rather than the younger sister herself. Those odd footsteps had been caused by boots plastered with mud and wisps of dirty straw. Wind and rain had played havoc with her brown hair, flattening those curls so painstakingly put in place by rag curlers almost every night. Dampness disfigured her worn wool cloak.

"Maude!" Aunt Hetty's jaw dropped at the sight, discomposing each of her chins. "You have not been in the library reading."

Clarissa rose and swiftly put the needlework aside. "Perhaps it was a book about a storm at sea which Maude took very seriously."

"I was at the pens," Maude said with no apology in her tone. "Jem Pendarran sent for me to say that Blossom was having difficulty with her offspring."

Aunt Hetty's small, plump hands soared in dismay. "I declare that this is the outside of enough! That a young female scarcely out of the schoolroom should have witnessed such an event, much less that she should assist a mere dairyman, is unsupportable!"

"Blossom is a dear creature and I didn't want her to suffer any more than necessary."

"Blossom is a cow," Aunt Hetty pointed out irrefutably. "All the livestock seems to be your domain—the ducks with broken wings, the sheepdogs with colly-wobbles, the kitchen cats with hairballs. You seem to think that you are a female Noah, and the farm is your ark."

With her affinity for animals, no onlooker could have denied that Maude's current expression was nothing less than mulish.

"And when I don't worry about you, I seethe about your sister, who wants nothing more than to be stolen by gypsies or pirates or both."

"I have never said—"

"Almost every word from your mouth deals with a longing for some great adventure."

Clarissa looked away.

Aunt Hetty wouldn't be stopped. "I owe the deepest apologies to my late brother. I have failed in the trust he put upon me on his deathbed. What one woman alone could do I have done, but it hasn't been enough."

Maude sneezed.

"If she isn't in bed immediately," Clarissa said, already gesturing for Maude to join her at the parlor door, "your responsibilities will be far more difficult."

Aunt Hetty was blessedly halted in mid-harangue. "Accompany your sister upstairs, my dear, like a good girl."

Clarissa waited until they were on the draughty flight of steps before saying lightly and quietly, "Your sneeze was most timely, sister."

Maude was still chuckling as she settled down for the night with a hot brick at her feet and a warming drink of milk with honey and cinnamon bark placed on the bedside table. Under those circumstances, it was pleasant to be indisposed.

Clarissa was not in such a good humor herself as she retired to her own room. She had listened encouragingly to the details of Blossom's accouchement and verbally applauded the happy ending. Left to herself,

9

though, she felt unhappy, pacing the mossy carpet to the drapes, then back and around once again. She seemed to have acquired endless energy for doing very little worth a mention.

Nothing is more difficult than for a young person to admit that some older person has been telling the truth. Aunt Hetty had done nothing else. Clarissa could no longer put off marriage. Already the first bloom of youth had gone. In a few more years she would have to resign herself to a situation in which life offered even less than it did now.

Spinsterhood, as Aunt Hetty often remarked, was largely undesirable. She said it feelingly, knowledge of local conditions being enough to offer many examples of unhappiness among females who were solitary. It was little consolation that she was better off than most of her kind, having taken over the guardianship of her two young nieces and becoming the mistress of Narborne House. She could pause to pat her own full stomach and sympathize lavishly with others as she preached against the sorry state of women who were unmarried and older.

Clarissa had no intention of remaining unmarried and unloved. She was always eager to attend county balls and festivals. Her aunt had taken her to London for the last season, that of '11, and she had been glad to go. It made her happy to meet young men and flirt, or to encounter acquaintances of the stronger sex, then dance a decorous quadrille. Her presence had made many an occasion far brighter.

Again and yet again, however, she found herself confronted by young men who had no ambition but to spend their lives in unrelieved grayness, as she thought of it. This one wanted to succeed in the House of Lords, that roosting place for the living dead. That one wanted to give his life to banking, an accomplice to dreary men of business. A third, rather than choosing to sail away to a life of adventure with a fitting wife

10

of a similar taste, wanted to fatten his coffers on the work of those who actually did so and sell maritime insurance. Small wonder that she was so often tempted to flee the presence of these stuffed gentlemen. Even their clothes were dreary.

Some young men were actually likeable, but nothing more. She could understand and sympathize with those friends who had married the latter specimens in search of companionship.

*Then why must I be different?*

She was aware of a sudden silence, and realized that the rain no longer beat at the panes of the tall windows. By this time, the heavy mournful clouds that had covered the sky over Narborne had been blown westward. The December moon gave an intoxicating glow to the long stretch of beach below the garden and the sea beyond. At this time, one wouldn't see anybody else while walking in fresh clean air.

Clarissa did not hesitate once she realized that Aunt Hetty must be secure in bed by this time. She changed her indoor muslin for a long-sleeved woolen dress of a dark shade that was currently called cinnamon. Over this she put on a black cloak and sturdy walking boots. One could think about the Duke of Mainwaring when attired so practically.

She walked through the garden, past stables and outbuildings that looked like so many hulks in the nighttime. Only then did she fill her lungs with the December night air and draw the hood of her cloak away from auburn curls. She felt free.

She contemplated matrimony with Aubrey Seldon, the Duke of Mainwaring, as she walked along. Certainly he was a catch, wealthy enough to own a townhouse in Berkeley Square, an ancestral home in Norfolk, and a shooting box in Scotland. Wherever he might travel on the island, it seemed, he would be near home.

He was personable and handsome, both, blessed

11

with the affable self-assurance that comes with wealth inherited, a man as much at ease with dairymen like Pendarran as with the Prince Regent himself. A fine fellow, the duke, admired by men and desired by other women.

Why, then, had not Clarissa accepted His Grace's offer at once? Why wasn't she aglow with triumph over her great luck? She had asked herself those questions when Aunt Hetty desisted from asking them. No reasonable answers presented themselves.

She was surefootedly venturing farther afield while her brow was creased by thought. A familiar rocky pathway took her to the beach and down to the sheltered cove that was part of the estate lands. As ever, she didn't stumble, so familiar was she with the land around Narbourne House, with the steep and rocky cliffs, with the sea birds and lulling waves and windshaped trees. She might have made this particular descent with eyes closed and in her sleep.

An unexpected sight pulled her up short. At the stick-thin entrance to Narborne Cove, she could see the dark outlines of a sloop lying at anchor.

The clandestine actions of the sloop's master and crew were plain to be seen. The master silently directed the unloading of cargo onto a dozen rowboats. The crew members, working by moonlight, were equally silent.

Clarissa, having been born and bred in this part of Cornwall, easily guessed what was going on. Smuggling had been a source of illicit income for Cornishmen over the years. Natives who weren't directly involved would assist relatives in "the trade." "Preventive men" were supposed to see that all smugglers went to Botany Bay or danced at the end of a hangman's rope, but actually encouraged their neighbors. The bringing in of a new cargo would have raised a muffled cheer from the cracked lips of that fabled vicar of Dymchurch, Dr. Syn himself. If the war with Napoleon ended and the repressive Corn Laws were suddenly put aside, many a Cornish resident would no longer retain any joy in living.

There was danger, too.

Not all the preventive men responded to violations of law by looking the other way. Clarissa still had a childhood memory of one particular carriage ride, in the course of which she caught a glimpse of what seemed like a scarecrow dangling from a crossroads gallows.

"Don't look," Squire Tregallen had ordered, and refused to answer his daughter's excited questions.

She found out afterwards that she had seen the body of a smuggler who had been tried at the Bodmin assizes, and who had been convicted.

Small wonder, then, that an unexpected witness to some act of smuggling might be in danger, too. That person would be the object of questioning that might grow vicious. Some of the smugglers were nothing less than ruffians, and one of these men could slit the top of a cargo box with the ease with which he'd slit a throat.

Clarissa pressed herself against a rock outcropping, her slender dark-cloaked figure shadowed in concealment. There was no better hope of safety than for her to remain still.

The desperate men came closer to where she was hidden, rowing ashore and beaching their small boats before wading through the waist-deep waves to the smooth sands of the cove.

The unmistakable sound of a donkey's bray issued from the north end of the cove. Clarissa started, then slowly turned her head to see a burly man proceeding toward the beach and leading a row of the small, strong beasts. They were soon being loaded down with the smuggled goods; kegs of French brandy or bales of fine silk were fastened to their backs. Eager to be done before the first revealing light of dawn, the smugglers

13

worked quickly and silently.

Her breath coming quickly, muscles tensed, Clarissa was aware of one man in particular. His face was no clearer than the others. The top of his head was hidden by a tricorne hat, the body by a cloak. He was the only man who watched the loading of cargo without taking part, standing away from the others with arms folded across his chest.

Two of the others approached him swiftly, arms gesturing in determination in the direction of the donkeys. The tall man shook his head. The others exchanged glances, then one man turned. Under the glow of moonlight, the other resumed the silent argument.

The tall man had shifted away from a view of the donkey train, so he couldn't see the approach of the apelike figure of the animals' driver. He came up stealthily. Moonlight illuminated the heavy stick he raised menacingly. Clarissa's hand flew to her lips to stifle her own involuntary cry as the donkey driver brought his stick down on the back of the tall man's head. The injured man swayed. His tricorne hat flew off, then he was eased, face down, on the sand at the water's edge. Everything was done with the least possible sound, even the disposal of their accomplice.

Clarissa's heart lurched. Had a night's walk caused her to witness not only smuggling, but a murder as well? Why hadn't she stayed indoors like a proper young lady?

Pity stirred in her while the smugglers went on ruthlessly with their illegal work. A man had been given no chance to defend himself before being felled, and no one was coming to his aid. In a different way she, too, was entirely helpless.

The smugglers began the process of leaving as soon as the last of the cargo had been loaded. Some men led the donkeys back in the direction from which the animals had been brought. Those few men who remained behind now waded back to the small boats and started rowing hurriedly back to the sloop. Except for the figure of the man lying prone on the sand, the beach was soon empty.

Clarissa moved away from the cold, wet rocks which had given her their protection. Not until she was almost upon him did she know that she had been walking toward the beach, toward the fallen man. Her head had given instructions which were being disregarded by her feet.

She forced herself to halt, and told herself autocratically that she would turn and leave. In the act of doing so, she was aware that the man had stirred.

With unsteady movements, he was pulling himself to his knees. He stood swaying, then fumbled and dropped to one knee. After regaining his shaky balance, he moved forward. He looked as if he were about to drop again, but he collected himself and walked ahead.

Clarissa didn't know whether or not she had been observed, although he was moving in her direction. Swiftly she retreated once again into the shadow of the rocks and waited, her heart hammering as never before. He was less than a foot away, but didn't call out or try to attract her attention. He moved to the left, convincing her that she hadn't been seen.

She decided against running away immediately, telling herself that he could carry a fowling piece and could wound her mortally from a distance. She wanted him to be in a place where he couldn't see her departure.

She knew the ground so well that she sensed where he was without having to look. He had blundered against the mouth of that cave known to her and Maude as the Egg. To the girls' imagination it was egglike in shape. He was scrabbling about the Egg, roiling the chill earth at its base. The pitch of sound confirmed for her that he was no less than ten feet

15

from the opening.

An escape was possible now. Careful to pick her steps, she moved in the direction of the path. A depression in the ground had gathered more moisture, and she stumbled. One of her boots struck loose pebbles that descended to the rock below in a series of showers.

He was out of the cave more quickly than would have seemed possible to a man who had been wounded. In seconds he was upon her, a hand closing on the folds of her cape with a grip that wasn't as strong as it would have been in a well man. As she drew back, the hood of her outer garment fell back to reveal her bright masses of hair, the moon highlighting her high cheekbones and rounded chin.

"Be still!" The man's voice was low and hoarse, his grip slackening further in surprise or accelerated weakness. "Why the devil is a female lurking in such a place at a time like this?"

He had spoken haltingly and it was hard to keep afoot because of the burden of his swaying body. Without thinking, she put a hand under an arm to steady him.

She didn't mean to say so, but heard herself insisting, "You need shelter!"

"Behind me . . . long enough to get my strength b—"

Aware of a change in the light around them, she looked warily up at the moon. A black cloud from the east had put it in shadow, a certain omen of more to come and probably of rain as well.

He was already ill. Being away from substantial shelter during a cold rain might bring results that could well be mortal.

Nothing was further from her intentions than giving thought to this man's well-being. Her wish to leave seemed to have no relation to her desire to offer assistance. Normal caution was being replaced by a foolhardy compassion.

Or perhaps she was giving in to a sense of uncertainty that she found gratifying, facing a genuine adventure with undisguised relish.

No common criminal, no ordinary smuggler would have aroused her sympathies. This one had the accents of a man born to the purple, a gent. His clothing, too, spoke softly but firmly of refinement. Under the boat cloak, with its fur collar, lay a shirt of white cambric and closely fitting breeches of buckskin. This companion of criminals had been well raised.

Softly she said, "I live close by . . . in the house at the top of the cliffs."

His voice was slightly higher with hope. "Are you suggesting—Are you good enough to suggest that I—I come with you?"

He realized that he was speaking too loudly. Because of the silence that followed, he and Clarissa heard another sound.

Hoofbeats from the distance were coming closer. They were a way off, but Clarissa could hear the riders call out occasionally, and she knew she would view them soon enough.

The riders might be official dragoons venturing from their position in Bodmin. Clarissa expected to notify them of this man's whereabouts, but she had no intention of exposing a wounded and weary gentleman (no matter how keen his participation in some minor crime) to the dragoons and their tender mercies.

That conviction was enough to resolve another difficulty raised in her active consideration of possibilities. She had thought of escorting him back into the Egg, where they'd wait till the riders were out of sight or hearing. Dragoons, however, might bring their steeds down to the beach as part of their hunt for smugglers.

On the other hand, if the riders were coming in this direction it would be some time before they would reach Clarissa and the gentleman smuggler. By then, if

17

they moved immediately, the two of them might be in Narborne House.

Plentiful risks were offered by either alternative.

Clarissa Tregallen, of course, decided to adopt the strategy that called for more daring, for greater adventurousness.

At his first step toward the rocks, the man nearly stumbled again. Clarissa pulled back, putting her arm around his waist and under the boat cloak, then put his arm around her waist to help him further in finding his balance.

Together, in the gloom of night, she and the stranger began their ascent to Narborne House.

## Chapter Two

There was a large pink cloth pig with a twist of cloth for its tail. A brightly painted wooden dog, with three smaller dogs painted in blue and black and orange, were arranged in a row behind it.

And there seemed a good chance that Bryan Deverell had lost his mind and would soon be observing the Prince Regent dressed in yellow shamrocks and singing "Rule Britannia" backwards.

Worse yet, his head was throbbing. The first light of morn, having waked him, did nothing to ease that pain.

Bryan closed his eyes hopefully. Nothing had changed when they flew open again. His head still felt like the village of Albuera must have looked after the famous battle, and the pig and dogs hadn't vanished.

"Of all the inf—"

"Hush," warned a soft, feminine voice. One quick look upwards showed that the voice belonged to a young female with high cheekbones and full lips as well as lustrous curls of auburn hair.

"The girl on the beach," he called out.

"Do speak more quietly, please!"

She showed concern, although she couldn't have been a timid priss. It seemed that the two of them were fated to address each other only in whispers.

"I put my arm around your waist and you put yours

19

around mine." The recollection caused him a certain amount of pleasure. "You insisted upon it."

The vision dropped softly into a chair at the right of the couch. She dipped a cloth briskly into a bottle of water, wrung it out with care, then eased it onto his forehead. Her touch was almost supernaturally gentle, her movements blessedly efficient.

"You led me to this house, I am sure," he continued. "We must have climbed a dozen flights of stairs."

"Two only."

"I never knew that heaven is a small room with wooden dogs and a cloth pig."

"I could not think of a better place to bring you. This room is no longer in daily use. It was formerly a nursery for many generations of the family, including my sister and myself."

"Then there are others in the house and I might be discovered. No wonder you ask me not to speak at my usual strength."

"I live with my sister and my Aunt Hetty, who took charge of this household after the death of my father."

She had said too much, Clarissa told herself, allowing this smuggler to know that he was in a household of females.

"We have several male servants about the place, naturally."

The flicker of understanding and amusement in his hazel eyes told her that he understood her purpose in making that last assertion.

"May I ask that you refresh my memory about your name? You did tell me last night, but I fear I was in no condition to be properly receptive."

"Clarissa Tregallen."

"And I am Bryan Deverell, your most obedient, ma'am, but not at this very moment."

"In these circumstances, Mr. Deverell, a lapse is understandable." Partly because of his excellent manners and gift for self-mockery, she recovered her poise.

The recent hours had been difficult. Most of the time since returning had been spent in this room watching over Bryan Deverell. Thank heavens he hadn't been afflicted by nightmares that would make him call out and inadvertently give away his presence, but she had never before spent time in a room with a sleeping male. The experience had been as provocative as it was harrowing.

She had made a point of changing into a violet morning dress as if the last hours had been ordinary for her. She then started the day officially by inquiring into Maude's condition. Exposure to rain and cold hadn't affected her younger sister's health. Maude was anxious about the welfare of some animal, as usual, in this case a pig named Nanette. It was good to see Maude in such fettle, but she seemed to have no idea that Clarissa was in a state of almost feverish excitement. In Clarissa's brief eagerness not to take offense, she imagined herself being seen as some retainer whose solicitude was appreciated in an offhanded manner.

Nor was relief from her agitation to be found during a brief breakfast. Aunt Hetty, from a position at the sideboard, watched balefully as Clarissa picked at soft-boiled eggs and ham and strong tea. Aunt Hetty talked about the Duke of Mainwaring and Clarissa's need to accept the peer's offer for her hand in marriage. The entire monologue was trivial as well as unsettling. Clarissa had no mind for much beside the great adventure which had taken place last night.

She made a decision before leaving the table. It was going to be necessary to look in on the visitor once again and determine his condition. Then she would instruct a male servant to ride out to Bodmin and bring back the dragoons, who would put the stranger under lock and key to wait for the assizes and its verdict. More than one arrested smuggler had been hanged before trial, but she warned herself against let-

21

ting that consideration prey on her mind. When a man took up smuggling, he could not cry out at injustice in the wake of the likely consequences. At any rate, Clarissa's mind was made up. It was Bodmin for this smuggler.

She could probably have brought herself to feel some sympathy for the gentleman in his choice of an occupation. So unlikely a smuggler might have merely wanted to satisfy a lust for adventure. It was a reason that Clarissa Tregallen, of all unattached females in the land, could certainly accept.

Wasn't it also true that he could have satisfied such a lust by joining the navy or the army? If his excuse for not doing so was merely that he would not accept necessary discipline, then he would stand revealed as a poor excuse for a Briton or an adventurer.

Clarissa was wise enough to be aware that if she gave much more thought to the matter, she would soon be reasoning that there must be a third side to this particular coin. He was a smuggler, and that put an end to all attempts to consider his behavior as justifiable.

When she had climbed to the uppermost level of Narborne House, Clarissa chose to enter the smuggler's refuge without using the passageway. To achieve that purpose, she walked softly into the schoolroom and through the connecting door to the nurse's chamber. Another connecting door took her to the nursery.

She was disappointed if she had hoped to find him cavorting or, best of all, prepared to leave. He had not stirred.

She discovered more about that young man than his name in the moments after he revived. Nature had blessed him with a strong skull in addition to jet black hair atop a wide forehead, and warm hazel eyes. Somehow he had acquired the faculty of keeping his spirits up despite physical indisposition. During their talk he remained amused as well as courteous.

22

"It will be difficult to conceal you here for much longer," Clarissa said after their first exchanges. "The household is stirring even now."

"You did say that there are no children," he reminded her. "Surely, then, this sanctuary should be free from outsiders."

"Part of the staff appears at some time during the day to clean every room."

"Inform them that the rooms are spotless and no work need be done till you give further notice."

"My aunt will hear of that and probe into the matter without delay." She hadn't meant to sound brusque, but having spoken in that vein she continued. "Nor can you sensibly expect that I would welcome a prolonged stay on your part."

As if reading her thoughts in those mobile features, Bryan Deverell said, "It is natural that you should think of me as a criminal. I can assure you that in my case such an impression is incorrect."

"If you are not a smuggler, then, might I ask why you were in the cove last night?"

He sighed. "Yes, you certainly may ask. I could not possibly prevent that."

"But you decline to answer. Nor will you admit that you must have been attacked by a fellow conspirator in a falling-out over the division of the spoils from the cargo that was brought in last night."

He smiled ruefully. "If you were a judge at the Bodmin assizes, you would now be putting on a black cap."

He suddenly shielded his eyes and shuddered.

She reached over mechanically to smooth the covering of the brightly-colored quilt with which she had covered him during the night. That done, she drew a hand toward the moist cloth which had proved so valuable.

"I don't require any ministrations," he said firmly but pleasantly after taking a hand away to show both eyes firmly closed as if to help reduce the impact of

23

pain. "My vision is clear when the eyes are open and I am not aware of any disturbing symptoms. Except for a roaring headache, which is surely understandable, I am as well as could be expected."

She did not know the truth of those words, accepting the possibility that he might prevaricate to put her at ease. By way of reciprocating, she was now determined against alerting the dragoons to his presence or sending him on the way before he was prepared to rise and put on the Hessian boots which she had removed from his feet during the night. For as long as she could help it, the gallant man would be safe. Caring for him was going to be her first (and perhaps only) great adventure. She found herself like Maude if her sister should ever be confronted by a wounded tiger.

"You say that you are better and I have to accept it as a possibility."

"Thank you."

"That is primarily why I will shortly be leaving you. I also hope to keep my immediate family from posing any questions as to my whereabouts."

"A sensible motive, Miss Tregallen. I applaud it verbally, given the circumstances."

"Should you hear voices in the passage while I am gone, Mr. Deverell, you must take those boots with you and conceal yourself in that cupboard over there."

"Easy enough," he said.

"And as soon as I am able to obtain food and drink to tide you over the next few hours, I will return."


No sooner had Clarissa reached her chamber on the floor below and closed the door on herself than she heard a respectful knock. She drew a deep breath to steady herself, called out, "Enter!" and was smiling in welcome as the door opened.

Lizzie, a sharp-eyed thin girl in her twenties, was the sister of Jem Pendarran, the dairyman who had done most of the work in delivering Blossom's calf on the previous night. A socially adept young woman, she was known to have kept company with the butler and underbutler, one of the two footmen, one coachman, both grooms, a gardener, and a gamekeeper. She was a girl who believed implicitly in the need to improve each shining hour.

"You're up and about already, Miss Clarissa," she said, exercising her famous gift of observation. "But your shoes are muddy and damp!"

"I have been out for an early walk," Clarissa responded, keeping her voice casual. "With all the recent rain and wind, I wished to examine whatever damage might have been done to the garden."

"Of course, miss."

"We will need considerable greenery to decorate the great parlor and the blue saloon, not to mention the halls and stairways."

"Naturally, miss, but in weather that's so treacherous, you must guard against a chill."

"Indeed I shall."

At Clarissa's nod of permission, the maid then addressed herself to caring for Clarissa's heavy auburn locks, repeating the flattering but simple arrangement with a center part and deep waves at the temples.

"Now I plan to prepare a list of tenants who are in need of food baskets at this time," she said cagily when repairs had been completed and she had changed into bow-knot leather shoes. "No doubt Granny Fletcher is still plagued by her rheumatics, for example."

"Yes, Miss Clarissa, and old Mr. Passy has the gout something terrible."

"I will have no time to arrange these matters if I don't do it now, but unfortunately I am famished."

"I will bring up a tray, Miss Clarissa."

"A pot of strong tea will be useful," said she, considering any possible internal difficulties which might have been inflicted upon her guest. "And a decanter of

25

brandy."

The well-trained servant accepted this last order un-blinkingly.

"Papa always said that nothing is more effective in warding off the repercussions from a chill."

It was gratifying that the maid put no questions, expressed no doubts. The normally astute Lizzie accepted every word of the story. Clarissa smiled to herself when she was left alone. Not that she looked forward to fooling other people, but it was good to know that she could take to intrigue the way a duck supposedly takes to water. She had apparently been born with a talent for subterfuge.

A surprise awaited Clarissa when she finally brought the tray stealthily into the nursery. Bryan Deverell was no longer prone on the sofa, but seated. He had fastened his cravat with some care, put on the slightly stained waistcoat which had been expertly cut to emphasize the breadth of chest and shoulders. His Hessian boots were now free of mud even if he wasn't yet able to put them on himself. Regardless of strain, he had valiantly attempted to put her at ease by improving his appearance.

Certainly the repast that confronted him was more than ample for rebuilding a body's strength. Three eggs were offered with a quantity of hot toast on a silver-covered dish, biscuits, a pot of honey, and another of damson preserves, steaming souchong, and a cut-glass decanter of brandy. Such imposing rations enhanced the likelihood of survival.

"Your hospitality, Miss Tregallen," he said courteously before his first bite, "is not to be faulted by even the most finical of men."

She was a prey to moody thoughts, however, as she looked away from him. It was hard not to wonder where a man like Bryan Deverell would be bound.

Already a hiding place would have been prepared along the coast. More than one, very likely.

Possibly, too, a young woman was anxiously waiting for him, a creature willing to associate herself with him only because he was handsome, gentlemanly, and not without intelligence. Some youthful members of her sex, Clarissa told herself disapprovingly, were easily pleased.

She was on the point of telling him that he could stay no longer. A little more sternly, she might add a few words against smuggling and its dangers. If an argument developed, she might indicate that she felt no compunction about sending an able-bodied malefactor with a full stomach off to the gallows.

Her mental preparations were needless. The repast concluded, he set the tray aside and rose to his feet in a careful manner. The first steps he took made him wince and draw a sharp breath, but his expression and breathing were soon under control.

"It may be that I will find an opportunity to leave the house before I speak with you again. Perhaps after dark tonight."

She nodded, feeling that the wind had been taken out of her sails. The rhetoric which she had been intending to use against him could be cast aside.

"I will take my farewell now, and tell you that you have my deepest gratitude." There was no missing the strong emotion in his voice. "I won't forget you, Miss Tregallen. I only wish that the circumstances of our meeting could have been different."

She felt the warmth of his strong fingers take her hand. It was as if her entire being had been touched. Within her, every fiber stirred. If she had not promptly pulled back, she didn't know what course might have been urged on her by her own feelings.

Even as she mustered a smile, she recalled that she had felt no such emotions on the rare occasions when she was touched by Aubrey Seldon. The Duke of

27

Mainwaring may have been as honest as the day was long, but his hand conveyed no warmth.

In the moments before she turned to go downstairs, it occurred to Clarissa that Mr. Deverell hadn't yet taken his departure. Perhaps he was offering an obligatory courtesy to the hostess to show that he wasn't lacking in sensibilities, while he actually meant to stay until hell turned into a picnic ground. It was certainly possible. If she had discovered in herself a talent for intrigue, the more experienced Mr. Deverell had very possibly developed a genius for it.

She was taken aback when she reached the ground-floor hall. Visitors had arrived. More astonishingly, to Clarissa's mind at that first moment, their effects were being brought inside. Only then did she recall that the Christmas holiday fell on Friday of this week and, as ever, Narborne House would be chock-a-block with guests.

She walked along the polished oak flooring and into the great drawing room. Aunt Hetty, attired in prune-colored silk, was looking away from the newcomers even as she spoke agreeably. At sight of Clarissa, the older woman signified that she desired a brief meeting. During a lull in the proceedings, Clarissa joined her near the fireplace, where the crackle of logs would hide any recriminations that might be forthcoming.

"I understand that you have been swilling spirits," Aunt Hetty began, her tone as quiet as her eyes were fast becoming icy.

"I . . . beg your pardon?"

"Your dear father did not approve of females who drink in secret, young lady, as you have been doing. Drinking as a social ritual cannot be carried to excess."

It was impossible to tell her that the brandy had been intended for a guest of whose existence Aunt Hetty wasn't even aware.

28

No doubt the news about her unprecedented behavior had been properly communicated by the alert Lizzie. Clarissa's action, although certainly well intended, had been an error. Perhaps the talent for intrigue had eluded her at birth, after all.

"It is not to happen again," her aunt said sternly.

"You have my assurances in that matter, Aunt Hetty."

She approached the recent arrivals who were now in conversation with Maude. Squire Farrowmere gestured excitedly as he spoke.

"Blossom has always been a good breeder," he was saying enthusiastically. A tall rangy man, his face had been reddened and his body made thick by outdoor living. "But you have to be careful when a calf enters the world hindquarters first."

"Mr. Farrowmere, if you please," his lady said reprovingly. Small though she was, the forceful Phoebe dominated her husband easily and it was whispered that she was able to control the servants, too. "Surely there can be no need to publicly discuss the travails of some animal."

Maude said fervently, "I am ever enthralled by hearing about the ways of our dumb friends."

That much was obvious. Maude's nature-loving tendencies even extended to her clothes — she wore a sack dress in white on which bird simulations were sewn close to the heart.

Clarissa took it upon herself to bridge the awkward pause. "I trust you will pardon my delay in coming down to greet you both."

"Of course," said Squire Farrowmere. "I very nearly put off my visit entirely because of the difficulties in arranging for the thatching of several tenants' homes. In the winter, one cannot delay these duties."

Phoebe was apparently disposed to make emendations to almost any remark of her husband's. "The weather hasn't kept smugglers from landing."

"Smugglers!" Aunt Hetty, coming closer, was round-eyed with shock. "Near Truro, was it, or perhaps Falmouth?"

"A good deal closer, if one can believe the talk. The dragoons caught one of them already."

"How do you know?"

"I heard it from Mark Elbottle on my way over this morning, and he got it from the captain of dragoons himself. The fellow's horse threw a shoe and Mark had to repair it. Captain Taggart said he expects to round up the other smugglers in no time at all. I understand that if you catch one of that ilk, it's not difficult to persuade him to lay an information against the others."

It was as much as Clarissa could do to keep from looking as if she wasn't concerned. A chill had risen in her bones, and only the folds of her olive green day dress concealed her fists formed by tension.

"Surely the other smugglers will have scattered over the length and breadth of the coast in going to ground." Did that detached voice really belong to her?

"Captain Taggart vows he'll have every one of them as his personal guest at the assizes." Squire Farrowmere's labored gaiety was intended to make certain that all the ladies would be reassured. "He has seen service in Holland and overseas in the colonies. If anyone can turn that trick, therefore, it is Taggart."

"I am sure we are all perfectly safe," Clarissa said, almost as if she were talking about some folk in far-off Devon. Tactfulness came to her further assistance. "Your presence by itself, squire, acts as a bulwark against danger."

"How good of you to say so, Miss Clarissa."

Maude put in, "The staff will protect us all in case of need. Jem Pendarran, the dairyman, for instance, is quite sturdy."

Clarissa would have said in amusement that she wasn't surprised Maude's first suggestion for help would use as a source a man who aided the animals.

30

She was, however, perturbed. It came to mind over and over that Bryan Deverell must shortly find a way to manage his escape. The arrival of additional guests would make that feat increasingly perilous.

She turned suddenly as the door opened, almost leaping into the air at this intrusion. It was only Old Creddon, the butler, advancing serenely into the room. He took no more than two steps, which clearly augured that he was going to make some announcement.

"Beg pardon, but the vicar and Mrs. Carteret have arrived."

The newest arrivals were soon at their ease in the drawing room. Aunt Hetty ordered strong tea for the gentlemen and weaker tea with puffin cakes for the ladies, making certain that all stomachs would soon be comfortably warmed.

The ladies prepared for a discreet gossip while the gentlemen regaled each other with tales of the journey to Narborne House, speaking as if each had displayed the greatest skill in evading certain death on the road. Mrs. Carteret was the first to break ranks, her eye having been caught by something on the other side of the huge bay window. She rose and looked out, heedless of mildly disapproving glances from the others.

"Do you see that?" the good lady began, excitement growing within her.

One of the residents of Narborne was duty-bound to join her at the bay window. It was Maude who accepted the obligation.

"Come here, Clarissa," she said after a moment. "See for yourself."

A huge carriage in three painted colors was standing in the circular path. This luxurious accommodation had been brought by coachmen in wigs and almost certainly in stockings of the best silk. The outriders seemed less human than like animated fixtures intended to display powder and plush.

Maude, of course, admired another aspect of the matter. "Those grays are hardly lathered, and their coats still shine like satin."

It was the crest on the door which had drawn Clarissa's fixed attention. This showed a silver-painted bulldog standing bemused in the middle of two turned-up indigo leaves. There was no motto, perhaps because the family felt that any addition would be needless.

Certainly that was true for Clarissa. She knew perfectly well to whom the crest belonged, and her heart, accordingly, sank. She had allowed herself to forget that Narborne House would be visited for the holiday by the peer who had made an offer for her. The Duke of Mainwaring had come to hear her answer.

## Chapter Three

"We had not expected that you would be able to reach Narborne until evening," Hetty Tregallen told the duke after the first salutations. "The condition of our roads is worse than usual after nearly a week of steady rain."

"I began my journey yesterday, ma'am, rather than trust to the vagaries of Cornish weather or roads."

"Indeed, Your Grace, our roads leave something to be desired even under the best of circumstances."

The duke had greeted his fellow guests, shaking hands warmly with the gentlemen and expressing his pleasure at meeting the ladies. He would have spoken as pleasantly to an earl or an urchin. This trait always suggested to Clarissa that under the affable manners and sunny smile he hid a lack of feeling for anyone.

Nobody could fault his looks. His hair, of so pale a shade of blond that it shone with silvery highlights, his light gray eyes, his long narrow head with its finely cut features — all gave him a look of distinction. Fashionable attire enhanced this quality. The lean waist was accented by the cut of his sapphire blue coat worn over a waistcoat of indigo and silver stripes. His cravat, arranged in the popular "oriental" fashion, was held in place by a single pin. A diamond decorated one of his long slender hands. The quizzing glass, worn about his neck, descended from an indigo band the same color as appeared on his family crest. He was dressed to the tens rather than the traditional nines. Mr. Brummell himself would have approved.

His eyes sought out Clarissa and found her standing on the fringe of the turkey carpet with a hand on the polished mahogany table at her left. He did not approach until he had first glanced at his image in the full-length mirror in the northeast corner of the room, as if judging his features to be appropriately cordial.

"And you, Miss Tregallen," he said in the exact tone of courtesy with which he had favored Aunt Hetty. "No matter how trying the journey, it was not to be reckoned any great matter as it has brought me once more into your presence."

Clarissa could think of no reply to match his overwrought prose. "You are most welcome to Narborne, Your Grace. And you, Lady Winifred."

This last had been carefully addressed to the duke's sister, who accompanied him on the expedition to this outpost of Bulldom. Winifred Seldon was dressed for a tea party in Mayfair. Under a scarlet-lined cape with a pink hood, of which she hadn't yet divested herself, she wore a day dress of cambric with a square-cut ruby between her breasts.

The ruby, however, had shifted to her right and the dress contained unexpected creases while the cape was no longer to the crack in London. Lady Winifred obviously cared no longer whether or not her rig-out was impressive. A woman with narrow gray eyes and puffy cheeks, her untreated complexion reminded Clarissa of nothing so much as boiled ham. She was one of those plain women with no hope of marriage whose very lack of comeliness had made her aggressive.

"I have no direct knowledge of gardening," she was saying icily to Mrs. Carteret. The latter had been trying in vain to find a common ground between them. "Nor have I ever attended the church of Little-Middleton-in-the-Dell."

Mrs. Carteret managed to retain her composure.

"You would be entirely welcome at services, I do assure you."

"I am certain of that," said Lady Winifred.

"All chambers have been prepared," Aunt Hetty interrupted loudly, stepping in to dispel the frost. "There is a suitable room for your valet, Your Grace."

"Thank you."

"I fear, however, Lady Winifred, that your maidservant will have to share our Lizzie's room. Lizzie is Clarissa's personal maid and a fine women of her class."

"Such an arrangement is unsuitable," Lady Winifred sniffed. "Sybil is not accustomed to sharing her quarters and will require a room of her own."

Hetty Tregallen was not disconcerted for long. "There is Miss Pratt's room, I suppose."

"Have I not informed you that my personal maid will not share a room with one of the resident domestics?"

"Miss Pratt has not resided at Narborne for six or seven years now, and was never a servant. Miss Florinda Pratt was governess to Clarissa and Maude."

Clarissa, feeling every muscle in her body suddenly turn into knots, tried to offer another suggestion.

"Nothing else available would offer comfort for a servant, dear, as you must surely know," Aunt Hetty pointed out, severely but not unreasonably. "Miss Pratt's room has not been occupied for some time, and will have to be aired and fresh linen provided."

She summoned Creddon with her silver hand bell and instructed the aged butler to send a pair of maids to attend to the necessary tasks on the third floor.

Clarissa winced at the prospect of someone occupying the room across the hall from the nursery. True, the servant would be spending precious little time up there, and would probably be too tired by bedtime to be wholly alert to the possible presence of someone else on the same level.

But that could mean little. Suppose that Bryan Deverell were to knock over one of the many objects that

35

cluttered his hiding place? An immediate search would follow. Was a man of his height and breadth of shoulders going to be able to conceal himself in the cramped nursery cupboard? Even if he accomplished that feat, wasn't one of the searchers likely to look there? Let him be found, a man in his weakened condition, and he would surely be detained for the dragoons, the assizes, and an unforgettable visit with the hangman.

Some way must be found to warn him at once that he had been placed in added peril.

The back staircase would be infested by servants struggling with haircloth luggage belonging to the duke and his infernal sister. Worse yet, logical reason did not offer itself for her having to rise to one of the upper levels.

Nevertheless, an attempt had to be made at resolving matters. "Perhaps I ought to—to make sure that all is in order."

"It is very kind of you to want to see personally to the welfare of our guests," said Aunt Hetty with a sideglance for the duke to make certain that he had noted this striking example of her niece's generous nature. "The maids are capable of attending to whatever small adjustments may have to be made, and they will be supervised by Jamison, the underbutler. Your presence, dear, by any standards, would be entirely superfluous."

Lady Winifred, having taken two sips of the tea and no more, rose. She turned her back to everyone else in the room except His Grace, who was offered a few words. "Sybil will join me in whichever chamber has been assigned to me and will lay out my effects."

His Grace turned to Clarissa, but not before aiming his usual friendly smile at his sister's rigid and disappearing back.

"Please join me in a brief walk about the room, Miss Tregallen. I wish to know how you have fared since last we saw one another. You no doubt have much to tell me about your activities."

He deserved more from her than airy persiflage. It was time for her to give an answer to his marriage offer.

She had no hope of persuading anyone that she was justified in giving the answer she preferred. She could imagine Aunt Hetty's unbelieving dismay some time in the future when she spoke in wonderment about a titled suitor having been rejected because he was too amiable, too courteous, too ostentatiously kind. In no other words could she justify her preference.

This was the time to hint her feeling. Later on, when they spoke together, he would at least realize that he had been gently prepared for the bad news.

She was distracted before she could start.

The drawing-room double doors had been left open by the heedless Lady Winifred. As the view out looked onto part of the hallway and the staircase, Clarissa was able to see what was descending the stairs.

It was, it must be, a supernatural manifestation.

Against that theory was the probability that a manifestation would be wearing neither dark cloak nor Hessian boots. Nor would it have difficulty maintaining a balance as it walked.

Her basic premise, therefore, must be incorrect. With that point conceded, only one answer remained. From a vantage point in her own drawing room, the crowded drawing room of Narborne House, she was looking at Mr. Bryan Deverell.

To see him was to realize what must have recently taken place. The gentleman smuggler had heard steps ascending the servant staircase, steps in quantity, so to speak. He must have known that in spite of the encouragment previously offered to him, it would be almost impossible to hide himself successfully. He had decided to brazen it out, to proceed down the front stairs at risk of discovery. Because of several circumstances in combination, fate had turned thumbs down on his action.

She was aware that the eyes of everyone else in the

room must have been following hers. All conversation had come to a halt and she could hear various levels of labored breathing. From Aunt Hetty's constricted throat there proceeded a watery gurgle of astonishment.

At her first sight of him, Clarissa's fingers had tightened on the cloth of His Grace's finely cut sleeve. She released her hold in spite of Mr. Deverell's advance. Never in life had she fallen into a faint. This was no time to make a beginning.

Without knowing exactly what she intended to do, Clarissa raised her head proudly. Her sense of adventure, having risen to the surface during last night's rescue of this man, was enough to match his boldness. In slow and gliding movements such as she had been taught by Miss Florinda Pratt, she put herself between Deverell and the parties in the drawing room.

Only then did she remind herself that in the view of the others, he must appear to be an invited guest.

"I did not expect," said Clarissa loudly as well as clearly and carefully, "that you would be able to join us so soon."

She was aware that those warm hazel eyes rested appraisingly on her. With a nod, he acknowledged that she was trying to be helpful.

From behind Clarissa came Aunt Hetty's tones, restrained but forceful. "Clarissa, I fear I do not understand. Who is this gentleman?"

"I am Bryan Deverell, ma'am. Your most obedient."

He gave a quick but impudent smile, leaving it to her to conceive of a suitable explanation. He may have been lacking in honesty, but not in nerve.

"I regret it, Aunt Hetty," Clarissa began, "but we have all been so happily occupied in anticipating guests and receiving them this morning that I did not have the opportunity to tell you of Mr. Deverell's arrival last night."

"Closer to dawn, I should say," Bryan remarked, apparently unaffected by finding himself in a situation that could reasonably be considered difficult. "Miss Clarissa was already awake, ma'am. She opened the door to me."

"Clarissa awake at so early an hour? Well, let us disregard that. There are limits to the number of phenomena with which I can deal at a given moment."

"If we return to the drawing room," Clarissa said evenly, "we will find a more comfortable area in which to discuss these arcane matters."

She did not see Deverell join them, but was aware that he settled himself in a high-backed chair beside the fireplace with an excellent view of its heavy caryatids and carved wooden chimney pieces. He reflected assurance just as the full-length mirror reflected features that were polite but frozen.

"I agree that, as you have said, you arrived." Aunt Hetty was settled in a royal blue monopodium chair that had been designed to accept her weight. "But where did you arrive *from?*"

"Abroad." Bryan Deverell smiled sunnily, showing not the slightest sign of any feelings but ease and comfort. "From far off."

"I must ask exactly where."

"Ah, from that area where the British branch of the Tregallens have relatives."

"There are no connections of ours as far off as you seem to indicate, sir."

He had suffered enough. Clarissa leaned forward and spoke slowly, as if to make matters clear. "Cousin Prudence lives in what dear papa used to call the sugar islands."

"Quite so. I had forgotten, briefly. Prudence married a Jamaica planter named Ransley or Ramsey. I have never met him and I saw Cousin Prudence only once, at a ball in Shropshire."

"The relationship needs no further explanation," Squire Farrowmere said calmly, preferring that social matters resume their customary tenor of unruffled placidity.

Aunt Hetty remained unsatisfied. "My brother told me that Prudence had given birth to three children."

"That is correct," Deverell agreed happily. "You are blessed with an excellent memory."

"Thank you. I was also informed by him on that occasion that all three of Cousin Prudence's offspring were girls."

"Which proves that even a good memory can fail," he said equably, without a pause. "Surely I don't look to you like a female."

Clarissa said hurriedly, "I think you should tell my aunt exactly what you told me a while ago."

He took time to sip some of the strong tea which had been brought in for him, but when he set down the sturdy white cup he was smiling. A possible explanation had come to his fertile intellect.

"I do truly beg your pardon if you think that I may have presumed for even a moment. It is disconcerting, however, to find myself being questioned skeptically as if my words were disbelieved."

Aunt Hetty waited.

"It is not easy to speak of, but after Mr. Rupert Ransley passed on—"

"I was not aware that he had done so."

If Clarissa had been in Deverell's position, she would have pointed out pertly that Mr. Ransley could hardly have been expected to take out an advertisement in the paper to notify others about his own demise.

"—his widow married Mr. Edgar Deverell, and I am their only son."

"Then you are a fourth cousin," Maude said, hugging herself in pleasure at the appearance of a hitherto unsuspected relative. "Are you acquainted with Jamaica? Have you ever seen a giant tortoise? Or a mongoose?"

"I have seen both," Mr. Deverell said, markedly more polite to the good-hearted young animal fancier. "It is fair to say that their lineaments conform to the illustrations in books."

Aunt Hetty, her attention fixed upon the major matter under consideration, took a moment to say, "I hope that your parents are in good health."

"Alas, they are gone." Bryan Deverell's handsome features had turned solemn. "I looked forward to writing them of my visit as you, too, would almost certainly do. I regret to say that fever is widespread in the West Indies."

"Please accept my condolences and those of everyone in the room." Aunt Hetty bowed her head.

"Thank you. Among my mother's last words was a request that I come here to meet others of my family, and I have taken it upon myself to do so."

The duke, having raised and lowered his quizzing glass, asked, "Would I be correct in assuming from what I have heard that you are engaged in trade, sir?"

"I ship tobacco, cotton, and tea," Mr. Deverell said, looking modest. "When needs must, I accompany a cargo to the shores of Bulldom—ah, to Britain, I should say."

Clarissa was not surprised that he had given himself an occupation that was highly respectable even in this sad era of war abroad and Corn Laws at home. Nothing less could have been expected by a man who claimed relationship with the Tregallens and mourned a family which had almost certainly never existed. One would have to travel long and far to find any equal for this man's cool impudence.

On the other hand he had not truly made sport of Aunt Hetty and had been entirely courteous to Maude. To that extent he had redeemed himself.

"Once you reached Britain, you arrived here most unexpectedly," the duke proceeded, having momentarily taken over Aunt Hetty's role of inquisitor. "You cannot be surprised, sir, if the mode of your entrance is such as to raise questions, even doubts."

Faced with this blunt assessment, Mr. Deverell fell back on the truth. Or at least on part of it.

41

"There are dangers not only in the West Indies but in Cornwall itself. As I was on my way down, I was set upon by a band of ruffians, as violent a lot as it has ever been an honest man's misfortune to meet."

Hetty Tregallen looked alarmed while the others, except for the duke, murmured among themselves. "I am sure you were not injured by these miscreants," Hetty said.

"I sustained a blow to the back of my head with a stick or cudgel," said Mr. Deverell. "My horse was stolen along with some letters and personal valuables."

"And may I ask about your health now?"

"I am much restored, thanks to the capable ministrations of Miss Clarissa." He smiled at her, perhaps not aware that the usually amiable duke was bristling at the thought of Clarissa's having been so close to him. "After a day's rest, I shall be perfectly well."

"Well, but without the ever-blessed needful," said the duke, making his sarcasm sound like sympathy. "You will require another animal and a fresh purse."

"I am glad to say that I carried a substantial sum of money concealed — ah — on my person. A traveler soon learns the wisdom of keeping his money in more than one place."

He had obviously taken the other's measure as soon as the talk turned to Clarissa's having ministered to him. If he depended on the wealthy peer for a loan, he would be a long time penniless.

The duke brought his quizzing glass into play, raising it skeptically. "I cannot understand why the footpads were so remiss as not to make certain of your impoverishment. That class know enough to search a victim thoroughly. Perhaps they would have — forgive me, ladies — stripped you to prove their efficiency."

Rescue for Bryan Deverell came from the unlikely person of Squire Farrowmere. "You are undoubtedly not aware, Your Grace, that a band of smugglers made a landing near here last night. As magistrate for the district, I was apprised of this some hours ago. Those men must have been the ones who attacked Mr. Deverell. The profits they stand to gain from their nefarious trade make it unlikely that they would commit robbery for its own sake. They would only want to make certain that no one had seen them. As an afterthought they seized his horse and his purse, and were on their way."

The duke fell silent, acknowledging Farrowmere's argument with a good-humored shrug.

Aunt Hetty was convinced that the physical evidence for Mr. Deverell's story had caused the squire and vicar to accept its truth. She would, as a result, follow the lead of these longtime friends, these ancients of days, with their accumulated wisdom.

"We will not hear of your staying only for another night, as if this were an inn, Cousin Brian," said Hetty Tregallen, generously compensating for unfounded suspicions. "To think of you coming this far and then not spending the holidays with your family! You will surely remain through Christmas week."

"I thank you, Cousin Hetty. It would be a great honor."

Clarissa's green eyes narrowed with a flash of anger. He had taken advantage of her aunt and younger sister, trading on their family feeling to gain himself a refuge and a false identity.

It was not too late for her to take the squire aside and inform him privately about "Cousin Bryan" and his true Satan-given vocation. No doubt she'd be able to justify her having concealed a rogue, perhaps by claiming that he had made threats against her and the other females of Narborne.

Handsome he may have been, with fine broad shoulders and strong chest, but he was a deep-dyed rogue all the same.

It would be the act of a savage (would it not?) to send away a wounded man who was still recovering, however.

43

A human being had to show the compassion of which so many revered books spoke highly. Compassion, as the vicar had once insisted in a Sunday address, made the difference between the lower orders and humankind.

Yes, this quandary had but one answer.

"It will please me very much," Bryan Deverell added, "to be seeing more of you, dear Cousin Hetty, and Cousin Maude and, of course, Cousin Clarissa."

He grinned conspiratorially at her, delighted that his last words had caused the duke to shift two times in his comfortable chair.

Only now did Deverell turn toward the peer. "I have observed that you look at Cousin Clarissa in a way that is adopted by young men toward comely females. As the only male relative of the family who is present, I must ask whether you have any intentions toward my cousin and whether those are honorable."

Aubrey Seldon, the Duke of Mainwaring, rose to his full height. It permitted him to look down at the interloper.

"You will be pleased to know that I have offered for Miss Tregallen, and I have every hope that my offer will shortly be accepted. I hope this prospective arrangement meets with your approval. And now, if you will excuse me, Miss Hetty and ladies, I will proceed upstairs to my chamber."

There was a long silence after the duke had left, quietly closing the door behind him. For a moment everyone in the room realized that the sun was lowering though the wintry afternoon had just begun, and even the roaring fire seemed sadly inadequate to provide much-needed warmth.

Phoebe Farrowmere, more alert to social interplay than the others, looked at Clarissa with admiration. The younger woman was being envied for having provoked enmity between two men who were sturdy and handsome.

Squire Farrowmere, his tanned features glowing with

approval, said, "The duke is friendly for all his rank."

The vicar made a steeple of his slender fingers and said consideringly, "His amiability is not spontaneous."

"I fail to see the difference."

"He reminds me of a former parishioner, a Mr. Gerald Hudspeth," Mr. Carteret responded. "Hudspeth was the type who smiled all the time, asked after your health, came up after the Sunday sermon to congratulate you upon its effectiveness."

"The duke, I feel sure, would do the same."

"That is my point. I soon discovered that Hudspeth was the leader of a faction wanting to oust me from my living. Even after he knew I had twigged his purposes, he continued to behave like the most loyal and faithful of my parishioners."

Clarissa, stirred and unsure of herself, spoke from a dry throat. "And you think the duke is that way, too?"

"One should choose carefully before making him an enemy," said Mr. Carteret somberly. "Such a man is — in my best opinion — dangerous."

*Chapter Four*

Fears for the safety of her self-appointed fourth cousin came to Clarissa's mind a short time after leaving the others. It suddenly occurred to her that the duke was not a man to shrug off any attempt to make him look like a fool. If Mainwaring could have his way, as Clarissa didn't doubt, Bryan Deverell would even now be spending his time decorating a spit above some roaring fire.

There was no help for it but to take Bryan aside and strongly direct him to vanish from the Tregallen house, even though Narborne would be a duller place by his absence.

As it happened, this new consideration came to Clarissa only after she was back in her own bedroom and on the verge of pulling the bell to summon Lizzie. Firmly deciding instead to keep further difficulties from taking place, she started out to the hallway.

Just as she reached the first step of the broad staircase, she came to a halt as unexpected as it was unwelcome.

Aunt Hetty was proceeding upwards, eyes fixed on Clarissa's features. Like her niece, the older woman was pursuing a goal to be gained immediately, and in her case she wanted a conversation with none other than Clarissa herself.

"We must speak," Aunt Hetty began, having distributed her weight gracefully as she reached the step below

46

Clarissa's vantage point. Enough breath remained in her body so that she could have promptly started an oration in Parliament.

"Perhaps we can meet afterwards, dear Aunt, in your room."

"I will discuss this matter very briefly."

Clarissa hadn't previously allowed herself to show impatience. "I need first to speak with Cousin Bryan, so I beg to be excused."

Hetty Tregallen didn't move an inch. "It is about him that I wish to speak with you first."

There was going to be no easy way to avoid hearing her good and loyal aunt. Clarissa kept her temper with the aid of an iron grip on the carved oak balustrade, not caring that the wood seemed moist to the touch after recent rain, as often happened. The gesture did help her to retain that civility which had been instilled in her from childhood.

"Aunt Hetty, I beg you to reach the point you wish to make."

"Certainly, if you will refrain from hurrying me." Aunt Hetty's tone made it clear that rushing at Narborne House was a tactic used only in fevered dream. "There is no need to hurry about this—oh, very well, young miss! One more moment of your precious time."

"Please, Aunt." Clarissa was reduced to speaking in a hoarse whisper.

"Very well." Aunt Hetty did hesitate, but briefly. "Do you think that Cousin Bryan has taken to Maude?"

Clarissa actually drew back in astonishment.

"Cousin Bryan? Does he like my sister?"

"Surely the question is simple enough and a girl in a great rush can give the answer in a very few words."

"Of course he feels kindly toward Maude." Clarissa spoke from a full heart. "How could anyone not love dear Maude?"

"My judgment is confirmed!" Aunt Hetty chortled in triumph.

47

"Maude is a darling young woman who is loved by the beasts in the field, the beasts in our property, and all of God's creatures as well."

"I fear that you don't quite take my meaning," Aunt Hetty said regretfully, and then spent more time rescuing her thoughts from obscurity. "You know just how strongly I feel that spinsterhood is a condition to be scrupulously avoided."

"My beloved aunt, I must —"

"Clarissa, although you have found someone you have delayed accepting, your dear sister has not yet found anyone. Distant cousins, of course, as I'm sure I need hardly remind you, may marry."

Clarissa ceased to be shocked. "Are you suggesting that Bryan Deverell might be anxious to marry my sister?"

"Do you feel it impossible?"

Clarissa wanted to say that she would rather see her beloved sister married to Napoleon Bonaparte's chief of police. She contented herself with shaking her head vehemently.

"Of course not!" Clarissa corrected herself in speech. "No arrangement along that line would ever come to pass."

Her vehemence was surprising. If Deverell turned out to be respectable, the Tregallen family could certainly make him welcome. The conception, however, of his being joined with Maude in the bonds of matrimony was appalling. The protest was being made for Maude's sake entirely.

"The best course to follow is for you to sound him out," Aunt Hetty suggested with the strained smile of a conspirator planning her first foray. "You must inquire about his circumstances. We want to know how much he earns, the extent of his savings, and what sort of enterprise he could fall back upon in the event of some fresh difficulties in his current business of importing. You do understand, Clarissa?"

48

"Indeed, yes."

"As for a dowry, you may assure him that the Tregallen lands would offer a substantial settlement that could be made upon him. At this time I see no need to mention a sum, even to offer an estimate."

"Of course not, Aunt. I shall carry on with this mission as soon as I am able to speak with Cousin Bryan."

"Good. I do believe that as Maude's sister and closest living relative, you are in a better position than I to make those preliminary queries which can be of such importance."

"Then if you will permit me . . ."

With her customary grace, Aunt Hetty stepped aside.

Clarissa proceeded down the stairs. She held onto the balustrade to keep from losing her balance as much as to prevent herself from keeling over with sheer dismay.

By the time she reached the drawing room entrance, her balance was restored. Her head high in anticipation of another meeting with Bryan Deverell, Clarissa opened one of the double doors with great swiftness.

She was doomed to disappointment. Deverell had left, as well as the other men in the room. Phoebe Farrowmere was deep in conversation with the vicar's wife. At some other time Clarissa might have been amused to see the perky Mrs. Farrowmere leaning forward to make a point without the constraints of a masculine presence.

The vicar's wife, having despaired of speaking for awhile, was the first to notice Clarissa's return. Moments passed before she turned her entire body away from Mrs. Farrowmere. Hope Carteret was a woman almost as large as Clarissa's Aunt Hetty, but without Hetty's pertness. She seemed always mindful of the impression her words and gestures might make, realizing that her husband's living depended on the amount of approval generated by her behavior. Her eyes were never fixed on any one person.

"Clarissa, how good of you to enliven this talk by returning."

49

"Thank you, but I came back in hopes of finding my cousin. Would you know where he has got to?"

Phoebe Farrowmere interrupted her friend's negation. "I wonder if I might ask you something, Clarissa. Quietly, of course, and in confidence."

Once again there was no rescue from doing the bidding of another. Clarissa closed the door behind her and took several steps into the room, but was careful not to sit down. Indeed, she made a point of placing herself before the fire so that Mrs. Farrowmere would hasten the tête-à-tête.

"Have you been previously acquainted with Lady Winifred, the sister of the duke?"

"We met when I was in London for the last season," Clarissa admitted.

"Is she always," Phoebe Farrowmere asked cautiously, *"quite* so sure of herself?"

"I believe so." Clarissa spoke with briskness, not even pausing to tell herself wryly that one of the same breed would immediately recognize another. "Might I ask in my turn whether Mr. Deverell informed you to where he was going?"

"Why no, not at all." A shiver passed through Phoebe Farrowmere's small person, and she tried to look around Clarissa to satisfy herself that the fire was still going. "I am sure you want to seek him out, my dear."

"If you'll excuse me, then, ladies."

"Certainly," said Mrs. Farrowmere.

"We excuse you with the greatest reluctance," Hope Carteret added instantly, hugging a merino shawl more tightly around her neck to keep herself a little less chilly till Clarissa was gone.

The library, which was close by, turned out to be unoccupied. Glass in the bay window rattled like a living thing, making a sound which had caused her to look in and then outside. One of the Mainwaring carriages was not in the grove where it had been left, she noticed. For some reason, the discovery made her move quickly in the hunt for Bryan Deverell. Without knowing why, she found herself feeling freshly uneasy.

Deverell was not in the dining room, either, but the wind had died down by the time she reached that location, fading into a series of plaintive murmurs that she could remember from childhood.

The vicar and Squire Farrowmere were at the table in the billiard room, the former poised to attack a white ball with a stick.

"Is something wrong, Clarissa?" the vicar asked, looking up.

Mr. Carteret would most likely hear her story with great sympathy after what he himself had recently said about the duke. He would strain himself to be of assistance. Clarissa, however, didn't want to run any risk of the vicar gossiping later on to his wife. The fewer who knew what was actually taking place, in her view, the better.

"Nothing is wrong, sirs," she said, turning. "Please pardon me for having intruded."

With a burst of inspiration, Clarissa returned upstairs to satisfy herself that Maude was not in her room. She smiled. No further probing was needed.

As if she had been a witness, Clarissa now felt certain of what had taken place. Maude had approached Bryan Deverell and had asked him to join her on one of those numerous trips she was always taking to visit the animals of Narborne. Deverell, sly of tongue when he wished, could no more find it in himself to deny a request of Maude's than anyone else who came within ten thousand feet of the property.

Clarissa stopped at her own bedroom long enough to change for the outdoors. Over a dark woolen dress she donned a dark cloak. She had already changed into her pitch-black boots which still felt a little moist on the inside after last night's downpour. Headgear was to be avoided, as it could be lifted from her person by an onslaught of December wind.

51

On the outside in midafternoon, she could clearly see the leafless trees standing against leaden sky. On the tops of several of those trees, deserted bird nests showed in bold varicolored patches. Fog was drifting in from the west, bringing with it a pervasive dampness. Fog and wind didn't often go together, but she had known them to appear in unison. Her father had once remarked ruefully that hell, like Cornwall in winter, made its residents' lives sadder by various grades of unpleasant climate. Very probably Squire Tregallen had been right.

Because the stables were closest, she began her second search in that area. The stables formed a quadrangle with a court in the center. She walked through the archway, looking in at various enclosures. The gray horses, with which she wasn't familiar, probably belonged to the Messrs. Farrowmere and Carteret. The sleek ones which had already been washed down and were now being fed were owned by the duke and his thorn-tempered sister.

In this particular search, impatience was its own reward. She turned a corner to find Maude inside one of the stables staring at whip marks on a rusty brown quarter horse named Spinner. Stubby fingers, roughened by work with the animals, traced the mark gently, but her eyes burned with anger.

"It was the tiger that did it," she snapped. "I know it was."

Bryan Deverell, who had been watching with friendly concern and nothing more, opened his hazel eyes wide in astonishment.

"I have perceived that you are fond of animals, but I cannot bring myself to believe that you would permit a tiger on the premises, and certainly you couldn't teach any tiger to use a whip."

Maude was still too angry to consider anything but the wound inflicted upon the animal. Clarissa, gingerly walking into the stable and feeling the crackle of straw underfoot, gave the needed explanation.

"You have been away from country life for so long a time, dear cousin, that you are not familiar with the current modes," she began easily. "Tiger is a name given to a small groom who usually rides a curricle at some point between springs."

"Oh." Deverell turned those strong eyes full on her. "I saw a small groom holding the horses when Lord Mainwaring descended from his carriage. At the time, I assumed he was one of the few of his kind to be employed at a great house."

It was a reminder. She had allowed herself to become forgetful of her mission. Speaking with Deverell again, being close enough to hear every word from his voice lowered in response to her, was truly exhilarating. Small wonder she had been distracted.

"I must raise a matter with you in privacy."

At those words, she felt her face flushing. She had thought of a second possible interpretation to her request, an interpretation that wasn't simple and clear.

Deverell glanced over at Maude, who was crooning some lullaby to Spinner while rubbing his flank with an odorous unguent.

"We *are* enjoying privacy."

"Will you accompany me back to the quadrangle?"

"Certainly."

It was unnecessary to take any prolonged leave of Maude and, in any case, it would have been beyond Clarissa's abilities at this time. Looking at Bryan Deverell, she was preoccupied in thinking that a wide forehead below dark hair was a sight that afforded the female eye a certain amount of pleasure when displayed by a gentleman. It indicated the presence of intellect, and the capacity to make mental efforts often accompanied with a talent for various types of physical efforts as well.

At this time, she warned herself, such a line of thought was not going to prove helpful. Best to concentrate on the goal that was in view, the need to make certain that he would soon find himself far from

53

Mainwaring's possible vengeance.

She was happily aware at the same time that a little color had come back to his fine features. He walked with only a hint of his previous hesitation. Instead of a man who was physically sick, he looked like one who had just wakened and hadn't so far steadied himself.

"I have a feeling that you don't want to congratulate me, even though everything is going so well."

" 'Going well'?" In spite of Clarissa's best efforts, her voice had grown louder.

"I wonder that no one asked in what room I spent the preceding night," he mused. "I suppose they were spell-bound by my skill as a narrator."

"You were largely successful," Clarissa noted, his amusement serving to cap her temper. She decided not to tell him about Aunt Hetty's plan for marrying him off to Maude. It was not of any real importance, certainly not now.

"A glorious triumph, in my opinion," he contradicted her, totally without modesty. "As a result, I anticipate a delightful Christmas week in the company of my surviving family."

Clarissa then realized for the first time that Bryan Deverell didn't have the slightest intention of leaving Narborne. Much as she welcomed his presence, it was more important to persuade him that he must quit the premises to save himself.

She wished she knew how to accomplish that feat.

## Chapter Five

Like it or not, the citadel had to be stormed.

"Mainwaring was not pleased by your behavior," she reminded him.

"He didn't think of me as heroic, no."

She wanted to say that she was the one who thought of him that way, no matter what else he might have done in his life. She made do with a fierce shake of the head.

"I greatly fear that my opinion of Mainwaring in turn was not of the highest. As for his sister, Lady Winifred has lowered the term 'high on the instep' to new depths of meaning."

Clarissa didn't want to rebuke Bryan Deverell. His easy humor was making her feel like some prissy nursemaid of great age, a woman who had never experienced happiness in youth and would always reprimand it in somebody else.

"You must understand what I am saying," she snapped. "You are not to deflect me. This is a matter of the utmost seriousness."

"In which case, you may be sure that I humbly beseech your pardon."

"Very well, then. Lord Mainwaring is not a man who accepts slights and overlooks them. He executes vengeance."

"And you think that he would try to wreak harm upon me? But I am a member of the family, as far as he knows, the same family which is hosting him and his sister for this stay. He can do nothing or very little. Oh, I suppose he might try to defeat me dismally at billiards, for example, but no other course is open to him."

"I tell you again that I have seen him in contact with others who have displeased him, and he will strain every effort against you. I need not remind you that you could be considered vulnerable to attack, sir. There is a chink in your armour."

"But Mainwaring doesn't know that."

"He is more than willing to probe until he finds it," Clarissa assured him confidently.

Bryan stroked his chin in a meditative way. He was now giving his serious attention to the difficulty.

To have accomplished that much was a triumph for her, but it was saddening, too.

"There are some difficulties," he said after a moment.

"What do you have in mind?"

"Well, 'Cousin Bryan' is going to disappear after everyone has been told that he will be staying through Christmas week."

True enough. Aunt Hetty would be only a little less disappointed than Clarissa herself. There would be no more adventure in her life as she would certainly never see him again.

His own view of the problem didn't involve individual attitudes. "Everyone will be convinced that the family is hiding something. More accurately, that the family had been hiding some*one*."

"I will confront that obstacle when it becomes necessary," Clarissa said stubbornly. "After you are among the missing."

He grinned. "You are a devil-may-care young female, aren't you? Unfortunately, Clarissa, that sort of planning is inadequate."

"I'm not planning."

"Of course you are. You may call it something else, but it's what you're doing. With my help, I may add. I was going to say that you have to determine in advance how you will handle any foreseeable difficulty."

She was on the verge of pointing out that the last hours had seen him deal with several obstacles for which no one could have made allowance.

"Clarissa, I was so well prepared for likely troubles that I was able to improvise when necessary," he said, anticipating the objection before it could be made. "You can be as impulsive as you wish, in these instances, but you must never be careless."

"Then what am I to say when asked what has become of you?"

"That's extremely simple." But he paused long enough for the first rueful smile to turn into a laugh. He was one of those men who could laugh heartily without losing dignity. "Indeed yes."

"You have found a solution? Give it to me then, and quickly, if you please."

"Tell Mainwaring that 'Cousin Bryan' has hared off to Bodmin, where he will lay a complaint against those miscreants who assaulted him."

"That's all very well up to a point. But what can I say when you don't return?"

"Inform all questioners that I will be putting up at the Goat and Grapes until the capture is made. I can therefore testify against them that much more quickly and speed their inevitable meeting with Jack Ketch."

She had looked approving until he mentioned that nickname which was applied only to a hangman. She felt a shiver at the memory of that scarecrow figure of her childhood, the one that had dangled from a gallows, the one she had seen in the course of a carriage ride with her father. Not for years had that memory caused her such a feeling of shock.

"I see," she said, trying to speak carefully so that he wouldn't sense the pain of memory or of her knowledge that he would soon be leaving forever. "That is an excellent thought. You are a liar beyond compare."

"I am only a man who thinks with the power supplied by a good imagination." Was he, too, feeling regret at going away? Did he feel badly about leaving a place of comfort and safety or about leaving the Tregallens? "In that case, nothing remains but to wish you a happy future and let you proceed with it."

She couldn't permit him to leave on foot. Hours ago, he had been badly hurt.

"You will take a carriage, of course."

"There is no need for that amenity."

"At the very least, your going in a carriage will lend my explanation a certain ring of truth."

"I came into your life without a carriage and will leave in the same style."

She already knew that when his voice reached a certain tone, countering some idea of his would be useless.

Her eyes darted to his lips. She wanted to feel those lips against hers, to feel that he was closer to her than any male had ever been. At the same time she was well aware that his eyes rested on hers, and she saw his shoulders move as if he was raising his hands.

"There is time enough, though, to thank the person who saved me," Bryan Deverell said, and swept her into his arms, lips lowered to hers.

She was aware of being slowly released. Stars danced before her eyes.

"You had better leave first," he whispered. "Someday, perhaps . . ."

"Someday."

And she knew that he would come back in the future if he could. Watching her so intently, he must have known that she would be waiting.

She gasped and turned toward the house, walking slowly, navigating a route that no one could ever have taken before this.

## Chapter Six

On her way into the square hall of Narborne House, Clarissa brushed away a tear. The sting in her eyes made it impossible to look ahead at every step, and she walked to the first landing and down a long hall which took her to the servants' wing. Turning back, she nearly stumbled into the so-called bachelors' wing. Before that mistake could be corrected, she was facing Lady Winifred Seldon.

The sister of the Duke of Mainwaring did not trouble to smile, but offered a cool nod. The gesture was enough to shake some of her faded straw blonde hair which hung down behind. She was wearing light blue muslin, which looked discolored, and a broad sash that ought to have been a virginal white but seemed at some point to have been defiled. Clarissa would have liked to take the imperious Lady Winifred to one side, for her own sake, and offer a few suggestions about keeping up a wardrobe. It would have been inappropriate to do so, as well as useless. Perhaps the casual destruction of one's good appearance was a current London style, but Clarissa rather doubted it.

Lady Winifred apparently wished to make some communication. She stood perfectly still, a hand raised and forefinger up as a way of demanding attention.

"Yes, Lady Winifred?"

Assured that Clarissa was alert, Lady Winifred began

firmly. "I see that you are not in his company."

"The duke's company, you mean?"

"No. That man."

"My cousin?"

"That is how he calls himself." Lady Winifred was prepared to doubt any information that Deverell might have offered. "He seems so different in manner from the Tregallens that a kinship is difficult to imagine."

Clearly she meant that Deverell bore no traces of country-bred sluggishness. Lady Winifred's normally glazed eyes were showing traces of animation. It seemed impossible to believe, but she was speaking of Deverell with an approval she would likely have withheld from members of her own family.

"My cousin is a visitor from a far-off land," Clarissa took some pleasure in remarking. "In this case, from Jamaica."

"Indeed?" Lady Winifred remained skeptical, like one of King George's physicians being told that His Majesty had performed some action associated with sanity. "The young man's behavior is so London-like that I would have taken him for a polished exclusive of the *ton*."

"It seems, then, that there are gentlemen as far afield as Jamaica, your ladyship."

"Perhaps."

This was the time to say that Bryan Deverell had gone off to Bodmin so that he could help see justice done. Clarissa had communicated lies of less importance in the past, but this time the words refused to leave her lips.

Lady Winifred offered further information. "I saw the young man briefly when he was leaving the drawing room and I had come down the stairs in hopes of enjoying a stroll with my brother. A forlorn hope, in the circumstances." She sniffed, considering the waywardness of brothers. "Mr. Deverell was in the company of your sister, who effected introductions. He told me that the two of them were hurrying off so that they could search for you."

Clarissa had vaguely wondered how Deverell had come to meet her ladyship. He had spoken of her not long ago with the grim knowledge acquired by anyone who had ever been in her company.

"Did he find you?" Lady Winifred proceeded.

"Yes," Clarissa said mechanically, and then realized she had lost the chance to relate casually to her ladyship the fable that Deverell had constructed to explain his absence. No matter how firmly she braced herself to say those few words, innocent in themselves, they refused to cross her lips. Could words, mere words, possibly have a will of their own?

Lady Winifred resumed pacing the hall, apparently having decided that there was nothing more she wished to communicate to Clarissa. Presumably her ladyship felt that the duke would see her and castigate himself for having been negligent of her wishes. In Clarissa's opinion, that was another forlorn hope.

She decided against excusing herself before she left.

Lizzie, the personal maid, appeared in Clarissa's room shortly after Clarissa got there herself. The maid noticed Clarissa's air of surprise at seeing her.

"You summoned me, Miss Clarissa."

Clarissa decided against remarking that she didn't recollect having done so.

"Of course, Lizzie. I need to dress for the late afternoon."

With the help of frequent advisories from the astute maid, Clarissa decided on a russet day dress with white and blue flowers illustrated upon its surface at the most discreet intervals. To this she added blue Moroccan leather shoes and a proper scent from the bottles displayed on her table. She felt justly confident in that effective combination. She looked that way, too, but the self-assurance she conveyed did not go deep.

She took time to inspect her gold-bordered dark blue

gown, deciding that it would be suitable wear for the come-out of her dear friend, Serena Dorward. This event would be taking place at the Dorward farm in Launceston some eight days into January. Many young ladies were looking forward to the affair.

Suddenly, Clarissa didn't feel that way. Music would be provided by several of the locals, dancing would be clumsy, and the young men of the vicinity would be callow and unsure of themselves. They would be apologetic when they weren't leering. None would seem natural. Finding herself physically close to any in a dance would be an experience to dread.

Circumstances would not be mitigated if she stayed with a small circle at her friend's come-out. She would have to do so if she were accompanied by the duke and his sister, but that would cause other problems. While Lady Winifred sneered, the duke would try to seem like a hail-fellow-well-met. During their return ride to Narborne, each reveler would be slandered. Listening to their comparisons of Cornwall farmers with the London nabobs would cause considerable teeth-gritting.

Nevertheless, she looked closely at the elbow-length white gloves which she would also wear to the dance, then at the gold-dusted reticule and slippers which would complete the ensemble.

She wished she cared as much as a tuppence about the occasion. If she didn't it was mostly because one certain male would not be on the premises to amuse her, to make her feel contented yet exhilarated, to convince Clarissa Tregallen that she was a female in youth's fullest bloom.

Lizzie may have seen a certain smile across the young miss's mobile lips. If so, she interpreted it correctly before speaking again.

"Your cousin, that Mr. Deverell, he has certainly turned the heads of a few girls belowstairs, Miss Clarissa, if I might say so."

"Of course you can say so, Lizzie. It means nothing

whatever to me."

"Yes, miss."

"I am not sure whether light blue gloves would be more suitable with this gown, Lizzie. Fetch me the light blue immediately so that I can examine the contrast."

"Yes, miss."

Aunt Hetty had changed to poplin when she appeared in Clarissa's room. The material added weight to her figure, but also lightened her gray curls and helped fade the crows feet under her eyes. All in all, a satisfactory exchange.

"I wish you wouldn't look out the window at clouds," Aunt Hetty complained. "Too much staring weakens the eyes and makes a girl look older than nature planned for her at a given time."

"Pardon, Aunt." Clarissa walked along the mossy carpet and paused before her carved dark chair on the north side of the bed. "Do you wish to descend?"

"In a moment. What I would like first is to know whether you spoke to him."

"To — Deverell?"

"Don't be a quiz! Did I not tell you to sound him out with regard to his prospects? He may be a suitor for Maude's hand."

"You did tell me, yes."

"And what did you learn?"

This was the chance to say that Deverell had left Narbone forever. As before, the words refused to come. She had not previously known that she might develop such an aversion to verbal embroidery.

"I spoke to him, but I had no chance to query him." Bitterly she added, speaking more to herself, "If I had done so, it would have changed nothing."

"How do you mean, Clarissa?"

"His feelings are taken elsewhere."

"What? He is due to marry another? Or do you mean

63

that he already has a wife in Jamaica or some other outpost?"

Clarissa said nothing.

"How wicked to flirt with Maude when all the time there is another in his life." Aunt Hetty's face reddened with anger. "There is a name for that sort of young man and it is not a compliment. I do believe that Maude is well out of the involvement."

Clarissa stopped herself before she responded that the involvement didn't exist anywhere but in Hetty Tregallen's mind. More importantly, Bryan Deverell had done nothing wrong.

She would have said so if not for hearing a series of hoofbeats.

"Perhaps the duke and his sister have gone out riding," Aunt Hetty suggested, seeing that the commotion had caused her niece to look startled.

"No, too many horses are out there."

Not caring at the moment if her aunt might disapprove of such behavior, Clarissa turned back to the bay window.

She was in time to see that twenty uniformed members of the light dragoons had appeared before Narborne House. Having previously observed that the duke's missing carriage had returned to its proper place with the others, she knew immediately who had called for the presence of law enforcers.

And she knew, too, for whom they would be searching.

# Chapter Seven

Clarissa courteously allowed her aunt to lead the way downstairs. For once, her good manners nearly led to an unfortunate consequence. Aunt Hetty, in a rush, came close to tripping over one of the many cats Maude insisted on keeping in the house. If Clarissa hadn't caught her in time, Aunt Hetty would certainly have been put to bed with a bad leg.

As it was, after only a muttered curse and a louder, "God forgive me," Hetty led the way to the square hall. Men could be heard in conversation, but the immediate area was unoccupied.

It was Clarissa who pointed to the open door of the library. Aunt Hetty proceeded firmly in that direction.

The lighted fire gave a glow to the scattered volumes on a few shelves, the gewgaws on small tables, and the newcomer.

Encased in the dragoon uniform of Hessian boots, white pantaloons, stiff white shirt, and a coat far redder than the flames in the roaring fireplace, was a fine figure of a man. His posture was magnificent, his face like an eagle's, his eyes piercing. He looked more like a drawing of a soldier from one of Clarissa's books than a human being.

As Clarissa came into the room, the dragoon officer was turning from Squire Farrowmere and the duke to examine the hostile older woman who stood before him.

"Am I addressing the mistress of the house?"

"You are."

"Allow me to present myself. I am Roderick Taggart, captain of the 12th Light Dragoons. Your most obedient servant."

"May I then make so bold as to ask why my most obedient servant chooses to make an operatic entrance at the head of a regiment of stick figures?"

"Ma'am, I did not 'choose' to come here."

The duke turned his long narrow head so that he was facing Aunt Hetty. "I am sure that there is a perfectly good reason for this visit. I was on the point of finding out what it might be when you suddenly appeared."

"Then perhaps *I* can find out." Aunt Hetty didn't quite put her arms akimbo, but she sounded as if she were adopting the same tone which accompanied that hostile stance when either Clarissa or Maude was causing some difficulty.

Lady Winifred had begun to speak disapprovingly as she walked into the library. At one pointed look from the duke, she subsided.

Mr. Carteret had come in behind her. "May I escort the ladies upstairs?" he began with clumsy gallantry.

Aunt Hetty and Clarissa shook their heads firmly. As for Lady Winifred, the sound that issued from her throat resembled a horse's whinny and would certainly have roused Maude's interest. Phoebe Farrowmere, who had reached the doorway on the vicar's heels, was standing with feet apart and doing her best to look immovable.

"We haven't yet been vouchsafed any answer to the burning question of the moment," Aunt Hetty said, placing herself in front of Clarissa to give unnecessary protection. "Why, Captain Taggart, have you and your men materialized at this time?"

The duke and the squire began to speak simultaneously, but it was Aunt Hetty who silenced them with a crisp, "Please, gentlemen, not now!"

Taggart, relieved that there was one person to whom he could explain his actions, smiled. Clarissa, stepping to one side, noticed that the captain was not quite as tall as her aunt. His lack of stature went far to justify that superlative posture.

"Ma'am, it has come to our notice that an unauthorized person came ashore at the nearest inlet last night."

Clarissa didn't ask who had brought that to his attention. The answer wasn't needed. She glared at the duke.

"That is horrible," Mainwaring said with a shudder. "I fear for your safety, Clarissa, and that of your family. A foul villain is stalking the land."

Taggart, grateful for what seemed like the support he wanted, smiled at the duke. "Thank you, Your Grace, for that encouragement."

Aunt Hetty said, "If an unwelcome person appears on the grounds of Narborne, you may rest assured that the staff can attend to the matter. I would not care to be an intruder who encounters, say, Jem Pendarran in the dairy — or anywhere else on the grounds if truth be told."

"This instance, ma'am, is unusual," Captain Taggart responded briskly. "The man is said to be dangerous."

Again Clarissa wanted to ask who had said so. Again, however, she realized that such a question was entirely unnecessary.

Aunt Hetty put the question, however. "Who said that the man is dangerous?"

"We have the testimony of a man who came ashore at the same time. He had no business in the vicinity, either. No legal business, that is. He is a member of the Brotherhood, if you take my meaning."

A smuggler, then.

Squire Farrowmere, going back to his occupational attitude of a magistrate, put the next query. "How did you come to obtain this man's testimony, captain?"

"He was ensnared when his horse threw a shoe," Taggart replied stiffly. "Somebody with no tolerance for the Brotherhood — there are many of those, contrary to

67

what most citizens think — brought him to us and we had to hear out his story."

"I assume that you would have let him go if he had not mentioned someone else coming ashore at the same time, a man he called dangerous."

Taggart managed to shrug without disturbing the straight back.

Aunt Hetty, of course, asked that question which was most pertinent. "How is this missing man a danger? What makes him dangerous?"

"Ma'am, I powerfully dislike to unsettle you," Taggart responded, "but I must reluctantly inform you that — ah — the man who came on board the smuggling ship at the start of its journey in Marseilles is a man who speaks French quite well."

"You are saying that the man is a spy for that detestable Bonaparte." Aunt Hetty tossed her head. "He will find no sanctuary at Narborne."

The men nodded in agreement while the women — all but Clarissa — exchanged glances.

"I am sure he won't," Taggart agreed blandly, "but there are questions which have to be asked."

"Proceed."

"Has any man you don't know been seen at Narborne since last night and during this day?"

"None."

Phoebe Farrowmere, interrupting from the hall, put in, "There was a man here today who spent last night at the house and who none of us knew."

Taggart wheeled on Aunt Hetty. "Would you care to explain now?"

"Mrs. Farrowmere is referring to a member of the family who came to visit and told us he had just been set on by marauders."

"So he said." Taggart blinked, digesting this information. "Had you ever seen him before?"

"I had not."

"He claimed to be a member of the family, you say.

Did he use a name with which you were familiar?"

"No." Aunt Hetty looked as if she had suddenly lost weight. Her head hung down.

"Why, then, did you accept him, ma'am?"

Clarissa took it upon herself to intervene. "No one could have listened carefully to my cousin without believing him, as I did when I found him, and I do at this time."

Aunt Hetty protested that her niece should not have to be heard in any proceeding of this nature. Taggart was looking consideringly into Clarissa's face even as he apologized to Aunt Hetty for doing what was necessary.

Clarissa was selective in telling the truth. She claimed that she had discovered Bryan on the road rather than at the inlet. As for his story which he had told their guests, Clarissa repeated it in such a way as to make it clear that she never considered doubting so much as one word.

Her true feelings would be of no interest to a captain of the light dragoons. She did not for a moment believe that Bryan Deverell was a French spy. Wasn't he so intelligent that he could see through Boney's cant and ambitions? A girl like herself certainly could. True, she didn't want to believe any horror about him, not after her strong response to his physical presence, his smile and strength and gallantry.

Taggart now asked, "Do you know where this man is to be found?"

If she repeated Deverell's fable about going off to Bodmin, the light dragoons would fan out over the countryside and possibly pick him up on foot.

"When I saw him last, he was at the stables helping my sister with one of the horses."

"How long ago was that?"

"Within the hour."

Taggart asked the pardon of everyone in the room before turning his back on them. From the window he shouted an order for one of his men to run out to the stables and find Miss—ah, Tregallen, of course—and her companion. At the last moment he decided to send two of his men on the mission.

At the very least, Clarissa could be grateful that she had persuaded Deverell to shake the earth of Narborne from his feet. The matter of a spy's identity would be cleared up in time and the very children in the road would be well aware that Bryan Deverell was innocent, a loyal subject of the King and his Regent.

She knew, even in her moment of triumph, that a difficulty might appear. When the dragoons who had been sent for Bryan returned empty-handed, Taggart would most likely order them to scour the countryside, which meant that Bryan might still be found and arrested ignominiously.

"I feel certain that we would all like to see the matter resolved," she began, showing far more coolness than she would have expected. "I can suggest a way to ensure greater speed in doing so."

"Pray do." Taggart's attention was caught.

"If my cousin is somewhere else on the property, I feel that a search for him should start in Narborne."

"You may rest assured that the tenant farmer enclaves will be covered in their entirety."

"Good." But not good enough for my purpose, Clarissa thought. "It does seem to me, however, that my cousin might have returned unseen to the main house itself, where he is staying. Therefore, a search for him should rightly begin here."

Aunt Hetty gasped. "I will not have soldiers, brutes, peering at my effects."

Phoebe Farrowmere avidly offered a suggestion. "I will accompany the men and go into every room first. When I leave I will be able to report whether Deverell is to be found there."

It was Squire Farrowmere's turn to look outraged. "I will not permit you to roam in the company of dragoons."

Judging from the glint in Phoebe Farrowmere's eyes,

she could have gotten her way with a vigorous argument. Because of the mass of people in earshot, she chose the way of compromise.

"I will ask Hope Carteret to accompany me."

The squire paused as if considering the matter, then glanced at his determined wife and nodded reluctantly.

Taggart said, "I will spare several men for that duty."

A small concession, Clarissa told herself, but it would result in a longer interval before the dragoons could mount a full-scale hunt for Bryan. Even a half-hour's delay was likely to help him.

Mainwaring said exultantly, "That rascal will soon be in chains."

Clarissa looked questioningly at the duke, but he didn't choose to clarify his remark. The duke was taking it for granted that Deverell's guilt or innocence would be established the minute the dragoons had him in sight, as if a French flag would be tattooed on his forehead.

"What His Grace means," Taggart explained thoughtfully, "is that the smuggler who was captured, and who I previously mentioned, is now in the company of my men at the west side of the house."

"A criminal?" Aunt Hetty was outraged yet again. "A known criminal has deliberately been brought to Narborne?"

"We have no intention of permitting him inside the main house, ma'am, you may rest assured of that much."

Taggart was extending himself to be helpful and courteous. "What we want is for him to look at the man. As soon as he does so, he will be able to tell us if Deverell is the one we seek."

The duke suddenly said, "Ahhh! Very soon now, very soon."

He was rubbing his hands and smiling as he looked out the window. Clarissa became aware of mounting apprehension as her eyes followed.

There was a slight rise near the main entrance to Narborne. Walking on this were two dragoons and

Maude. Her sister's head was turned, allowing her to speak with someone else.

Clarissa strained her eyes to make out the identity of the fourth person in the party. That face in profile was almost hidden by a darkening cloud, but she was able to see a male's broad shoulders and muscular build as he moved. The passing of that dark cloud permitted her to see his jet black hair. His appearance was far too familiar.

Rather than follow the best possible advice and take himself off, he had chosen to stay, to flirt with imprisonment and possible death. Bryan Deverell was cheerfully returning to Narborne, possibly to his doom.

Clarissa Tregallen keenly regretted the moment she had ever seen him. That regret continued to occupy her mind when the front door opened.

# Chapter Eight

"Miss Tregallen," said Deverell, pointing to Maude, "left the stable with me to assist one of the hounds who had acquired a stone in his paw. I am happy to say that we were successful in removing it."

Maude, having seen the dragoon uniform of Captain Taggart, was entirely elated.

"I had no idea that you could act so quickly after a crime was discovered," she said, smiling up at him.

Taggart, basking in approval, looked gratified. Instead of seeing a young woman with straight brown hair and rough, stubby fingers, he saw a shining-eyed young female who was blessedly shorter than he.

Clarissa responded to their mutual admiration with reluctant hostility, not able to help herself at this particular time.

"What on earth could you be talking about, Maude?"

"Why, this officer must have come to haul the tiger away to the assizes because it was the tiger who thrashed Spinner."

Clarissa did remember hearing her sister talking about the woe that had befallen one of the horses. In Maude's world, anything that happened to some animal was unequalled in importance.

"That infamy will never be forgotten," Clarissa said, "but it is not the difficulty we are here to discuss."

"I should have known," Maude said sulkily.

Taggart, not wanting to cause unhappiness to the younger girl, said, "We will discuss the matter with your tiger in time if you want my assistance in this, Miss— Maude is it? A lovely name. Perhaps it is because I have trapped so many humans in these last years, but I, too, feel considerable interest in the welfare of our dumb friends."

Maude only nodded, as if she could expect nothing less from a fellow human.

Taggart's voice was sharper when he looked away, not willing to be so thoughtful now.

"Your name is Bryan Deverell? Are you aware that a French spy landed ashore nearby late last night?"

The duke put in needlessly, "That was just before he appeared at Narborne."

"Indeed?" Bryan Deverell looked startled, his eyes wide, jaw slightly dropping in wonder. "The spy must have been aided by cohorts. Fellow conspirators must have waited for him and spirited him away."

"How could you know that, Deverell?"

"For the simple reason, captain, that I was set upon last night by more than one marauder, and those must be the fellows who did it. Unless, of course, there are clusters of law breakers loose in Cornwall every night. One group may be on its way to bring a spy in from the coast, another planning to rob someone for his money, a third on its way to do I don't know what."

It was the start of a long discussion in the form of questions and answers. Taggart would put forth some probe that didn't seem to allow room for evasion, then press for even more accurate details of Bryan's story. He confirmed several statements by pausing to question others in the library. If he missed any details given to him about Bryan's recent past, no one in this room but Deverell and Clarissa could have known.

Bryan responded with an appearance of openness. He could have passed for a young man trying to tell everything about the crime committed against him, willing to

74

answer any question put to him even if it didn't make sense.

Clarissa, watching him, didn't stop to tell herself that Bryan Deverell might be a traitor to his country or a Frenchman who spoke the Regent's English as if to the manor born. She saw a tall and handsome man who was having a great adventure. She shared in it, but only at second hand. It was impossible to keep from feeling envious.

Taggart, having developed a slight crick in his neck from looking up at Bryan Deverell, became quiet if only briefly. Clarissa realized soon enough that it would be a mistake to convince herself that this serpent had lost any of its cunning.

"I understand you to be saying, Deverell, that you feel all the miscreants should be made to suffer."

"Hanging would only be barely adequate," Bryan Deverell said. "I would prefer to see them executed in some mode that was popular during the Middle Ages."

"And it is your wish to encourage me and the light dragoons in helping such a wish to come to pass?"

Clarissa wanted to urge Bryan against committing himself further. Her breath would have been wasted.

"That is a point I have been trying to make over the last minutes," Bryan said patiently, falling that much more deeply into the trap.

Mainwaring, having grunted whenever Taggart spoke and made sounds of disapproval at every answer, was now smiling.

"In that case, Deverell, I am going to ask you to join me briefly."

"If it will help, I am only too glad to accompany you." Bryan straightened himself. He had been leaning against a bookshelf as he still couldn't remain on his feet too long.

"I appreciate your cooperation," Taggart said a little surprisingly, risking another crick in his neck to look up at Bryan. "You see, there were obviously other men on the ship that brought the spy to these shores. One of those men has been captured."

Clarissa's hands were tightly held down at her sides as if to help her from calling out with dismay. She knew the snare had been set. Worse yet, she didn't see how this device could possibly fail.

"That miscreant is waiting with my men at the western entrance to the building." Taggart sounded relieved now that the hunt was nearly at an end. As he had said not minutes before, he found no pleasure in the trapping of human beings.

The duke said drily, "The two of them will be able to exchange opinions."

Just as Bryan turned to the door, Clarissa called out, "Don't go!"

There was a moment of complete silence in which Aunt Hetty and the Farrowmeres as well as Taggart looked embarrassed. Maude, of course, didn't realize what had taken place because she was staring at the captain as if she had never seen a man before. Lady Winifred and her brother were most likely not capable of feeling discomfort, and it was impossible to guess at the vicar's feelings.

The duke spoke mildly when Lady Winifred gave a sniff of disapproval. "Miss Tregallen is a delicately nurtured young woman who cannot bear the idea of so unsettling an episode."

Clarissa wished she could have told Mainwaring flatly that never in his life had he been more mistaken.

Aunt Hetty smiled hesitantly at the duke. "That is so true, Your Grace. My dear girls have been kept sequestered from the world and its rough edges. I fear that such a circumstance as we face cannot but have a bad effect upon them."

"My apologies, Miss Tregallen and ma'am," the captain said, sparing a look for Maude before he left the library.

Clarissa had been unable to catch Deverell's eye for

one last look. Her despair over that matter was short-lived. Just as he reached the door, Bryan looked back quickly toward her and winked.

The wink was meant to be encouraging, to tell her that there was no cause for worry. No reason for optimism presented itself, either. Bryan Deverell was a man who would probably dance the Caledonian just before he went to the gallows.

At that last thought, Clarissa nearly called out again. How she managed to still the gasp she would never know.

The vicar left sadly, his head cast down.

Squire Farrowmere turned away shortly afterwards and said to his wife, "Let us take a turn about the drawing room, my dear."

Phoebe Farrowmere started to shake her head. The squire took her hand and applied pressure, however gentle. For once in the course of their marriage, it was his will which prevailed.

Lady Winifred, not having troubled to offer respects to anyone, was already mounting the stairs to her chambers. She wasn't bothering to raise her mauve day dress to keep its hem from drawing up dust. Either she wanted to give more work to her maid, Sybil, or she cared as little for her appearance as for the feelings of others.

The duke, of course, took the trouble to pay his respects to Aunt Hetty, to Maude, and to Clarissa. Only Aunt Hetty answered in kind.

With the Tregallen women alone in the library, Clarissa started to take to her heels.

Aunt Hetty trumpeted, "Where are you going?"

"I want to—" No lie occurred to her.

"Young woman, you cannot go out to the west entrance," Aunt Hetty said firmly. "Whatever takes place out there is men's business and does not concern us."

Maude, having picked up one of the numerous cats of Narborne and stroking it behind the ears, buried her face briefly in the tabby's fur.

"So handsome, so handsome," she murmured.

As the animal was female, it didn't seem that Clarissa's younger sister was speaking in its praise.

That was one of the many philosophical questions Clarissa was in no temper to pursue. She hesitated with a hand on the door.

Aunt Hetty sounded shocked by even the hint of impertinence.

Clarissa came back, the habit of years not entirely forgotten. She suddenly drew in her breath and hurried toward the window that faced the west side of Narborne.

"What are you doing now, child?"

"I wish to allow some fresh air into this room."

"There is absolutely quite enough air during Christmas week."

Maude came to her sister's support. "I agree with Clarissa, dear aunt. We could all use a little more of nature's clean air."

Aunt Hetty threw up her hands, but didn't leave the room. The sturdiest of guardians proceeded to the fireplace and stood close to it, not forgetting to look sternly at her nieces as she searched their features for added traces of rebellion.

Clarissa repaid the forbearance in part by turning to the window over the main entrance and swinging it shut. With that done, she turned to the window on the west side and flung it open.

Aunt Hetty said firmly, "You must not be seen or heard close to the window."

Clarissa obeyed again, but took no more than half a dozen small steps away. She made a point of facing the older woman.

"I hope that you are not indulging some vulgar curiosity," Aunt Hetty said carefully. "Young ladies must never do so."

Clarissa looked surprised. Hetty Tregallen was apparently well aware of what her nieces were doing even if she didn't know the reasons for their behavior. She was human enough to allow for young girls' curiosity, as well as her own. Most importantly, she didn't want to be showing her authority in an unreasonable way. It occurred to Clarissa that some once-young man had done himself a considerable disservice by not marrying Hetty Tregallen.

There was the sound of footsteps on yielding earth, louder than might have been expected.

The duke's voice could be heard first. When he was taking part in face-to-face conversation, he never sounded so keen, so alert.

"Here, you!" He might have been talking to a dog. "This is the spy!"

# Chapter Nine

Clarissa was shaking her head, trying to make it clear with every fraction of her will that the unseen witness must respond with a firm *no!*

Captain Taggart put in smoothly, "If I might be permitted to handle this interrogation, Your Grace."

Mainwaring coughed once, apparently to hide anger. He had remembered that he was supposed to be gracious and affable to social inferiors.

"Certainly, captain. Didn't mean to take over your duties. I just wanted to get this whole, ah, unpleasantness over and done."

"That will happen in good time, sir."

Clarissa noticed out of the corner of an eye that the moment her sister heard the captain's voice, Maude's spirits seemed to rise. She hugged the cat so tightly that it squeaked to be let free.

Taggart's voice was raised. "Now, Jossy, do you see the man who was on board the ship that brought you to the shore?"

"Yerss. I sees him."

The voice was high, and there was a whistle in it whenever its owner pronounced the letter *s*. Clarissa had dealt with tenants on Narborne often enough to know that the defect was caused by an absence of teeth and an unwillingness or inability to buy new ones.

As for what the rascal was saying, she had to accept

unvarnished truth. Certainly Deverell had been on the ship, but that wasn't a reason to doubt he was an Englishman and a patriot. But that, of course, was a question yet to be settled.

"Was he acting as a spy?" Mainwaring snapped, no longer able to show self-control.

"Yerss, Your Worship," the witness answered, taking it for granted that the duke was a local magistrate. "I 'ears 'im talkin' in frog when we're filling up the old ship."

"Aha!" The duke was triumphant. "You can take him away now, you men!"

"One moment, Your Grace, if you please," Taggart said smoothly. "I am sure you will appreciate that certain forms have to be followed. It makes a conviction that much more certain."

Clarissa was shaking her head over and over.

"Now, Jossy," said the captain, resuming the questioning. "Did you hear this man say anything about spying against Britain?"

"That I did not," the man Jossy responded, for once without that odious whistle to accompany his words.

"Do you know of anybody else who did hear him say anything of that sort?"

"No, I doesn't, but there 'e was! What other business could 'e 'ave on the ship if 'e 'adn't paid to be brought out 'ere?"

"Ah," said the duke approvingly. "Well reasoned, my man."

"Thank you, Your Worship."

Taggart said carefully, "Your presence on a smuggling ship does need some explaining, Deverell, and there remains a case to answer. For that reason, I am bringing you in to Bodmin."

Bryan spoke at last, sounding as if he were mildly amused. "I wonder if I might ask this man a few questions."

The duke exploded. "Of course not." Then, having considered, he added, "I have no wish to usurp your

81

functions, captain, but your duty at this time is entirely clear."

"Indeed it is, Your Grace." Taggart sounded as if every inflection had been washed out of his tones, perhaps by the recent rain but more likely by Mainwaring's high-handedness. "Ask your questions, Deverell, but do it quickly."

"Indeed I shall. First off, Jossy, I want you to look directly at me."

Clarissa hadn't realized that Bryan Deverell's voice was so strong. Not intimidating at all, but its pitch forced any listener to focus attention to the major point that was being considered. If he had been a speaker in Parliament, Clarissa found herself thinking, no session would drone on for weeks or months. Parliament would likely adjourn on the same day it met.

She was still encountering facets of his character, as she was becoming well aware, but this was no time for speculation.

He was speaking again. "Do you still claim that I am the person who was on a certain smuggling boat?"

" 'Strewth you were!"

"When was the last time you saw this person you think is me?"

"It was you, awright. Jemmy Smithers, 'e come up be'ind you when we was taking cargo out the ship, an' 'e 'it you so 'ard I figgered you for bein' in the choir with the angels."

Mainwaring sighed. No doubt he was wishing that Jemmy Smithers had been blessed with a stronger arm.

Clarissa, realizing that much, felt her teeth collide and start burrowing into their mates. She had never known it was possible to be so angry.

Taggart said, "It doesn't sound to me as if you have any more questions to ask, Deverell."

"Of course not!" Mainwaring once more. "Reserve a place for him on the gallows."

"Just one more moment, captain, if you will be so

82

kind," Bryan Deverell said calmly. "This man, Jossy, is making a mistake and I can prove it in a few more minutes."

The duke said instantly, "This is some sort of a trick, captain! You mustn't let yourself be gulled by the likes of a spy, a traitor."

Taggart, again apparently irritated by the duke's hurry to hang someone who must have made him angry in some way, said, "I think that I can allow Deverell a few more minutes without seriously affecting the course of justice in the realm."

The duke's opinion hadn't been asked and wasn't necessary, but no one could escape hearing it. "This is a mistake, captain, and I shall reluctantly take up the matter of your dereliction with your superiors."

"Your Grace is at liberty to do so," Taggart said. "Well, Deverell? Get on with any proofs if you have them to offer, man! You mustn't waste His Grace's time."

"I certainly wouldn't do anything like that," Bryan agreed, drawling. "Now, Jossy, you say that you saw me in various situations that make it probable I have betrayed my country. I, on the other hand, am convinced that I saw you just before I was struck on the head in the road late last night and my valuables were stolen from me."

" 'Old yer 'osses, now!"

"The more I think of it, the more I become absolutely certain you are one of those I saw by the moon's light. The same ferret face and squinty eyes and broken nose and receding chin. 'A human weasel,' I remember thinking to myself at the time, Jossy, just before I was set upon. The passing hours and a second meeting have not caused me to change my mind."

" 'Ere now, this hain't right!"

"As a smuggler, you are subject to few penalties because the population at large is sympathetic. But when it's proved that you have aided in the assault of a man whose social rank is higher, your career will not sail as smoothly (so to speak) as it has previously."

" 'Ere now, what's this? Gor! I never did nothin' like what 'e says. You have got to be fair with me, guv— Your Worship."

Deverell was speaking a little more quickly. "If I am accused of treason, I shall stand up in court and accuse you in turn of assault upon my person. One of us speaks the King's English and makes a good impression. One of us does not."

The duke protested swiftly. "This is a barefaced trick to intimidate your only witness, and it's been allowed to happen because you've given Deverell the time he needed."

"It would have happened otherwise, Your Grace, but this way Jossy is able to protect himself."

"And you miss the chance to send both men to the gallows, as they most assuredly deserve."

Bryan, ignoring the dialogue between officer and peer, asked, "Well, Jossy, what is it to be? Do you still recollect seeing me on the smuggling ship? Are you still absolutely sure I am the man you saw, the man who might have been a spy?"

Clarissa's spirits had been lifted with every word he spoke. Deverell *was* actually the man on board ship, but she felt more certain than ever that a man with such a skill at handling himself in an adventure, such a gift for easing himself out of a tight place, must have acted originally from the most exalted of motives. She couldn't think of one at the moment, but found herself feeling enormous confidence in the honesty of a man who was so verbally adroit, so physically handsome.

Mainwaring snapped at Jossy, "The truth, you verminous rascal! You'll get no mercy if you lie!"

"I'll get no mercy from Jack Ketch, either, beggin' Your Worship's pardon."

Deverell, having heard that title once too often, put in swiftly, "This man is a peer, but not a magistrate, Jossy. He has nothing to do in a courtroom."

84

The duke took time to let Taggart know that he could still rectify his error by taking both villains off to Bodmin and a fitting justice.

Jossy cleared his throat with a sound like a rock falling down the face of some cliff. "I wonder, sir, if I might get a closer look at you just to be absolutely sure if I'm not by any chance mistaken."

Taggart laughed.

The duke called out as though he had been wounded in battle.

Clarissa didn't hear the arguments that took place afterwards. She was beaming at Maude, who was satisfied to grin back.

"Isn't he the smart one?" Clarissa said admiringly, but in a low voice.

Another participant in the recent meeting had won Maude's admiration. "That officer isn't letting himself be trampled on."

Clarissa, thinking about her sister's personal feelings, said, "I suppose you're convinced that any trapped man should escape, just like an animal."

Maude looked briefly puzzled, not making the connection between human and animal. Probably it was just as well she didn't.

"This is a serious matter," said Aunt Hetty with the sternness of an Old Testament prophet.

"Indeed it is, Aunt," Clarissa agreed, and kept her face as straight as a poker.

Aunt Hetty escorted both young females up to their rooms to dress for supper. She said not a word.

Arrived in her own room, Clarissa sank down on the bed and prepared to enjoy the recollection of the recent occurrence. Her pleasure did not last long, being destroyed by a thought as unpleasant as it was painful: Bryan would not ever again appear at Narborne.

He was a brave man, Bryan Deverell, but not foolhardy. Knowing that he might face further danger on account of Mainwaring, Bryan would leave immediately. Narborne had seen the back of a fine man whose life was one long adventure.

It occurred to her that she might be able to talk with him once more, but she realized that he was likely to depart as soon as Captain Taggart went off with his dragoons.

The thought sent her to the window in hopes of seeing him at the west entrance. There was no sign of him. The dragoons, too, had returned to wherever they were stationed. She didn't see so much as a trace of wind causing one tree to stoop, one leaf to flutter. Without so much as another wink, he had departed from her life.

In the far future, a letter of thanks might be sent from him, intercepted by a glacial Aunt Hetty. Any letter addressed to Clarissa would be interdicted. Never would she have so much as a scrap of handwriting by which to remember him.

She sat down slowly at her mahogany desk, pushing away the foolscap and quill pen for composing her own letters. She added a book to the pile of foolscap, volume one of Miss Jane Austen's *Sense and Sensibility*. Like Aunt Hetty, she was inclined at the moment to say nothing favorable about any modern novel.

In a spasm of self-pity, she saw her future as a round of parties she would enjoy less and less. A time would come when her age would insure that she was no longer invited as one of the young females, but to help chaperone others. She and Maude would live out their days under one roof, Maude becoming further obsessed with the welfare of all animals and turning Narborne into a dry version of Noah's Ark. She could imagine no further life for either Maude or herself that wasn't bereft of the slightest joy.

Lizzie, the shrewd and lively maid, arrived in time to help Clarissa change for supper. Every suggestion that was put forward to assure a cheerful appearance was turned down by the listless young woman.

Some decision had to be made. "I will wear the cerulean."

"The blue? The cerulean blue? Beg pardon, Miss Clarissa, but you hate that cerulean."

True. Aunt Hetty had insisted on buying it for her. Having taken a dislike to it in part for that reason, she seldom wore the garment. That high neck and those infernal long puffed sleeves made her look like the hanging judge that Bryan Deverell might shortly have been facing.

Further consideration didn't result in her mind being changed. The grimness of that sardinian was entirely suitable for her current mood.

She rejected the opportunity to use lip gloss, disdained scent, and permitted only a brush-through of the auburn crown rather than a change of its current pattern, curled over the forehead and hanging down behind.

In a cheerless mood, as if on her way to a funeral, Clarissa walked downstairs. Like a participant in some mourners' procession, she passed the library, the drawing room, billiard room, and breakfast room.

She paused for a deep breath in the hall, looking impassively up at a suit of armor which had been mounted on a dais as if some medieval knight was on the verge of making a speech. As she turned the corner, she was facing the closed double doors of the dining room.

One prospective diner had gotten there first. Standing with perfect ease (was she truly surprised?) was none other than Bryan Deverell.

## Chapter Ten

Clarissa's first impulse was to whirl around and run upstairs to change her clothes, but it was already too late. His sharp hazel eyes had lighted with pleasure, and his lips thinned in a smile.

"Miss Tregallen," he said loudly for the benefit of anyone nearby, "how well you look!"

She managed to smile in return. When it came to an appreciation of clothes, she expected nothing but wrong-headedness from any man. There was, of course, the exceptional Mr. George Brummell of London town, but Aunt Hetty insisted discreetly that Mr. Brummell suffered from other flaws of character.

Deverell was wearing black, with a cravat so rigidly starched that it might have come out of a foundry. His knee buckles were of gold, his socks tan and his pitch black shoes half the size of most footwear for males. He certainly hadn't been togged in such splendor when taken by surprise near the smuggling ship.

"Where did you acquire all that?"

"These articles of wear are a loan from my good friend Aubrey, as he insists I refer to him from now on."

Clarissa had been sure that she could no longer be taken aback by occurrences involving Bryan Deverell. In this, she'd obviously been mistaken.

"Aubrey Seldon loaned those to *you?*"

"Yes, and they come close to being a good fit, I must

say. If you ask why Aubrey experienced a change of heart in his feelings toward me, I can only tell you that I have his assurances that he is gratified to know I am not, after all, the villain he expected me to be. In other words, he accepts the statement of Jossy that I wasn't the spy on that ship."

"Nonsense!" Clarissa said with spirit. "He is trying to lull you so that he may strike out at you yet again."

"I really cannot accept your strictures against Aubrey," Deverell said before lowering his voice. "Certainly not if they are spoken so loudly."

She brushed his remark to one side. Now that he was free of danger from the hangman, at least for the moment, she wanted to quarrel with him. He'd had no reason not to quit Narborne when she clearly warned him against staying longer.

"Why didn't you leave?" she whispered fiercely. "I assured you of the urgency, but you ignored me. Look what almost happened as a direct result!"

There was an expression in his eyes she had never seen in anyone but a parent. "If you don't understand that much, Clarissa," he said softly, "I marvel at you."

She wasn't sure what he meant, but felt herself flush from the neck upwards. Over the next minute, remembering how warmly he had kissed her, it was impossible to speak. She found herself flushing more deeply at remembered pleasure.

The sound of footsteps was coming lightly toward the turn in the hall. She took advantage of the moment and said in a low tone, "You came back a second time after knowing you might be in further peril."

Once again, his eyes filled with that look of amused tenderness. Clarissa turned away, unable to look at him and breathe evenly at the same time.

"There you are!"

It was Aunt Hetty who made an appearance. In spite of her weight she stepped deftly between Clarissa and Deverell.

"You are looking very well," she said to her niece. "You don't wear that rig near often enough, and it does wonders for you."

"Thank you, Aunt."

Clarissa stepped to one side in order to see Deverell and her aunt at the same time. She moved just as Hetty wheeled around.

"I am a plain-speaking woman, Mr. Deverell, and I must tell you that I am angered by your having played the courtier for my other niece."

"For—Maude?" He recovered quickly. "I can assure you that I had no such intention."

"I have warned Maude against you, explaining that you are married, with a wife in Jamaica."

"Another secret of mine has been brought into the light of day, it would seem." Deverell's glance at Clarissa took less than a moment. "Dear Clytemnestra!"

"I beg your pardon."

"My wife's name."

"Indeed! Her family must have been rather eccentric in its taste for nomenclature."

Clarissa realized that opportunity was knocking loudly. "Be that as it may, Aunt, I feel that Mr. Deverell, cousin though he is, has behaved in a way that is unacceptable in the boundaries of a family."

"Agreed, my dear. I wholly agree."

"Indeed, Bryan Deverell has betrayed every known principle of hospitality and should be asked to leave Narborne immediately."

"I am delighted by your good sense and heartily concur." Aunt Hetty drew herself up, and the square neckline of her bib-front evening dress quivered in reflection of her anger. "Mr. Deverell, you are to leave Narborne without delay."

Deverell did no more than shrug. "In that matter, ma'am, though I respect your feelings, I very much fear that I cannot carry out your wish."

Aunt Hetty would have drawn herself up even further

if that had been possible.

"I demand to know why not."

"Because, ma'am, after the confrontation at the west entrance, I was put under orders by Captain Taggart."

"Orders? What kind of orders?"

"The captain clearly instructed me to stay at Narborne until matters are cleared up in regard to the missing spy. I may add that I told him that staying at Narborne as long as necessary would be a great honor for me."

"And if you are forbidden to stay?"

"The captain indicated that if I leave before being permitted to, I will be hunted down like a mad dog. My blood will be on your head and Miss Clarissa's, I regret to say."

"Must I, then, entertain a guest against my clearly expressed will?"

"I have often been told about Cornwall hospitality," Deverell said blandly. "I must say that it is an experience."

Clarissa, who was used to Bryan Deverell's skills at improvisation, made a contribution. "I suggest, Aunt, that you send one of the footmen to the dragoon barracks, where he will be able to speak with Captain Taggart and learn whether or not we have just been subjected to a fable."

At which point the venerable butler, Creddon, barely managed to open the double doors of the dining room.

"If it pleases you," he quavered, "supper is on the table."


During this meal, almost everyone was under a strain.

Aunt Hetty, her face made pale by the Chinese lanterns suspended from the ceiling, spoke little. The duke smiled impartially to all, but wouldn't speak unless someone addressed him. Lady Winifred didn't utter a word, but kept a hand out toward the nearest vase as if to keep her body in balance.

The neighbors were no more at ease. Phoebe Farrowmere's attempts to make conversation with anyone but the duke and Clarissa were politely rebuffed. Even the squire looked embarrassed. Mr. Carteret, the vicar, was used to awkward situations and distracted himself by murmuring quotations from the *Book of Common Prayer*. Mrs. Carteret looked down at the food self-effacingly.

Maude's attitude caused others to feel awkward. She was in one of those occasional fevers during which she wouldn't eat meat. She waved away the haunch of venison, the boiled capons, and the fricandeau of veal. It was possible to make do with sea kale, asparagus, a cheese soufflé, a charlotte russe, and strong hot pekoe tea. Experience reminded her that she would receive the rough edge of Aunt Hetty's tongue if she tried to publicly justify her predilection.

Two of the diners, however, appeared totally at ease. Deverell ate as if enjoying every mouthful. Clarissa, unwilling to show that his presence was disturbing, tried to do the same. She made a point of not looking directly at him, although she couldn't help it if she saw his image in one of the silver wall mirrors which reflected the scene. She spoke warmly to Mrs. Farrowmere and showed politeness to the duke, an act which didn't seem to stir any jealousy in Bryan Deverell.

She happened to be looking in the mirror again as Deverell smiled. She wasn't the one who was being shown that recognition. Nor was it any other female at whom he was looking. Glancing swiftly around the table she saw the answering smile on the Duke of Mainwaring's face, as if each were sharing some knowledge of which no one else had any inkling.

It occurred to Clarissa, after a slight chill, that she wouldn't have wanted someone smiling at her with that particular unwholesomeness, like two fighting cocks examining each other.

* * *

Mainwaring walked into the drawing room with the other men after twenty minutes together over brandy. He noted that Clarissa was speaking to the bubbly Mrs. Farrowmere, then turned to the nearest female. In this case it was his sister.

Lady Winifred, seated by herself, of course, opened her eyes at his approach.

"I assume that you are planning to deal further with that man Devilment or whatever his name is."

The duke made sure that the man in question was on the other side of the room speaking with Mrs. Carteret. "I have no specific plans as yet."

"Something will come to you," Lady Winifred remarked. "Looking forward to such a confrontation, my dear Aubrey, gives a certain salt and savor to the joyous holiday season."

"And for me," the duke admitted frankly. "But I can remember when your primary interest in life was to find a polished exclusive of the *ton* who was suitable to marry you."

Lady Winifred couldn't deny that her brother's arrow had found its mark. "With the passing of time, one's interests change."

She smiled as he started to turn away, taking her revenge by speaking to his back. "That man, Deverell—"

"So you do know his name!" Mainwaring turned back long enough to say sneeringly.

"—is not as frivolous by nature as he may appear. Judging from today's little adventure, he is not nearly as vulnerable, either. Who is to say that he might not exact revenge?"

The duke gave one of his nastier smiles. "What a delightful Christmas the both of us are having," he said.

Aunt Hetty drew Clarissa to one side. "Before the night's entertainment begins," she said quietly, "let me ask you something."

"Of course, Aunt."

"I want to know whether you are interested in that . . . Deverell man."

Clarissa eyed her aunt warily, putting off the answer.

"I saw your face when he was with the dragoon captain, but your feelings became far more clear to me in the hallway before supper," Aunt Hetty proceeded. "When you looked at him, it was as if you were looking at the gates of heaven."

"I can assure you, Aunt, that I want Bryan Deverell away from Narborne as soon as may be."

"Very well. Now that I have been answered indirectly, permit me to remind you of something. Both you and your sister face a lifetime of unhappiness if you remain as you are. A husband is more effective than a warming pan, Clarissa. The best hope for both of you is if you make a brilliant match. Aubrey Seldon is certainly available for that purpose."

"The dastardly duke?" It was a name that Clarissa occasionally used in conversation with Maude, but had never before dared to speak before Hetty Tregallen. The presence of Deverell was enough to bring out her impulsive side.

"As the wife of a peer of the realm, as Lady Mainwaring, you have a chance to find a suitable match for your dear sister. You know perfectly well that unless influence is brought to bear, Maude may go through life as a useless woman."

"I see."

Aunt Hetty had spoken similarly in the past, but never before had Clarissa been struck so forcibly by the thought. Looking at Maude in a badly-fitting gown and too-large shoes, watching her broadly imitate a farm animal, Clarissa saw proof beyond doubt that her angelic guardian had spoken nothing less than the truth.

She turned to her aunt, features stricken by remorse, but stubbornness, too. She wanted to say that the price for Maude's future happiness was more than any devoted sister should have to pay.

Those bitter words were due to remain unspoken, though. Hetty had raised her voice to address the guests.

"My dear niece, Clarissa, at the specific request of the Duke of Mainwaring, has agreed to entertain us on the pianoforte."

Aunt Hetty interposed herself between Deverell and the musical instrument, giving the duke a clear field to walk up beside Clarissa and turn the pages while she played.

As she was interpreting one of John Stevenson's melodies, a modest interruption took place. The sight of Jamison, the underbutler, approaching Aunt Hetty on tiptoes was the distraction she needed. Clarissa happened to love music and this instrument in particular, but lacked the strength in her hands to play with the best effect. Maude's fingers had the necessary strength and span, but the possibility of making beautiful music left her indifferent.

Clarissa stood after the third selection, accepting polite applause from everyone but Lady Winifred. The duke, of course, paid warm compliments.

Maude was now called upon to entertain. The guests were polite while she read aloud from one of Sir Walter Scott's greatest poems. Judging from her own feelings at Maude's clumsiness, it wasn't only the Lady of Shalott upon whom the curse had come.

She left the drawing room to locate her aunt and saw Hetty coming out of the billiard room. Her usually placid features seemed downcast and as she walked she was shaking her head grimly.

"I have just spoken to Penwallis, the underfootman," Aunt Hetty said. "It was he who was sent by Creddon for an interview with Captain Taggart."

"You sound as if Penwallis failed to bring the news we wanted to hear."

"Indeed. Taggart admitted that he warned Bryan

95

Deverell against incurring severe penalties by leaving Narborne without permission."

Clarissa found herself responding with different feelings, each opposed to the other. On the one hand, it could be fatal for Deverell to become a guest at any different location. But he seemed able to keep an alert eye on his own interests, meaning that it was the Duke of Mainwaring who could very well find himself exposed to unpleasant consequences.

She walked back to the drawing room with uncertain steps.

It didn't seem at first that the night's social hours would turn out suitably. The duke and Deverell played against each other in the game of whist that followed Maude's reading. Deverell was the partner of Lady Winifred, who had been silently ordered by her brother to join the table. Clarissa found herself at the duke's side. It was an arrangement, she suspected, that Aubrey Seldon had determined upon. Somehow he had again gotten exactly what he wanted.

The duke was doomed to disappointment if he expected the game to follow a pattern of constant victory for his side. He was particularly set on winning any hand in which the suit of hearts became trumps. The first time it happened, Deverell and Lady Winifred took the trick easily.

"You play in a capable manner," Lady Winifred was moved to admit to her partner.

"With you on my side, Lady Winifred, it is easy to look capable."

Clarissa had noted that after the first pair of tricks, Deverell apparently understood the pattern of Lady Winifred's play and was able to gait himself so that they were indeed formidable. Clarissa would have been feeling antagonism to the ancient spinster in her early thirties, but was more concerned that an aura of peace

96

prevail at the table. It was too much to expect outright camaraderie.

The duke made a point of accepting victories with modesty, and congratulating his sister and Deverell on their six victories. The great test of his forbearance came after the thirteenth and deciding trick. Again hearts were trumps. After some hard and anxious play, the trick and game were taken by Lady Winifred and Deverell.

The duke rose slowly from the table. He may have been aware that the Carterets and the Farrowmeres, having finished their own game, were watching warily. Aunt Hetty had paused on her way to a chair. (Maude, of course, had celebrated the completion of her ordeal of reading aloud by a swift rush out to the animals.)

"That was well played," Mainwaring admitted through lips that had become stiff.

"You and Miss Tregallen are foes worthy of our steel," Deverell responded, after a pause that may have been brief but was noticed by all.


Clarissa looked out her window at a typical Cornwall winter morning. There was no trace of wind. It hadn't rained, and rain looked unlikely. A wedge of December sunlight peeped out behind a cloud that was shaped and colored like last night's charlotte russe. A miracle for the day before Christmas!

It added to her feeling that these few days might proceed in a civilized manner.

Last night had ended pleasantly, the ladies going off to bed at about ten-thirty. The gentlemen had been left in the smoking room. Clarissa had felt concern that there might be some eruption between the antagonists, but no voices were raised. She slept fitfully, but the mirror confirmed that she looked rested.

The feeling of serenity stayed with Clarissa while Lizzie helped her out of silk and into sprigged muslin. Because she felt contented, she agreed to let Lizzie comb her hair in a slightly different style. Lizzie had a gift for combing a woman's hair, and was often asked by Aunt Hetty to do it for her. Maude showed not the slightest interest.

"Do you really think this looks attractive?" Clarissa asked, staring into the glass. Her auburn hair had been drawn back, exposing her ears before ending in a long coil.

"Men care for it, Miss Clarissa."

It was no surprise that such a consideration should dictate Lizzie's choice of a hair setting. It was even less of a surprise that the maid sounded as if she were experienced in the matter.

"Why do they care for it, Lizzie?"

"It gives a girl the appearance of having had it freshly combed for the morning, and that she'll change it for the afternoon. It has a feel of the morning about it, if you know what I mean."

"And you tell me that men find such a feeling desirable?"

"Oh, yes, Miss Clarissa."

She had to bite her tongue to keep from asking for a clarification. The strong conviction came to her that it wasn't a maid who should give her the answer.

Clarissa came downstairs looking eagerly from right to left in hopes of seeing some male and hearing a reaction to the temporary coiffure. She suddenly paused in alarm at the sight of the captain who stood ill at ease in the large square hall. Had he come back to do some harm to Deverell?

# Chapter Eleven

Capt. Roderick Taggart showed no interest in Clarissa's hair. He looked restless, glancing behind her and drawing his lips together when he had turned and seen no other person in the hall.

Jamison, who had let him in, noted Clarissa's nod and returned to his various duties.

"Perhaps I may have a moment of your time, captain."

"Of course, Miss Tregallen."

She led the way into the drawing room, which was otherwise unoccupied. He stood, giving Clarissa one more opportunity to examine the superlative posture with which he tried to make up for a lack of substantial height.

She promptly brought the conversation to the subject on her mind.

"Have you come to find Mr. Deverell?"

The captain looked startled, his sharp eyes widening. "Oh yes, to be sure. I happened to be passing and I thought I would take the opportunity."

"You can be sure that he has remained at Narborne as you instructed him to do."

"Oh yes, yes." Was he disconcerted again? If so, it didn't often happen.

"Perhaps you should make certain that he is well," Clarissa mused aloud. "The duke is far from being kindly disposed toward him, no matter what he might say to the contrary. The duke thinks highly of taking extreme vengeance for a trivial slight."

Taggart allowed himself a smile. "Mr. Deverell cannot only protect himself, but give back as good as he may get. The man is quick-witted."

"Then you want him billeted here (no other word would do) to provoke a small-scale war with the duke."

"No, of course not."

Clarissa felt that her silence would be an effective retort.

The captain's attention was elsewhere. He turned briefly to look out the half-open door as if he expected to see someone else.

Clarissa drew a sudden breath in surprise. An explanation for the captain's behavior had occurred to her. She was inclined to put it to the test.

"Perhaps Mr. Deverell has joined the others for breakfast. Would you care to see?"

"I don't want to cause any disturbance, Miss Tregallen, but on the other hand—"

"If you haven't yet eaten, perhaps you will join us, too."

An officer who was more aware of his social position would have responded differently. He'd have refused politely, saying that he didn't want to make anybody uncomfortable. Then he'd have apologized for coming inside the house without being asked and say that he'd wait outside for Mr. Deverell to speak with him at the latter's convenience.

Captain Taggart smiled gratefully. "I would be honored to take tea."

The breakfast room, with windows facing west and south, was the brightest on the lower floor of Narborne. Mrs. Carteret had left the dark mahogany sideboard with a platter of eggs and bacon, and a mug of steaming tea, intended for the vicar who was sitting with other diners at the bright mahogany table. Mrs. Farrowmere and the squire stood together at the sideboard, putting food on plates.

Aunt Hetty's surprise at the sight of the visitor didn't last long. She nodded and approached the captain, who made his apologies after a quick look around.

Clarissa said pointedly, "I'm afraid Mr. Deverell isn't here yet."

Taggart's attention was on the door and stayed with the new arrival, who happened to be Clarissa's younger sister.

Maude's day dress was buttoned from the top down, for once. She had made attempts to smooth out her brown hair. Graciously, she greeted aunt and sister and the married guests. At sight of Taggart, she smiled shakily and flushed before speaking.

"Captain Taggart."

"Miss Maude."

*Miss Maude.* As if the two of them were social equals.

Clarissa raised a forefinger to her lips to prevent Aunt Hetty from expressing disapproval at the military man's presumption.

"Captain Taggart, you must take a plate before you can eat."

"Yes, of course." He didn't move, though, and Maude put a bone white plate into his left hand. He forgot or didn't care that he had assured Clarissa and Aunt Hetty, too, that he would accept nothing but tea.

"You must take some of the kippers. Mrs. Rankin always goes to special pains with them."

"Thank you, Miss Maude."

"And the ham is generally splendid."

"Thank you."

"Do you prefer boiled eggs or soft?"

"Yes, Miss Maude."

"One boiled, then, and one soft. You must take four or five muffins. They're hot."

Taggart offered his thanks yet again.

"Do you like strawberry jam? Splendid, so do I. And the butter comes directly from Blossom, who gave birth

101

only last night — no, the night before."

One would have thought that Maude, of all people, was obsessed with food. Clarissa had anticipated what might happen, but if Blossom the cow had suddenly learned the waltz, Aunt Hetty could hardly have been more surprised.

Deverell walked in quietly as the captain was saying his fifth or sixth or seventh thank-you. He was unnoticed by anyone except Clarissa, and no comment was made when he reached the sideboard and took nothing more than a mug of hot chocolate.

Clarissa and Aunt Hetty were talking once again about Clarissa's future and, on this occasion particularly, the future of her sister. This talk was taking place in the yellow and gray barouche with two up, the carriage in which the Tregallens took gift baskets to their tenants on the day before Christmas.

The talk began in spite of Clarissa's best efforts. She had tried to avoid conversation by looking pensively at the vacant space next to her in the carriage.

"Maude wouldn't let herself be talked out of spending time with the animals," Aunt Hetty sniffed, interpreting that pensive look correctly. "She departed with that dragoon officer to show them to him."

"He was glad to accompany her," Clarissa pointed out gently, resigned to yet another discussion about young spinsters and their goals. "He has genuine feeling for animals."

"He'd better have, if he wants to be noticed by your sister. And nothing else matters to her, except that she now also seems to have lost her head over a uniform."

Clarissa didn't point out that the uniform in question was occupied by a man. Aunt Hetty might not have swooned at an observation that verged on bawdiness, but she would certainly have been discomposed.

"I have been told nothing about her feelings," Clarissa

pointed out.

"But you have observed her, and so have I."

There was no time for Clarissa to nod in agreement. Several feet after the carriage passed a manx cat on its way up a tree, they came to a stop before the property that was tenanted by Granny Fletcher and her sons, daughters, and grandchildren.

The visitors were greeted with respect as they gingerly entered the thatched cottage with its squeaky floor and shabby furnishings. Clarissa knew that every house had its own distinctive odor, but in the homes of Narborne tenants the odors were so strong that she felt she could almost reach out and touch them.

The basket was given over and thanks and season's greetings offered. Conversation between Aunt Hetty and Granny Fletcher concerned health and the marriages of both Tregallen girls, which Granny hoped she would live long enough to see.

On their way back to the carriage, Clarissa couldn't help asking, "Is there a great difference in age between you and Granny Fletcher?"

"No more than eight or ten years, I think." Aunt Hetty saw the chance to repeat a previous lesson. "You see what happens to a woman without her husband."

"Granny Fletcher is a widow," Clarissa pointed out more tartly than she had intended. "Her back is bent because she spent many years in hard toil."

Aunt Hetty was silent, but discussion of Maude resumed as soon as the carriage was once more underway.

"Maude has made an unsuitable choice of a young man in whom to show interest, Clarissa. You must admit that much."

"The interest may soon fade, Aunt."

"Possibly, but Maude is not one to freely give of her affections. At least, not to another human. She is no coquette."

"It is a hopeful sign that she is showing interest in a male."

Clarissa should have known better than speak optimistically.

"As a match, he is impossible," Aunt Hetty snapped. "If he had any important social connections, relatives would have purchased a commission for him in the army and he could be sulking in his tent while the troops fight with that Corsican."

No answer suggested itself to Clarissa.

"It leads me to believe that he may be after money such as she will have when she reaches her majority."

"Maude will know if his feelings are genuine," Clarissa said firmly and confidently. "My sister is unworldly in some respects, but no one will ever fool her about the degree of caring for beasts, which would be the strongest common interest between her and any prospective husband. It would be difficult for that reason to fool her about other important matters."

"Let us assume that this underling's feelings for your sister are genuine, Clarissa. Let us be crazed with generosity and assume further that he cares nothing for the needful, that he wishes to marry your sister for love alone and that he would make Maude as happy as one of her own birds."

"I am willing to assume all that, dear Aunt."

"Certainly you are, Clarissa, because you are not responsible enough to make certain that Maude's future and your own will be suitable."

Clarissa flushed and looked down in embarrassment at her white-gloved hands.

"Furthermore, even on those terms, you are not anticipating the greatest difficulty which would lie ahead."

No details about this obstacle could be offered until respects had been paid to the Wadley family and suitable apologies made, as before, over Maude's absence.

"The difficulty," said Aunt Hetty almost as soon as she and Clarissa had been helped back into the carriage and resumed their places, "is quite simply going to be posed by the duke."

Clarissa wasn't surprised, having already imagined the duke's likely reactions. Her aunt didn't know that the images could offer considerable pleasure.

"The Duke of Mainwaring will certainly think carefully before marrying into a family in which his wife's sister may plight her troth with a mere officer in the dragoons."

Clarissa decided to take the path of honesty. "If those are the duke's feelings, I think I can somehow face the prospect of being rejected by him."

"And you intend to live out what is left of your years with a warming pan in your bed instead of a husband?"

"That is not so."

Aunt Hetty fell silent, remembering the high spirits of her own long-ago youth. "Clarissa, you have great confidence in your ability to find the perfect man."

"Time will prove whether or not I am right," Clarissa remarked, making sure that the image of a certain man didn't come to mind.

"And you have a candidate for the situation?" Aunt Hetty's talent for divining the thoughts of her nieces still flourished. "It is that—that spy."

Clarissa herself didn't know if her aunt's guess was the truth. "Cousin Bryan is a visitor whom I have only just met."

"My opinion is that you are carried away by a sense of adventure which Bryan Deverell wears the way other men wear cloaks," Aunt Hetty said, with more perception than her niece expected. "You will have to realize that romance is not love or marriage."

"Very well, Aunt."

"I am doubtful of your not wanting to be a duchess. Perhaps it is only a young woman's first frightened response to the prospect of a future that involves . . . being settled."

"Perhaps, Aunt."

"However, there is a difference between a future as a duchess and a future with some night bird."

"Yes, Aunt."

"I hope that you marry a man who will make you happy, Clarissa. I am convinced that your feelings about Bryan Deverell are entirely wrong, but I hope that all may work out for you with someone worthy, and am prepared to help in any eventuality."

Clarissa smiled warmly and reached out a gloved hand to press the back of the older woman's hand.

"Dear Aunt," she said fondly.

Christmas dinner was always the occasion for which Mrs. Rankin felt she earned her generous salary of thirty pounds a year. For Christmas Eve, too, her cooking was at its showiest.

Roast goose and turkey were offered along with sea kale. The meat dishes were garnished with rosemary and bay. A mince pie with tongue, chicken, and egg was the final delight before a fruit pudding that rivaled some mythical beast in size.

"That was splendid," said the Duke of Mainwaring after the last sip of hot orange pekoe. "There is a saying that one should always be a little hungry when drawing back from the table, but your cook makes it extremely difficult to follow that advice."

"Thank you," said Aunt Hetty, eyes downcast as if accepting praise for a meal she herself had cooked.

Lady Winifred's praise consisted in not conveying disapproval.

Squire Farrowmere had overindulged, but it was his good wife who had drawn a mild reproof by eating little. As for the Carterets, they had returned to the vicarage where the vicar could add finishing touches to his Christmas Day sermon.

Bryan Deverell, dressed in the rig-out he had been offered by the duke, was letting his eyes roam over the others. They lingered on Clarissa.

The duke, observing that most of Deverell's fruit pudding remained on his plate, was moved to an observation he considered amusing. "Do you fear poison, Mr. Deverell?"

"Not any more than I fear obesity," Bryan Deverell replied.

Squire Farrowmere lifted his brows, which may have been all he could raise after his meal. "I hope I am not being indirectly taken to task for being a good trencher-man."

"Not at all, sir," Deverell smiled. "As a young fellow I was on the heavy side and learned that a man shouldn't butter his bread on — ahem! — bloat sides."

"A worthy riposte, sir," said Squire Farrowmere. "The point is made to good effect, we all smile, and no one takes offense. You have the skills of a diplomat."

Deverell's lips were briefly pursed, and he blinked rapidly to hide that brief burst of annoyance.

"Mr. Deverell does indeed eat sparsely if not always with wisdom," Clarissa said, giving him another moment to recover his poise. "Breakfast, judging by his actions this morning, consists wholly of hot chocolate."

The duke said mildly, "You not only observed him, but what you saw has not left your memory."

There was no change in his tone, but Clarissa saw the hands quick to make fists.

Aunt Hetty intervened. "Ladies, we shall leave the gentlemen to their port wine."

Clarissa felt confident that at least two of the men looked closely at her slender bare arms and tight waist in the brocade with its faint yellow stripes. It wasn't cut low at the neckline as she'd have preferred, but among her rig-outs, this dress for evening remained her very favorite.

She paused briefly in front of the closed dining-room door. No man's voice was raised, nor was there any sound of flesh striking flesh.

More slowly than the others, Clarissa proceeded to the drawing room.

Mrs. Farrowmere didn't speak until she was certain that Lady Winifred was sitting in a monopodium chair out of earshot.

"What do you suppose the gentlemen will be saying to each other?" She leaned forward eagerly.

The thought hadn't been out of Clarissa's mind since she left the dining room, but in response to the direct question she was silent.

Maude looked mildly puzzled. She had insisted on wearing green, not heeding the opinion of sister or aunt that it didn't become her. The choice of gown was a gesture of defiance brought on by Aunt Hetty's firm refusal to issue a Christmas dinner invitation to Captain Taggart of the light dragoons.

"They will behave like gentlemen who are visiting in someone's home," Aunt Hetty said coolly. "This is the season of peace and goodwill."

"But you saw how angry the duke was!"

"If any difficulty should materialize, I am certain that your capable husband will act as peacemaker."

Phoebe Farrowmere looked as if she wanted to put in a few disparaging words about her husband's abilities. Under Aunt Hetty's glacial gaze, the impulse fled.

"I'm sure you are right," Phoebe admitted, but she sounded regretful.

The men arrived before twenty minutes had passed. The duke's fine features showed strain, but his breath came evenly. Bryan Deverell, walking behind him, looked up approvingly at the hanging mistletoe and the inevitable bay leaves and rosemary, not caring that they caused the indoors to have a scent which resembled the outside on a spring day. Only Squire Farrowmere, hurrying to catch up, looked tense around the eyes. His normal sun-tinged features were a little gray with tension.

Aunt Hetty attempted to ignore the antagonism which hung in the air, as plain to see as the decorations.

"I believe it is time to exchange gifts," she said.

The Duke of Mainwaring looked sharply at that other young man in the room, unable to help himself. It seemed clear the sort of token he would have liked to have given Bryan Deverell.

There was an interruption from outside. This took the form of a clearing of throats, perhaps a dozen of them. The servants had gathered — dairymen and coachmen, grooms, butler and underbutler, footmen and underfootmen, valet, gardener, ladies' maids and laundry maids, kitchen maid and scullery maid, all joined for the annual caroling.

"God Rest Ye Merry, Gentlemen" sounded out. One would have expected the Pendarren brother and sister, Jem and Lizzie, to carry the melody, but Clarissa knew from experience, it was Creddon and Mrs. Rankin who were most clearly heard no matter what was sung.

The first selection was followed (at a considerable distance, what with more time for throat-clearing and whispered discussion about what to sing next) by "Deck the Halls," "Good King Wenceslas," and "The Holly and the Ivy." A pause indicated that the proceedings were about to take a more serious tone. "Adeste Fideles" ended the performance.

When the servants had been thanked, Aunt Hetty suggested firmly that it was time for giving out the gifts.

All but one in the room began busily taking packages from the rows against the southwest wall. Deverell didn't move. It was understood that he failed to take part because he hadn't had time to make any purchases.

"I understand that the Westphalians keep their Christmas gifts under small trees in their homes."

The duke responded to Deverell's tone of admiration. "Barbaric people!"

The ladies were busily exchanging accessories to go with clothing. Fur muffs, shawls, hats and feathers were happily received and given. The men, except for Deverell, received opera glasses and a two-ounce bottle of almond-flavored orgeat.

The duke noted idly that Lady Winifred had looked at her gifts without touching them and then put the boxes down to one side. Clarissa Tregallen's behavior wasn't much better in regard to the gift he had given her. The perfume fountain ring had been accepted and thanks spoken, but it hadn't been put on a finger. To his mind, the drawing room of Narborne was overflowing with females who accepted gifts somewhat gracelessly.

There would be an exception, however, he was certain.

"For one person I have not put down a gift," he said, "but I do have something for Miss Maude Tregallen, and it is of a special nature."

Without asking permission, he rang the bell three times. There was a soft knock at the door and his valet appeared with a crate held by a handle. From inside the crate there issued a series of animal noises.

Maude smiled as the crate was given to her. She opened it eagerly. A brown and white spaniel puppy bounded out, took one look at the delighted young woman, and started to lick her face.

It was a sight that moved Clarissa and Deverell to hearty laughter. Mr. and Mrs. Farrowmere looked vaguely bemused. Aunt Hetty urged Maude to thank His Grace and keep the beast quiet. Only Lady Winifred turned away in disgust.

The duke smiled coolly, as if he were looking at himself in a glass. He expected that he would at last be sincerely thanked by one of the Tregallen sisters. Maude's happy gratitude was more than likely to shame Clarissa.

When Maude looked up she was dewy-eyed with happiness. All she said was, "Roderick will love him, too."

## Chapter Twelve

*Clarissa and Deverell were alone in a glade. Greenery surrounded them — grass grew hip-high, trees bulged with leaves. Wildflowers presented a kaleidoscope of colors and variety: bluebells, cowslips, Solomon's seal, white thorn, wild cherry blossom, stitchwort, trumpet-shaped convolvulus, and speedwell, white traveler's joy, poppies, and forget-me-nots. Every flower seemed to be displaying Clarissa's favorite colors.*

*Bryan Deverell took her in his powerful arms, his head lowering to hers. For the hundredth time, they exchanged passionate kisses and she could feel his strong but gentle hands moving, moving . . .*

She was in her room alone when she awakened. After a moment's regret, she recalled with amusement that her dream had not been precise about which of her dresses she was wearing for the great occasion.

Clarissa didn't linger in bed. She rose and pulled back the half-curtains on her window. The morning deserved to be inspected. Bare trees and earth glistened with overnight rain, but the morning sun would soon cause the moisture to dry and result in a Christmas day that would be notably pleasing. To mark this day contentedly was no more than the world deserved.

Her brief reverie was interrupted by the sound of barking and the tap of knuckles against her door. She guessed easily who was on the other side.

Maude's new cocker spaniel, followed by Maude entered the room. Her sister's brown hair was in the usual morning disarray, and she was wearing an unlovely nightgown that might have withstood the bite of a gorgon, let alone a spaniel puppy.

"You will have to send the dog away, Maude, if you want to talk."

That took time, but was eventually accomplished. "Isn't it sad to think that in the future he will want to sleep for most of the day?" Maude said wistfully.

Looking around at the wreck of her usually tidy quarters, Clarissa wasn't at all saddened.

"I don't have a name for him yet," Maude continued. "You have to know an animal's temper before you can give him or her a suitable name."

"Absorbing as all this is," Clarissa said drily, "you don't generally come in at such a time to discuss the care of pets. Something else is in your mind."

"Quite right," Maude nodded. "Clarissa, you must teach me how to dress well."

Several sarcastic remarks hovered on the tip of Clarissa's tongue. She herself hadn't been impressed by Capt. Roderick Taggart's handsomeness but Maude had been deeply stirred.

"How much time can I take to accomplish this miracle?" she asked calmly.

"Time? Clar, dearest Roderick told me that he plans to visit Narborne this afternoon and I simply must look my best for him."

"I'm not sure what can be done in so short a period."

Her sister's wardrobe was made up of ill-fitting and inappropriately colored garments. Maude had always been too occupied by other matters to clothe herself with any competence.

"You can offer me the loan of a dress for the afternoon."

"I am so glad to hear you talk about clothes in a favorable manner that I would cheerfully give in."

"I like the gray day dress with the red sash," Maude

began eagerly.

"It wouldn't suit your coloring, dear. Cherry red, royal blue, or turquoise will bring out your eyes best."

"Don't you have anything in one of those colors that you could lend?"

"I did purchase a cherry red before I knew better, and Aunt Hetty wasn't able to change my mind. You may have it, of course, but there is not enough time for Mrs. Penman to expand it to your size."

Maude looked crushed. "Well, then, I could have a pair of pointed shoes at least."

"Do you think you can squeeze your feet into shoes that were made for me?"

"Silk stockings, then. I could certainly wear those."

Maude's feet were slim, and so were her ankles. Clarissa's stockings would fit.

"These are a loan, of course, Clar. I will return them tomorrow, if you like."

Clarissa knew perfectly well that before the day's end the stockings would be shredded.

"I expected nothing less," she said gallantly.

"Stockings, of course, are not generally visible, however," Maude pointed out softly. "Do you think that a rice straw hat would look suitable? You have one, I know."

Clarissa had owned five *paille de riz* hats at the height of the fashion when they had been purchased, but had since then given the hats to servants and the daughters or wives of tenants.

"I have none now, but I could let you try one of my leghorns."

The hat's dark color was adequate, but any slight movement would cause it to slide down Maude's face or the back of her neck.

"Aunt Hetty and I, dear, can help dress you over the next week or two," Clarissa said as Maude finally gave the hat back. "You don't know Madame Thion in Launceston, but she is a dressmaker devoted to her craft and will be only too happy to deal with a convert."

"I'm not a convert. I only want to look well."

Clarissa didn't explain the contradiction. She was still ruminating over the difficulty when her maid's gentle knocks sounded at the door.

"Good morning, Miss Clarissa and Miss Maude," said Lizzie cheerfuly, "and a happy Christmas."

Greetings were exchanged and compliments offered for last night's singing. Lizzie was flushing with pleasure when Clarissa suddenly called out, "The hair, of course!"

Both the others looked puzzled.

"Hair that is neatly coiffed can make a favorable impression. Along with lip gloss and scent, it can be useful in hiding other imperfections from the masculine eye. Lizzie, I realize that today is Christmas, but I hope you can take the time to do Miss Maude's hair."

"Oh, yes," said Lizzie, her sharp features blurring as she gleefully contemplated the prospect of straightening out the tangled growth which confronted her. "It'll be my pleasure to be of service, Miss Maude."


A new Maude was not shown to the world until after breakfast. Her hair had been parted in the middle with almost mathematical precision. It had been combed into thick and glossy ringlets ending in a line just above the ears. Lip gloss, borrowed from a startled Aunt Hetty, was dark in shading. Her brows had been reduced in size so that they took the form of straight lines rather than shaggy ones. If Maude failed to recognize herself in the glass, she gave no sign.

There is a belief that the color white is suitable for everyone, but Maude's day dress called this idea into question. Wide at the waist and tight in the skirt, it had been designed for her when she was younger and had not been altered as her body changed. She was aware of the incongruity, judging from the blush on her cheeks, but kept it to herself.

Aunt Hetty and Clarissa said that the improvement was considerable, adding that much work remained to be done. Maude was thinking only about the day's prospects, but made it clear that she would eventually submit herself to the ministrations of some infernal dressmaker.

The other women made favorable comments about Maude's comeliness. Mrs. Farrowmere was complimentary, but avoided looking down at the day dress and shoes. Lady Winifred's brows rose at seeing Maude, but she said only that she would not be attending church this morning.

Maude was still looking a little green when Clarissa busily kept the young girl from giving more thought to Lady Winifred's disapproval.

"Your partial transformation will not be observed as such by the gentlemen," Clarissa pointed out. "They will behave, though, as if you have suddenly become of greater importance."

Squire Farrowmere, who had just accepted carriage transportation with the duke, was his usual polite self.

"There was a glint in his eyes," Clarissa said after the brief greetings when they were alone. "He was piqued."

"Who cares about the squire's feelings? I'm not out to impress him."

"The squire," said Aunt Hetty, who had overheard, "is masculine. His reactions must be considered."

The Duke of Mainwaring remarked that Miss Maude looked rested, and hoped that she was still fond of the spaniel puppy.

" 'Rested.' " Maude was sarcastic. "I let myself be mistreated for the sake of beauty, let myself be harrowed, and he says that I look rested."

"I should tell you that not every male is perfect," Aunt Hetty remarked slyly as the Tregallen ladies waited for the family barouche.

Clarissa's heart suddenly pounded when she saw Bryan Deverell coming closer. He was not dressed to the nines, which caused Clarissa to raise her brows even while she looked eagerly at him.

"I cannot leave Narborne," he said upon reaching them, looking directly at Clarissa. "That was my promise to the dragoon captain."

Aunt Hetty sniffed, indicating that no one on the premises would find prayer of greater use.

Clarissa was confident that Deverell would notice the change in Maude and sound appreciative without making himself foolish. She could trust her Bryan—those last words made her flush to the roots of her hair.

"Cousin Maude," he smiled, "I will give your regards to the animals when I walk over to see them."

Maude beamed, knowing that he had made it clear that he knew and appreciated her efforts at being turned out so as to look more comely.

Maude was due to see one animal, at least, before leaving. The floppy-eared brown spaniel came running out eagerly after her and capered joyously around her feet. Deverell picked him up and escorted him back to the house, where he was less likely to get into trouble.

Maude turned to her sister. "One man did recognize that I look different. If one man is aware of it, then I am sure Roderick will be, too, even if he doesn't say a word."

Clarissa smiled at her sister as the approaching barouche came to a halt before them.


There was no reason for Maude to have thought that Captain Taggart would be a congregant at the church of Little-Middleton-in-the-Dell at Launceston. When it became clear that he was not among those present, she became irritable and restless. The vitality in her features was lost.

Clarissa sat with her on one side and Aunt Hetty on the other. The duke sat next to Aunt Hetty, looking over her head at Clarissa. Clarissa, under prodding from the older woman, returned two of his looks and then pointed to the pulpit, where Mr. Carteret was speaking.

Mr. Carteret did speak clearly despite the whispering among congregants about worldly matters. His sermon was not worthy of the great occasion, as it never had been. But he was a fine man and, as Clarissa's late father had once said about him, "The Lord must be pleased with Mr. Carteret if not delighted."

The duke, who had listened indifferently but with a respectful air, congratulated the vicar at the end of services. Mr. Carteret stood just beyond the doorway, greeting the many farm families who had also come. At the sight of Maude, lifeless despite her altered features, his eyes widened with satisfaction.

"My dear Maude," he said happily, "you look radiant."

Not until the three Tregallen women had returned to their carriage did Maude turn to look at Clarissa and then join her in peals of joyous laughter.

As the Tregallen carriage drew up, Taggart was talking to Bryan Deverell before the main entrance to Narborne House. Aunt Hetty and Clarissa left first. Maude, blushing, was last to emerge.

Taggart's eyes lighted upon her and he had to force himself to remain polite in greeting the others. He showed his usual courtesy and deference to the duke, but was addressed in return by only a few impersonal words.

"Has the spy been caught yet in the great world beyond Narborne?"

"Unfortunately no, Your Grace."

The duke turned pointedly to Deverell, but said nothing.

Reluctantly, and at Aunt Hetty's urging, Clarissa followed the duke inside. She was in time to see him brush the spaniel puppy negligently out of his path. He directed Creddon to see that Lady Winifred was asked to join him in the drawing room.

Clarissa, looking out the window, saw Deverell returning to the house. To judge from his movements,

Deverell's health was largely restored, and she rejoiced for him. It did seem, too, that for as long as Captain Taggart was apparently courting Maude, there would be no call for Deverell to leave.

The duke nodded at his sister as she entered, looked keenly at her features as if to make sure she wasn't fractious and troublesome, then turned his attention to Clarissa.

"Well, my dear, would you like a stroll about the grounds?"

"Yes, we could accompany Maude and the captain." Clarissa had been speaking her mind rather than trying to make him irritable.

Mainwaring's fine features were colored a murky red as the drawing-room door opened on Deverell. He nodded to all and warmed his hands at the fire, a place where he was able to turn his head to the left as if it was a habit. He was looking directly at Clarissa.

"I was suggesting that we walk by ourselves," the duke said, a little more coolly, "and you might determine if the fountain ring looks well in daylight."

Clarissa realized she hadn't put on the perfume ring that he had offered as a holiday gift. She couldn't remember before ever committing such a discourtesy, and must have looked unnerved.

"We can keep a distance behind the others," she said.

No doubt the duke's unwillingness was caused in the main by the prospect of being in a party with a social inferior. He fell silent.

Help arrived from an unlikely source. Lady Winifred, briefly forgetting that she was a person of rank, suddenly spoke.

"I had considered a stroll, but I do not feel that I should venture upon the grounds by myself," she said.

The duke looked as if he had suddenly swallowed something sour.

Lady Winifred's voice was different in tone now, sunnier, almost friendly. "I know it is the very worst of bad

118

form, Mr. Deverell, but may I ask if you would take the time to accompany me?"

The duke let out a deep breath, but said nothing. He must have been aware that his moods could only cause a limited impact on his regal sister. If he had pointed out that she was asking for the company of a possible British spy for Napoleon, her country's great enemy, he would have been dismissed with a wave of the hand.

Bryan said calmly, "I was hoping that you would consent if I asked, Lady Winifred."

"Mr. Deverell, you need have had no fear on that matter."

Clarissa glanced directly at the duke's sister. To hear another woman being coquettish with the man she herself craved was dismaying. She envied some gentlemen who could call each other out in a duel.

"Very well," said the duke, resigned to his fate. "We shall be two pairs."

"Three," Clarissa said firmly.

Lady Winifred was the one who kept the discussion from turning rancorous.

"Of course, two pairs shall be ahead of anyone who may choose to take the same path," she said. "I have decided upon that."

No doubt Deverell was supposed to be taken by her gentility and skills as a peacemaker. Lady Winifred's search for compromise made no impression whatever on Clarissa, at least, who knew very well that Lady Winifred was setting her cap for the handsome and impudent Bryan Deverell.

## Chapter Thirteen

Clarissa found herself exploring areas of discomfort that were new to her. Never before had she walked with a man to whom she was cool while a man who was of great interest to her had to stay behind with another woman.

True, the woman was older. All the same, Clarissa found herself thinking in terms of images that were appalling and that flatly refused to go away. It took all her force of character to smile at her escort, to make pleasant and trivial conversation, to give the clear impression that she was withholding a decision about marriage.

She wore a russet cloak of calcutta cloth which was supposed to keep out coolness, but was useless against the short temper in which she found herself. Good weather had continued, so that it almost seemed as if the spring season would not be far off.

"So I am to be put off even further," Mainwaring said, trying to sound resigned and even amused. It was a pose he could generally carry off with ease, but the good humor was fraying, the man of the world getting ready to bare his fangs in a snarl. "You must realize that I am unable to accept hesitation much longer."

"I do realize it, yes."

"And what are you intending to do about it?"

"Why, to give you my firm decision as soon as is convenient for all."

The duke, still looking unruffled, fell into another one of his irritable silences. He could deal somehow with the presence of Deverell near his sister, of a social inferior with someone who might very soon be a relative. With Clarissa, however, his true nature came closer to showing itself.

She was intending to do no more than put off the inevitable. The prospect of marriage and life with the vengeful cold fish of a duke was disturbing, but she would have to agree to it. Wasn't that a family obligation? This alliance would make it easy to arrange a dazzling marriage for Maude.

In the last day, however, Maude had finally been awakened to the happiness of male companionship. With or without the ruler-straight Captain Taggart, she would find her own way, her own happiness. A girl as direct and as uncomplicated as Maude wasn't going to need any help arranging her future.

And Clarissa had met Bryan Deverell.

She had known after only a short time in his presence that a woman could feel powerful and unreasoning affection. No one could say it was based only on a man's handsomeness or intelligence, the sound of his voice or his warm wit, his heroic acceptance of adversity or his understanding of someone else's emotions. It was all these and it was something more that had caused the change, something she couldn't put a name to. It was a factor she hadn't appreciated until these last days.

Now she was in the position of having previously said nothing to contradict the duke's impression that she was only being coy and that she would soon agree to marry him. For the duke to labor under such a misunderstanding could not be fair to him.

Perhaps she could explain now.

"Aubrey, I don't know if I can make you understand my feelings and why I am distraught."

"I'm waiting." He had dismissed the struggle within her.

121

"Very well, then. Aubrey, I must—"

There was an interruption.

Behind them, even behind Deverell and Lady Winifred, some twenty-five feet off, Maude was calling out. All heard a series of barks as well. Clarissa knew what was causing the disturbance. The spaniel puppy, the duke's gift to Maude, had escaped from the house and was eagerly following his new owner.

Maude came into sight now, concerned, stooping for the animal. The puppy capered away. Captain Taggart chuckled and brought his own best efforts to bear, but the puppy wasn't used to him and skittered off. He was probably the only one of his species who didn't always rejoice at the prospect of sealing a new friendship. Maude kept calling out, fearful that the puppy might venture too far.

Bryan left Lady Winifred to reach a spot before the cliffs in order to capture the animal if it came to grief. Lady Winifred, dismayed at losing Bryan's company, had held out a hand to keep him in place. Now she looked down at that hand as if hoping to see why it hadn't arrested Deverell's movements.

The puppy seemed to have made up its mind to avoid anyone trying to save it from its own folly. It started toward Lady Winifred, who threw up both hands to ward off the beast and turned her back.

Clarissa had decided that the best way of dealing with this matter was to follow Deverell's example. Like him, she set herself in front of the cliff ledge, determined to keep the puppy from sailing down to oblivion.

Maude lost her head and ran after the puppy, calling out at the top of her lungs. She didn't realize that nothing could have been more repellent to even the brightest and friendliest of puppies. No-name (Clarissa didn't know how else to think of him) was friendly enough as a rule, but not highly intelligent.

The Duke of Mainwaring looked from one to another of the participants in the struggle to keep the little animal from destroying itself. Clarissa and Deverell remained ready to tackle the small beast. Maude ran after him while Taggart tried a frontal attack in vain. Only Lady Winifred, appalled by the waste of effort and time going on all around her, was not tense. The duke started over to his sister, the only one whose attitude he would have called correct.

The puppy was moving toward him. It circled the duke, who made a dismissing gesture with one hand. Everyone but Lady Winifred and Deverell shouted for him to catch the animal. The duke simply continued walking toward his sister. The dog raced toward the ledge and a better world.

Bryan, who was closest, moved for him with a speed which picked up at each step. Only his previous injury kept him from moving quickly enough to hold the animal. As it was, Deverell almost caught its midriff in one hand. Before he could bring his free hand to the animal's spine to keep him in place, the puppy vanished over the cliff ledge.

Clarissa and Taggart were entirely still. Deverell straightened himself without complaints, but cursed the bad luck under his breath. Maude, who might have been expected to burst into screams of rage, stood entirely still for only a moment. She suddenly turned and hurried to the ledge, where she could look over.

Clarissa felt proud of her sister. Maude wasn't going to waste time bemoaning the animal's fate, nor was she ready to give up hope. She was a Tregallen right down to her stubby fingernails.

Clarissa became aware of the duke's eyes upon her. His tone, when he spoke, was mildness itself.

"Now that it's over, shall we resume our stroll?"

Clarissa knew the duke well enough to feel no dismay at his callousness. Aubrey Seldon judged everyone by their capacity to remain impassive. In time, and after a marriage, he would do his best to turn Clarissa into a person who kept all feeling to herself, a person who was no more lively than a stuffed budgie.

She was firmly shaking her head when Maude let out a gasp.

"He's alive!"

Clarissa, on one side of Maude, looked down. Deverell, on the other, did the same. Taggart hurried to the ledge.

The puppy had struck a lower ledge that was perhaps a hundred feet down. The watery sun revealed the muddy beast as he ran back and forth. The dog knew enough now to keep from leaving solid footing, but it was yelping in fright.

Maude shouted, "It's all right, it's all right!"

The duke, who hadn't taken the trouble to look down, spoke clearly and briskly. "Not in the animal's opinion, I feel sure."

Lady Winifred's lips parted and she let out the beginnings of a chuckle.

Maude, incensed at the peer, whirled on him.

"He could very well drop to the rocks below and be killed!"

"Possibly," the duke agreed, but not as if he had given the matter a moment's thought. "It is unfortunate, as the beast proved costly because of his pedigree."

" 'Costly'? 'Pedigree'? Is that all you can think of? A creature might very well die and all you regret is the cost of having bought him? Is that all?"

Clarissa was aware of Deverell urgently glancing at her and inclining his head in Maude's direction. She didn't need that warning in order to move close to Maude to keep her from becoming angry enough to hit out at the peer. The duke would brush her away, of course, but mark her down as a lifetime enemy.

Maude continued venomously, "You let him go over the ledge because you didn't want to stoop and get your cloak soiled."

The duke shrugged and turned toward his sister. "Winifred, I think you might care to accompany me back to the house."

Maude demanded, "You must save him!"

"*I* must? You're most unsettled! Do you really expect me to climb down there and risk my suiting?"

Lady Winifred once again produced the sound that was supposed to be taken as a chuckle.

"And all this to rescue some *animal?*" the duke added.

"You must! It was your fault that he is there, so you are the one who has to atone for it."

" 'Atone,' indeed! Look here, miss, I realize that you are in a wax because of this development. I will be glad to buy you another pedigreed animal when I accompany your family to London after the holiday, as I promised your aunt a while ago that I would do."

"But you won't help an animal after you caused it to perhaps lose its life?" Maude was stunned, not having realized that anyone would be so base.

The duke's lips were suddenly thinned by a notion he must have found amusing. "I am certain that Mr. Deverell would be happy to risk his life for some inf— some animal. He will surely compensate for my deficiency."

Was the duke expecting the wounded Bryan to amuse him still further by dropping to his own death?

Clarissa said crisply, "You know that he has very little chance of success. Not in his current physical condition."

"So you fear that Deverell may lose his life, but you don't fear for me. Is that correct, Clarissa?"

Deverell, who had been watching the puppy, suddenly looked over a shoulder. "The duke's assistance won't be necessary and neither will mine."

Clarissa feared the worst for the animal, but it was Maude who understood immediately what was taking place. She turned to see Captain Taggart remove his cloak and uniform coat, giving him the greatest possible play for his arms when he climbed over.

"Don't fear for me, Miss Maude," the dragoon said softly. "It is heartening, perhaps, but not necessary. I have maneuvered over these cliff faces from childhood

125

on."

The duke drawled, "Very kind of you to save me the expense of purchasing yet another dog."

For once, Captain Taggart paid no attention to a remark made by the visiting peer.

"I have only one request to make of you, Miss Maude. I have always fancied the name of Buttons for a dog, but have never prevailed upon anyone to let me name a dog accordingly. Let us consider from now on that the animal below is named Buttons. Would that be satisfactory?"

Maude couldn't bring herself to speak.

"Good." The captain smiled. "Then the game is worth the candle."

Maude, angry at everyone, said through clenched teeth, "It is not a game."

Clarissa suddenly felt a greater sympathy for her sister. Even Maude, who had shied from dealing with her equals, would have to learn one of the sad truths of the masculine nature. To a man, and it was a trait which the duke carried to an extreme of ruthlessness, obstacles were to be made little of, drawbacks to be shrugged off. It was unreal. It led to challenges like this one. On another level entirely, it helped to cause war. No other trait did Clarissa associate with almost every man born of woman.

Taggart started to climb down with care. He didn't look away to find out if his movements had drawn the others' attention. His own faculties were entirely given over to the business at hand. A good sign.

"He may fall," Maude whispered. She had begun the vigil by clapping both hands over her eyes. After a moment, she cautiously removed one. Soon, both hands were at her sides.

"I don't think he will," Clarissa countered.

"He won't," Bryan told them decisively.

"Do you know it for a fact?" Clarissa prodded, wanting to hear him speak and take their minds off what was taking place below.

"I'm not absolutely certain that the sun will come up tomorrow, but Taggart seems very well aware of what he's doing."

"He's out of my sight," Maude suddenly put in, horrified.

"Don't call him! He might find it impossible to lend his full attention to the task at hand."

"But he is nowhere to be seen!"

"Of course he is. The sunlight faded under a cloud for a moment and obscured him," Clarissa said impatiently.

"I suppose you're right, sister, but there is no need to sound all-knowing!"

"I was *not*—"

"Oh, do keep control of yourself, Clarissa! Don't you realize what he is trying to do?"

It was one more of those occasions without number in which Maude was entirely deaf to logic and sense. Clarissa prayed silently for the strength to overcome feelings that ranged from irritation to black despair.

Her solemn request was answered in part over the next minute. The duke and his sister started to walk away from the area.

Lady Winifred turned back briefly, her voice never losing the pitch of a well-bred aristocrat. "You must let us know later on whether or not he survives."

Clarissa heard a chuckle from the duke as he and his sister walked off.

She looked toward Bryan for a chance to show silent indignation. Mr. Deverell's features bore no flicker of expression. He was staring out at the cliff, eyes riveted on the further adventures of Roderick Taggart of the dragoons.

But he spoke from a corner of his mouth, "We can be glad they have gone."

"Indeed."

"They added nothing whatever in the way of a tone to the occasion."

Still another example of male understatement!

Clarissa gave the response he fully deserved, which was none at all.

Maude asked fretfully, "How long do you think Roderick has been down there?"

"It seems like all of two days," Clarissa answered fretfully.

Bryan assured them, "He will persevere and conquer."

"How can you be certain?"

"He is a dragoon, the finest flower of British military life. He has enough forethought to be far from the battlefield and enough diplomatic skill to fawn over his superiors whether they be military or civilian. Such a man will accept any challenge to which he can successfully lower himself."

Maude didn't look away from the captain's struggles, but her face was turning red with indignation. If Bryan's plan called for her to be thinking of something beside Taggart's current peril, he was succeeding brilliantly.

Clarissa made her voice level. "I think you've said enough."

"You must both remember the military man's motto as he charges through life, the credo by which a military man flourishes. Briefly it is this: 'In retreat, disappearance. In victory, vengeance.'"

"You've said enough!"

Her tone may not so much as ruffled a hair of Bryan Deverell's head, but he desisted from further speech along those lines.

"Roderick has reached Buttons," Maude whispered.

"Now he has to pick up the animal."

"What's the matter with the beast?" Clarissa interjected.

"Buttons must think this is some sort of a game, now that Roderick has descended."

"The animal is running back and forth and making it harder for Taggart," Bryan observed.

"Doesn't Buttons know what's at stake?" Maude was fretful. "I have loved animals for as long as I can remem-

# 4 FREE BOOKS

## TO GET YOUR 4 FREE BOOKS WORTH $18.00 — MAIL IN THE FREE BOOK CERTIFICATE T O D A Y

Fill in the Free Book Certificate below, and we'll send your FREE BOOKS to you as soon as we receive it.

If the certificate is missing below, write to: Zebra Home Subscription Service, Inc., P.O. Box 5214, 120 Brighton Road, Clifton, New Jersey 07015-5214.

# FREE BOOK CERTIFICATE

## 4 FREE BOOKS

### ZEBRA HOME SUBSCRIPTION SERVICE, INC.

**YES!** Please start my subscription to Zebra Historical Romances and send me my first 4 books absolutely FREE. I understand that each month I may preview four new Zebra Historical Romances free for 10 days. If I'm not satisfied with them, I may return the four books within 10 days and owe nothing. Otherwise, I will pay the low preferred subscriber's price of just $3.75 each; a total of $15.00, *a savings off the publisher's price of $3.00.* I may return any shipment and I may cancel this subscription at any time. There is no obligation to buy any shipment and there are no shipping, handling or other hidden charges. Regardless of what I decide, the four free books are mine to keep.

NAME

ADDRESS                                                              APT

CITY                                              STATE          ZIP

(      )
TELEPHONE

SIGNATURE          (if under 18, parent or guardian must sign)

Terms, offer and prices subject to change without notice. Subscription subject to acceptance by Zebra Books. Zebra Books reserves the right to reject any order or cancel any subscription.                    099002

ber and I am deeply fond of Buttons, but a person can be pushed too far. . . . He has him! Oh, Clarissa, I knew that when it came down to things, Buttons would be reasonable."

"So far, all is proceeding nicely."

"He should wait longer before he starts up. He should get back his energy," Maude said worriedly.

"He will do what is necessary," Clarissa told her sister through gritted teeth.

"Buttons is in his right hand, so he can only use one hand to raise himself."

"That won't be too much of a difficulty," Clarissa replied.

"Look! He started to take a step and he had to pull himself back. . . . Now he is starting to rise!" Maude sounded less apprehensive.

Bryan said, "He has a firm grip and is in good control of himself. He will be joining us shortly."

Clarissa could tell from his tone that for some moments he had not been sure of the outcome, but his doubts had now been eased.

Taggart was close to the top when Maude raced over and took the dog from him. She held the animal firmly, but instead of crooning over it and asking it about its feelings, her eyes remained on Taggart. There was hope for her sister after all. She did have a sense of the importance of human life.

Taggert sounded as if he were breathing easily, which explained why Bryan didn't try to help him up. The dragoon brushed his clothes with both hands as best he could, removing as much dirt as he could.

"A pleasant experience gives any day a certain spice," said Roderick Taggart, his upper lip stiff as a post.

## Chapter Fourteen

Squire and Mrs. Farrowmere took their leave of the Tregallens early in the afternoon. The three Tregallens — Maude had, for once, insisted on taking part in a family rite — stood in front of the Farrowmeres' chaise and said their farewells.

Others of the house party weren't in view. Bryan had spoken to the Farrowmeres before they left the house. The duke had taken a horse for a canter. Lady Winifred was resting.

It was Phoebe Farrowmere who suddenly smiled at Aunt Hetty and the girls and said, "Why, there is no need to make a ceremony of this leave-taking! We will all be together tonight at the Hatherly house."

"So we will," said Aunt Hetty.

Clarissa was stricken. For the first time in memory she had forgotten about the ball to be held on Christmas night, as usual, at the Hatherlys. In the rush of these last days, it was almost a surprise that she remembered to dress.

Maude didn't make any reference to the matter until the Farrowmeres were gone, and Clarissa had asked Colton, a footman, whether the Farrowmeres had left satisfactory compensation to the servants. In answer, she had received a hearty, "Yes, Miss Clarissa," followed by a shrug.

Maude was the last to start coughing at the dust pockets from the departing carriage that were rising in the air. She was the first to stop. Evidently, something beside animal welfare was on her mind.

"I'll go to the Hatherly ball this time," she said, "if I can take Roderick with me."

"You cannot expect the Hatherlys and their guests to accept an officer in the light dragoons as an equal," Aunt Hetty said magisterially.

"But he's done so much for us!" Maude wailed. She had found it difficult to make her previous good-byes to the captain after that heroic rescue and had spoken of little else: his posture, his athletic skill, his Voltairean wit.

"What he did was to rescue a dog that belongs to you," Aunt Hetty remarked.

"If Roderick cannot accompany me to the Hatherly ball, I shall not attend, either."

"Oh yes, you'll attend," Clarissa said grimly. "I have seen to it that your best gown has been cleaned and that time has been taken to tuck it in here and let it out there. I gave those instructions upon returning from the recent excursion. Your coiffure needs only some slight renewing, and with the usual accessories I am sure you will do us proud."

Maude had previously tried to counter Clarissa's will, but always found the experience daunting. She pouted, accepting the inevitable.

"When I am married to Roderick," she said, ignoring the sudden gasp from Aunt Hetty, "the Hatherlys and everyone else in Cornwall society will have to welcome him as an equal."

"Until that happy day," Clarissa said blandly, "it is time for you to gather some experience in social matters."

"Yes, Clar," said her sister weakly.


Clarissa found Deverell in the drawing room. It was

eight-thirty, and she was already dressed for the night; a ball in the country had to begin and end early because of the time needed in traveling back and forth.

She was well aware that she had never looked more attractive. She wore a closed violet gown, the bodice hidden by a ruffled panel on a ribbon which passed through two loops under the arms. No more than a hint of gloss adorned her lips, a trace of kohl on her brows, and behind each ear was a drop of scent. Modesty and discretion on her part, she felt certain, would promote a lack of scruples on the part of one male.

Bryan was dressed informally, which meant that he was still obeying Taggart's warning and staying close to Narborne.

"You had best leave the door open," he said at the first sight of her.

She closed it, smiling confidently.

"I cannot be certain of retaining my manners when left alone with a young woman dressed as you are."

Clarissa felt her own heart pounding faster. She'd had it in mind to spend time with him in the closed drawing room, not caring whether the duke learned of it. She could imagine herself and Bryan leaving Narborne that night to hide until the war with France was over.

Bryan stood. "Clarissa, I have to tell you that if you do not turn and leave, I will disclaim responsibility for my actions."

"I am prepared to take the risk."

"I . . . cannot." He circled her and then opened the door. Instead of leaving, however, he turned around and walked back halfway.

"A man doesn't retreat from the field of honor," she grinned.

He confirmed his recklessness, proving that he cared not at all which enemies he might make because of some action. With the door open and the sound of steps moving gracefully in the hall, he brought his head down to hers and kissed her. She felt her arms rising till they

132

circled his neck, felt her lips returning the pressure he had put upon them. She was unable to breathe, to think, to do anything but glory in the moment's pleasure.

He released her. There was a singing in her ears and she fell back, unable to stand. Fortunately for her balance, her left hip struck the dark brown sofa table.

In the doorway, she heard Aunt Hetty saying, "I thought someone else was in here with you, Mr. Deverell."

Bryan, who had stepped in front of Clarissa, glanced behind him to make sure she was upright and only then moved to one side.

"Cousin Clarissa was good enough to show me her ball gown," he said easily.

"We can but hope that it meets with your approval," Aunt Hetty remarked drily. "Ready, Clarissa?"

"Y — yes, aunt."

"Then let us not keep, ah, Cousin Bryan on his feet beyond the call of courtesy. Come, Clarissa."


The Hatherlys were located on the other side of Falmouth. The Tregallen women, reaching the main house at the fashionable hour of nine-thirty, alighted gingerly from the Duke of Mainwaring's brougham. It was one of those coastal nights with hardly a trace of breeze, but with bracing air that caused the skin to prickle.

The duke helped his sister out of the carriage. Lady Winifred spared one look for the Hatherlys main house and then smiled thinly at her brother as if sharing a humorous observation that had to remain unspoken. Clarissa, flushing at the sight, could guess the nature of those insults in both their minds.

Lady Winifred kept up her silence in the dressing room, with its striped white-and-black wallpaper, flickering candles, tables and chairs. Her maid, Sybil, had been brought along to make certain that she looked as well as possible.

"*You* look fine," Clarissa said pointedly to her sister.

Maude, changing shoes in a dispirited manner, nodded. She was wearing white-striped bombazine with puffed and banded sleeves that had the effect of lessening oversized arms.

"What a wonderful night this would be if Roderick had been permitted to come."

Clarissa was on the point of saying that she felt the same way about another male.

"Let us proceed," she said instead.

Aunt Hetty, who looked imposing in silk with floss trimming, was on her feet. "Yes, let's do."

Lady Winifred was not ready as yet. She brooded at the cheval glass, unsatisfied with Sybil's hair ministrations. She fretted about the shading of lip gloss which had been previously chosen and actually tried two others. When she stood at last it was only to approach the full-sized glass in the northwest corner. She scowled at the cerulean blue satin in which she was clothed. Clarissa had never before seen Lady Winifred show the least interest in what she wore, and maliciously supposed that the older woman was trying to decide how her rig-out would look in the eyes of Bryan Deverell.

"I suppose it will have to do," she said finally. "When I return to Berkeley Square, Sybil, I will pay my first visit in years to Madame Fanchon's emporium, and buy a wardrobe with a more modern cast."

"Yes, Lady Winifred."

Aunt Hetty asked mildly, "Are you ready to proceed, Lady Winifred?"

"As ready as I can possibly be." She examined the clothes of each Tregallen woman, her eyes pausing the longest on Clarissa's gown. "Two of you are dressed adequately," she decided.

In the hallway they found the duke, who had been waiting impatiently. As usual, he was dressed without fault and looked as if he were posing for a portrait. Aunt Hetty led the way to the bottom of the stairs, where she gave her name to the footman and heard it shouted to another on the first landing. That one shouted the name up to the butler, who was standing outside the drawing-room door. The family name as announced by the butler wasn't quite that which the ladies had received at birth.

Clarissa made the voyage upstairs after Aunt Hetty's light and graceful ascent. She was greeted by the shy Mrs. Hatherly and her daughter, Penelope, who had been a friend for many years. Mr. Hatherly was to be found off to one side talking about Parliament and crops with longtime friends.

After Maude had joined her, Clarissa stepped to one side. "Let us wait and see how the Seldons respond to their reception."

Mrs. Hatherly told the duke — and, later, his sister — that she hoped each would find pleasure in this evening under their roof. With that done, she turned away to the next guest, leaving the duke and Lady Winifred to look at each other with brows raised in incredulity.

"That is hardly how members of the peerage expect to be received by the provincials," Clarissa said with mock disapproval.

"Almost as if they were human beings," Maude agreed.

The sisters walked about, speaking to friends. Maude behaved sensibly, letting others speak rather than show herself as naive by only discussing the welfare and habits of animals. Possibly Maude was convinced that her feelings on that subject were only to be shared with one special male. If that were true, her feelings about Roderick Taggart of the light dragoons must be serious indeed.

Maude was whisked away for a waltz. She had never performed that dance or any other worth the mention, but she was a quick study. After the first half-dozen steps, she grasped the pattern and followed it.

The Duke of Mainwaring appeared at Clarissa's side. "I didn't think that *la valse* had already reached the provinces."

"The provinces these days are rife with surprises, Your Grace," Clarissa said formally.

"If you can dance it more gracefully than your sister, perhaps you would care to join me."

"First, Your Grace, you have to gain permission from my aunt."

"I had forgotten the provincial mode in these matters."

"More importantly, the dance will soon be coming to a halt."

When that happened, Clarissa expected to see Maude being armed back to Aunt Hetty, but the young man stayed with her.

"I assume that a quadrille is going to be played," the duke said. "We can gain your aunt's permission and join your sister and her escort."

There was no escape.

Maude picked up the various figures as they were being performed, acquitting herself capably at *la pastourelle* and *la trenise*. Her difficulties with *le pantalon* were of short duration. Maude was giving the lie to the truism that dancing has to be slowly learned.

For the next foray on the floor, the duke insisted that Clarissa stay at his side. He refused to escort her back to Aunt Hetty. Clarissa became his partner in the square dance, which the duke performed easily and well.

"I would like you to arm me back to my aunt," Clarissa said at the conclusion.

"There is no need." Mainwaring was speaking casually. "It is true that if we continue to dance, questions will be asked about my intentions toward you, Clarissa, but I can assure anyone that those are honorable."

"Nevertheless, I ask you to return with me to my aunt."

"A waltz is being played now." He pointed to the half-open door at the end of the room. "Surely you don't wish to deprive me of the opportunity to lead you across the floor in *la valse*."

She ought to have been pleased. Other females were

136

looking askance at her, the daughters enviously and the mothers with speculation. The duke showed an almost unheard-of skill at doing a reverse step, causing a gasp to rise from the throats of various witnesses.

"I thought that only in foreign lands could the reverse be done."

"In as continental a setting as London, all the black arts can be mastered."

It was the closest to a humorous observation that the duke had ever made to her, and even in this case there was more than a hint of condescension. During the dance, near the conclusion, he touched her at a point just below the back. It had not been done by accident, as his grin testified.

"And now I really must be armed back to my aunt," she insisted at the conclusion.

"The next dance will be another quadrille," the duke said as if he hadn't heard. "I look forward to improving my skills by sporting a toe with the only suitable partner to be found on the premises."

He didn't have the least intention of letting her spend time with anyone else, female or male. The Duke of Mainwaring would protect his rights to property, whether it was inanimate or alive.

"I must return to the dressing room," she said instantly, in a tone that would brook no disagreement.

Without waiting to see or hear the duke's reaction, Clarissa walked toward the staircase, passing the room where the late supper was being laid out. Smells of baking fish followed her.

She nodded and smiled at the friends among those young ladies who stood on the staircase because they hadn't been asked to dance. There was supposed to be a rule that three young men were invited to one girl, but either it had been forgotten this time or many young men were deep in conversation among themselves.

There was a double-size window in the hallway on the other side of the dressing room. Looking out eagerly,

Clarissa saw that the duke's brougham was plainly in sight.

She acted almost without another thought. Sweeping up her cloak in a hand and changing to boots, she hurried out to speak with the coachman.

"Take me back to Narborne," she said, imperious as Aunt Hetty at her worst. "Then you may return."

The coachman didn't want to raise difficulties with the future Duchess of Mainwaring. He nodded at the two footmen who rode with him, and they nodded back.

"Yes, miss," said the spokesman.

Clarissa sank back in the coach seat and looked in front of her at nothing. A dusty mail coach passed in the other direction, causing horses to shy and drivers to curse spiritedly.

Emerging at Narborne, she walked off as the horses were being cared for. She was in a mood like none other in her life. The duke had been troublesome in his arrogance, Maude was prepared to start a tempest if she wasn't having her way, and Bryan Deverell was—well, Bryan Deverell. Himself, as the Irish said.

The main house confronted her. Bryan was in one of the rooms. For a reason she couldn't make clear to herself, Clarissa didn't want to go into the house with Deverell inside and none of her family close by.

She looked up at the nearly full moon, which was yellow with dark flecks of gray. A moon to bring on thoughts of romance, as one of the novels she enjoyed had put it tactfully. The lightest of breezes had come up, and she found herself thinking about faraway places to which she would go with that man who she—

Enough!

If she went to any room on the lower level of Narborne House, she was in danger of finding company that would unsettle her. Going to her own room and reading was enough to cause other disturbing thoughts. Sleep wasn't a possibility at this time.

She would walk.

Almost instantly she knew she was leading herself down to the cliffs and the path to the coastline and the Egg itself, that almost circular shelter so close to where she had first met Bryan Deverell by moonlight.

The downward climb, in spite of her gown, was easy. She wasn't inclined to take a path that offered greater adventure. She'd lived through quite enough uncertainty in the last few days.

She couldn't keep Bryan out of her thoughts. His face appeared in her mind's eye. She saw his jet black hair and wide forehead and hazel eyes, noticed his broad shoulders as if for the first time, and heard his fine strong voice.

Another matter took first place in her consideration, though. She would have given a good deal — no, anything; she would have given anything to know whether he was a loyal Englishman or the other thing, as she was thinking of it. There must be a way to solve that difficulty, to reassure herself beyond doubt.

*Someone was nearby.*

She had heard a scrabbling in the earth. The wind wasn't strong enough to cause that sound. No animal was likely to scrabble for moments, stop, then start again, stop, start, stop, start.

No one was in sight.

Only one area could hide movements such as these. On the tips of her toes, she began walking in the direction of the Egg.

At the entrance, she paused. Enough moonlight poured into the cave so that she could easily see what was happening.

Bryan Deverell, on his knees, was scrabbling at the wet earth. As she watched, not knowing that her breath had stopped, she saw him suddenly reach deeper into the earth and pick up a buried pouch wrapped in oilskin.

She knew that he had hidden something from her and everyone else, and knew that he had stayed behind so he could retrieve that infernal pouch at a time when the dragoons were no longer on full patrol in the area.

And she knew something more: that which she was trying hard to tell herself was not so. She believed the evidence of her eyes. Bryan Deverell had never been straightforward. He had lied. He was pursuing some secret goal. And he was doing this after coming to Cornwall from a port in France.

The man she knew she loved, the only one she had ever loved, was a jackal, a traitor, a spy for Napoleon, a spy for the greatest enemy England had ever known.

In her anguish, she cried out.

## Chapter Fifteen

She turned around to run, eyes blurred by a surge of salty tears. She didn't move more than twenty steps before she felt a hard hand on a shoulder turning her around. Through a mist of tears, she looked up to see a tight-eyed Bryan Deverell.

"What are you doing here?"

"Spying." Bitterly she added, "Like you, I'm a spy."

"Stop that blubbering of yours!" He was holding the precious oilskin packet in his other hand, unwilling to let it down needlessly. Small wonder she hadn't been gripped more tightly on both shoulders.

"I can't . . . can't stop!" She would have liked to demand whether he knew just how badly he had hurt her, in a place where she could find no defense. Caution made her take a deep breath, made her say what he wanted to hear and then find out that it was true, indeed. "I'm myself, now."

"Good." He was brusque. "I take it for granted that you don't want to be mistreated in any manner whatever."

"I won't stand for it!"

"One of us is stronger, and you're not that one. If you force me to see that you won't stand for it, you will. But I think I have been understood."

She asked the same question he had put to her. "What do you want?"

"For you to promise you'll tell no one what you've just

141

seen, and not mention this pouch."

"You want me to turn into a spy? Or a spy's apprentice?"

"I want you to keep your lips tight about this."

"Why should it matter? You surely plan to take your information to the French. You came to England for that oilskin packet, which was left for you by another spy, and now you are free to leave for France."

"Clarissa, you are entitled to use your lively imagination in any way you like," he said irritably. "But you have to do what I told you."

"And if I wait till I am out of your reach before I speak to someone like Captain Taggart, what can you do?"

"Nothing, Clarissa, because I may well have been hanged first." He was back to smiling. "I don't think you will rest contentedly with the knowledge of having been responsible for my introduction to Jack Ketch."

Of course he was right. She could hardly have borne the notion of his being hanged, guilty or not, no matter who might be responsible. Only in part was it because of her feeling toward him as a man. There was also the certainty that she would experience a powerful constriction in her neck when the noose tightened on him.

Prison, yes. Traitor that he was, let him stay in prison till those magnificent hazel eyes turned sightless, for all she cared. She would never see him again under any circumstances, never have anything more to do with him. In which case, his fate hardly mattered to her.

"I see the fresh coolness in your demeanor," he said evenly. "It is an undeserved punishment for any man who has acted from my motives."

"Those words mean nothing to me, Bryan Deverell!" Never before had she known that her speaking voice could seem so flat. "I take it that you will surely be leaving Narborne now that you have what you wanted."

He drew his lips tight. Words that he would have liked to have said remained unspoken.

"As you will be gone from Narborne House, that is

where I want to be, 'Cousin.' I hope there is no misunderstanding about this."

"None at all."

She had been looking up at his lips, which were in motion. "But you don't want to see me hanged," he said. "You still have that much feeling for me."

She was not prepared for his next movement. For the second time that night she was in his arms and those lips were coming down on hers. She made a move to pound the arm, but didn't go through with it. Instead she returned the pressure gladly, wanting him close to her and on the other side of the world simultaneously. Dismayed and even revolted as she felt about his actions, it was impossible to hold him close enough.

A half-sob escaped her lips when he freed her.

"Go now, Clarissa," said Bryan Deverell. "Turn around and go."

She did and then whirled halfway back.

He was speaking before she could face him. "Don't look at me, Clarissa. For your own sake, don't look at me any more."

Sobbing, she ran away and up the familiar rocky path to Narborne House.


Candles were lighted in the drawing room, flames flickering in their glass cages despite the calmest of indoor weather. The fireplace had been banked, resting the eyes but bringing dampness in its wake.

"Leave me alone now," she told a footman who had hurried in with a taper. "Everything will do as it is."

She touched a chair which Deverell had used, eased her fingers around a mahogany table which he had leaned against. Restlessly, she stalked up and down the huge room, hands in front of her and ready to do her bidding by touching any other part of the room which had known his body in the last two days.

It was possible to move about and not recognize a

single thought or a single feeling. That one feat she had never before accomplished. The skill involved would be useful to her in the later years, the dead years that would follow this recent farewell.

She did not know how much time had passed before she heard the duke's brougham arriving at the front entrance. The door opened. Four sets of footsteps sounded on the heavy floor.

It was Aunt Hetty who asked, "Did Miss Clarissa come home? Where is she?" After a respectful answer, she spoke briefly but pointedly to the duke. "I would appreciate it if you waited in the smoking room, Your Grace, while I speak with her. Maude, you need not accompany me."

Aunt Hetty's footsteps proceeded in the direction of Clarissa's refuge. As ever, in spite of her weight, Clarissa's guardian walked softly.

"Well, Clarissa?"

She had not heard her guardian cross the threshold, and only turned in surprise as Hetty Tregallen closed the door.

"I was indisposed," Clarissa said, "and returned home."

"You have always been a poor liar, except when you and Bryan Deverell were agreeing on what you both called facts." Aunt Hetty looked as if she would have appreciated holding one of those quizzing glasses which were worn by London males. "Did the duke give offense to you in some way?"

If she had told the truth, she would have won Hetty Tregallen's sympathy at once, but would have been subjected to another speech about the nature of men.

She shook her head.

Aunt Hetty looked keenly at her, then suddenly turned and opened the door. She ordered the nearest footman to light the fire. There was a pause before flames crackled and the room was invaded by an odor that reminded Clarissa of singed meat. She was always grateful for the summer, when no amenity made her uncomfortable.

144

"Now, miss, why did you return home at such an early hour?"

"I wanted to decide whether or not to accept Lord Mainwaring's offer for my hand in marriage."

Hetty Tregallen didn't doubt that.

"And have you decided?"

"Yes."

"I'm glad of that much. There needn't be any more hesitation and mooning."

"None whatever."

"I am not going to ask the nature of your choice as you are unwilling to tell me now," Hetty Tregallen said. "I need only remind you that feelings of attachment to another, feelings that spring up instantly, can be mistaken for eternal love."

"I am aware of that much, Aunt."

"Feelings of that nature will not last over a lifetime. Even a spinster like myself is aware of that. I am blessed by having many friends and have heard much about the goings-on in Cornwall society."

"Of course, Aunt."

"Very well, then. Let me ask this: do you wish to speak with Aubrey now?"

"Yes."

"Do you want me to stay nearby while you do so, Clarissa?"

"Thank you, dear Aunt, but I cannot feel that it will be necessary."

"Ah! In that case I know what your answer to him will be. I urge you to have no further hesitation. A husband in your bed is far more satisfying, as I've said before, than a warming pan."

Clarissa looked down modestly.

"Lady Winifred has inched her way to her room, but Lord Mainwaring is nearby. I will ask a footman to request him to join you."

"Please do," Clarissa whispered.

145

* * *

The fire diminished when the door was opened, and the Duke of Mainwaring closed it only partway. He had been drinking, but not to the point where he might have lost his cool judgment.

"I am told that you wish to see me. Have you made the decision to accept my offer? Splendid."

She asked herself briefly why he didn't apologize for his recent unseemly conduct. Almost as soon as that question was asked, the answer came. Regrets were not expressed by His Grace the Duke of Mainwaring, as he was officially styled. Regrets were expressed *to* him.

It makes no difference now, she told herself. Without the only man she loved, a decision she made was as good as any other. Hetty would feel, as she had pointed out more than once, that half of her guardianship had come to a satisfactory end. Arrangements could later be set, if necessary, to make certain that Maude's future, too, was founded on a suitable marriage.

"I accept your offer," she said in a voice without the slightest inflection. "I will marry you."

### Chapter Sixteen

Clarissa woke before dawn on the next morning, a rare happening. She got out of bed right away, walked toward the door and pulled the desk back to its usual place at the right of her bed.

She had changed its place for a few hours because of what happened the night before. As soon as he was accepted as a husband, the duke told her that the two of them had to get away from the others and go up to her room or his. There, as the duke said, they would disport themselves at long last.

"It is the way of sealing our agreement," he added firmly.

She had been so startled by this statement of her duty, allowing no opinion from her, that she instantly refused. She'd had to invent one lame excuse after another. All the while, the duke stared as though she was an undercooked fish that had found its way to one of his supper plates.

"Oh, I understand the truth," he'd said at last. He smiled, which proved that he understood nothing of the sort. "Your problem needn't put you at a disadvantage in this situation."

Gladly she accepted the excuse which he offered.

"It is a disadvantage to *me*," she said with a demureness she was far from experiencing.

The duke looked startled, as if wondering how his

pleasure could possibly have anything to do with her feelings.

"Very well," he gave in sulkily. "If you wish it."

The drawing-room door was opened wider, to indicate that the duke was now prepared to accept congratulations.

Aunt Hetty offered them from a happy heart. Maude glowed briefly, asked whether she would serve as the maid of honor and then grinned.

"You will be congratulating me soon enough in my turn," she added.

No doubt she was thinking of herself and the ramrod-straight dragoon officer. Clarissa felt that that moment was no time to discuss the matter.

Clarissa's precaution with the desk would have given warning if the duke had tried to force his way inside. The desk had been set at such a curious angle in the morning that Clarissa could guess what had happened. At some time during the night the duke had come to her door, tried to push his way inside, and made up his mind that he didn't, after all, want to cause a disturbance. The others would hear about it. Their opinion of him was very likely to plummet.

Clarissa found herself unwilling to go downstairs after Lizzie's arrival. She decided to take a bath first. Swiftly she made her way to that small attic room where the rite would take place. She sank down into the copper-lined tub and bathed serenely in six gallons of hot water and two gallons of milk.

Back in her room, she chose a day dress of Irish poplin, which was not a sought-after material. That dress had been purchased for her by Aunt Hetty as a punishment of some sort. Oddly enough, Aunt Hetty had been sure it would help prove that if Clarissa didn't do what she was told, she'd never marry and would always be poor in spirit. Clarissa hadn't worn the particular dress until today.

She was of two minds about whether or not Lizzie should do her hair at all. The maid looked scandalized at the thought of any neglect. Clarissa gave in.

Nine-thirty had come and gone by the time she reached the breakfast room. Aunt Hetty was glancing indifferently at correspondence. Maude, who was on her way out to the stables, paused long enough to chuckle.

"You must have been delayed by a marvelous dream," she said.

Aunt Hetty called her a saucebox.

Maude made her sister promise to talk about wedding plans before the day was over, and hurried out. Aunt Hetty finished the last of her letters.

"The rent rolls have been collected and the moneys banked, according to Rossiter." Gerald Rossiter was the Tregallen solicitor. "I do think that Aubrey is pleased that he will be receiving the lion's share of five hundred per year in rents."

Clarissa had been approaching the kippers, but now she put down her dish and decided to make a breakfast out of strong pekoe tea.

Aunt Hetty sniffed. "At least you won't take hot chocolate for breakfast, like that Deverell man. Truly that is the sort of a barbarian or a Frenchman, one being the same as the other."

At the mention of Deverell's name, Clarissa's tea felt even warmer through the saucer.

"Which reminds me," Aunt Hetty added. "Before breakfast itself, I was confronted by Pendexter, who is serving as Deverell's valet. He tells me that Bryan Deverell's bed was not slept in last night."

Clarissa caught herself on the point of saying that she knew it. She stopped herself in time.

"He comes like the wind and leaves the same way," Aunt Hetty remarked, addressing tea and a scone the size of Mr. Cartaret's rectory, or so it seemed. "Perhaps

149

that is all for the best."

*In this best of all possible worlds,* Clarissa reminded herself, echoing the words of a satiric novel by Mr. Voltaire.

The duke entered briskly, favoring Aunt Hetty with a nod and Clarissa with a half-smile. He approached the sideboard before saying a word.

Asked a direct question by Aunt Hetty, he admitted that he had slept poorly. He threw a glance at Clarissa, making it clear that she and no one else was to blame.

Lady Winifred was dressed for riding when she came into the breakfast room. As ever, she would speak to no one till she had swallowed her second cup of strong tea. The others knew enough by then to offer no conversational opening intended for her until that particular sublime moment.

Aubrey finally said, "I have good news, Winifred. Clarissa has agreed to marry me."

Lady Winifred inclined her head. Was she pleased if only because she felt certain that now she could draw the interest of Bryan Deverell? Lady Winifred would hear some unsettling news about him before she aged much further.

"That is what you wanted," Lady Winifred allowed.

Aubrey's eyes grew chill, though he continued to speak civilly. "I know that my bride-to-be would appreciate your good wishes."

Lady Winifred did turn to Clarissa, but not till she had poured herself a third cup of tea that was almost hot enough for bathing.

"I understand that you are to be a member of my family."

"Yes, Lady Winifred."

"You may certainly forget my title when we are speaking in a situation like this."

"Thank you."

"I can but hope that you will be able to accommodate

your ways to those of my brother." She looked around her as an indication that she had her doubts about Clarissa.

An acknowledgment was in order, but Clarissa chose not to offer it.

"I would think that a husband and wife must change their ways. Both husband and wife."

"A typical conception of rustics, I fear," Lady Winifred lectured. "Some little time after marriage in London, you should be seeing the error of your ways."

Clarissa put down her teacup noisily.

"Which reminds me," Lady Winifred added, having cast her eyes up and down at the Irish poplin day dress. "You must urgently be taken to London, where you can be introduced to those fashions which are being worn in the precincts of civilization."


Maude was being unreasonable. It had been pointed out to her several times that the family had been planning a London trip after the Christmas holiday.

"I thought we were going to see in the year at home," she protested. "That's the least we could do."

"There has been a change in plans," Clarissa said irritably. They were on the second floor of Narborne House in Maude's room, with its green-and-white striped wallpaper and drawings of animals in their natural settings. The furniture had been scratched by cat claws, the fabric bitten by dogs' teeth. This was certainly the proper abode for the queen of animal lovers.

"Who will take care of the beasts?"

"The indoor animals will be seen to by Creddon, and the outdoor ones mostly by Jem Pendarren."

"Buttons was just given to me, and he'll be hurt by my departure."

"I agree that he'll be puzzled," Clarissa nodded, proceeding to the window and looking out at a morning

151

that had just finished being soggy. "The family cannot make its choices because of one animal."

"I know what has soured you," Maude said shrewdly. "You are disappointed by Cousin Bryan's failure to pay you more attention, and now you don't care what happens to anyone else."

It was the time to say temperately that she herself wouldn't have put it so strongly. A certain honesty was desirable, but it ought to be flavored with optimism. She fell back on silence.

"I want to see Roderick," Maude proceeded, "and will stay alone."

"You are forcing me into Aunt Hetty's role, and then you will be angry at me for sounding tyrannical. Nevertheless, you are too young to stay by yourself. The idea of your doing so will be strictly and rightly forbidden."

"I must see Roderick to tell him that I am leaving."

"When do you expect to see him next?"

She confessed sadly, "He wasn't sure when he could make the time for another visit."

"I believe that even on *your* desk there is a sheet of foolscap, an envelope, and a steel-tipped pen. You only have to write a letter and one of the footmen will deliver it."

Maude thrust out a lower lip as if holding back tears, something that Clarissa hadn't seen from her since childhood.

"Very well."

"Do it after you have instructed Dilys about your packing."

Dilys was Maude's personal maid, a thin and pimpled girl who breathed through her mouth and appeared to speak through her nose. She must have had more qualities than those to have won the loyalty of Shane O'Hoghie, one of the undergardeners.

Speculation about the sevants' lives was beside the

point at that time.

"I don't need to take any clothes except the ones I will stand in," Maude said, stubborn to the end. "I won't instruct Dilys to pack for me."

"In that case, I will do it," Clarissa said firmly.

"Leave my effects alone!"

"It is going to be done by one or the other, Maude, and you have the right to choose if this chore is to be accomplished quietly or not."

"Very well." Maude let out a sigh. "Dilys will be instructed to pack and I'll write to Roderick, just as you say."

"Good, and you shall have your reward long before arriving in heaven. You will be receiving new clothes, as I will."

"Why should I care, if Roderick doesn't see them?" Maude pouted. "I suppose there is time for him to see my dresses after we return to Narborne."

"Indeed there will be time. As soon as I leave you, Dilys will come and the good work can begin."

Maude, having been sulky for the last minutes, suddenly turned thoughtful and met her older sister's eyes. "Do you know what is wrong with you, Clarissa? You have no romance in your soul, none at all."


Maude happened to recall that some months ago Aunt Hetty had despaired of ever again being able to wear a riding habit. She had owned it since girlhood, and it had been let out any number of times. As the years grew short, Aunt Hetty decided that time spent on riding was so much time wasted. The rig-out remained, useless. Maude had been disinterested in clothes since childhood. Clarissa felt that the habit in question would have suited a wife of Methuselah's, but not Clarissa Tregallen.

A servant could not refuse the offer, and such a gift

might be considered an act of generosity. The riding wear had found its way into Dilys's hands. Dilys had been a little less than overawed, but tactfully wore the rig-out during holidays.

Maude, having remembered this bit of history, rang for Dilys. Night had fallen, and the maid had been looking forward to rest, but tried to show her usual willingness to serve.

"Dilys, I want you to bring me the riding clothes which my aunt gave you as a gift," Maude said. "I will return them in the morning."

"Yes, miss."

"No one is to know about this including others on the staff. I hope I make myself entirely clear."

Dilys, who had never seen the young mistress in such an imperious mood, nodded twice to emphasize that the warning had been understood.

The outfit was in Maude's hands within moments. It was made of slate-colored cloth, with a full skirt finished up the front by braiding. The accessories caused her to flinch. There was a small round hat which Maude's teeth convinced her was made of cork. Gray leather boots were a size too large. Maude inspected herself and disliked what she saw, but the clothes had been expensive at one time and she doubted that their deficiencies would be noticed in the darkness.

She heard Dilys, who was watching, let out a gasp.

"I forgot to bring the gloves, miss."

It was one of Maude's many convictions that gloves were instruments of oppression, keeping a female from direct contact with animals or nature. In this instance, though, she put them on. She had previously set herself to mend her ways.

The gloves turned out to be made of some material called limeric, as Dilys remarked. Inside them, Maude's hands itched. She took them off and put them in the tops of her boots to be worn afterwards.

"I won't be gone long, Dilys, and you had best wait at the rear door till I return."

The maid thought disapprovingly that Miss Maude was starting to take to herself some of the less winning traits of Miss Hetty. Ah, well, the people with money were all alike, wanting their way about everything. It was only to be expected.

The gloves were on Maude's hands as she stood at the shore, not far from the Egg. She could feel the weather chilling the habit she wore and causing the cork hat to feel icy. If the chill hadn't taken her mind off the itch in both hands, she would have felt miserable.

"Maude!" It was Roderick Taggart speaking. The dragoon officer had walked into the Egg itself, where he had waited. Shortly after receiving the letter Maude had written, the captain had come to meet her as she had requested.

In the light of the moon, he looked even better than usual, like an eagle who had just received an inheritance. His features were sharp, his eyes probing as ever, but he was exhilarated by her presence.

He would not be exhilarated much longer.

"You seem cold, Maude. Would you like to come into that shelter?"

"No." She wanted to look at him more clearly, so she would remember his face over the long stretches of time that loomed ahead in the depths of London.

"You wrote that you wanted to give me some news you couldn't bring yourself to communicate by message."

"Terrible news."

Were his eyes twinkling? "Is it a plague? Fire? Flood? If not that, I see no need to feel upset."

"I am going to London."

His fine eyes blinked two or three times. "Forever?"

155

"It will seem that way."

"And I will feel the same. But, of course, we will see one another when you are permitted to return."

"You don't realize it, but that will take time. Possibly until my sister's wedding to the duke, possibly even longer."

"The passing time will seem even drearier than it is." He reflected. "If you would like me to look in on the farm every other day and keep an eye on your animals, I will be only too happy to spend time in your usual surroundings."

"Jem Pendarran will do whatever may be necessary," Maude said, having given the matter some thought. "We disagree about any number of matters, Jem and I, but he cares for the beasts as living creatures and is concerned about their well-being."

"You seem resigned to being away from them, but not from me."

Maude hadn't thought there was a smile in her, but she found one and displayed it. A rueful smile, certainly. A smile that didn't convey happiness.

"I am deeply fond of all my animals," she said quietly, "but my feeling for you is of a different type."

"I am a different animal." He smiled. "A ferret, perhaps. When I am primed to capture a rabbit, that rabbit had better look to its laurels."

She smiled again, but turned briefly to give a hurried look back toward the house. "I had best return shortly if I want my maid to let me in. She looked half-asleep when she came to me earlier."

"Animals like myself want to get some sign of affection," Roderick said softly. "They want to know that someone else cares for them."

"I have no idea what you mean."

He took her in his arms and fervently kissed her. The experience was new to Maude, but she found it of interest.

"I had never known of this," she said hoarsely.

"It is quite common among the higher animals."

"I would not have put you in their class, Roderick. Your instincts are low."

"Like a snake?"

"A wombat, perhaps, but then I am not sure—"

He kissed her again, his lips strong against hers. She found herself returning the kiss with more enthusiasm than she had ever felt.

"A lizard, perhaps," she murmured when she could speak again. "But now I *must* leave."

"Only one more demonstration for tonight, then." And he followed words with the deed.

This time, there was a smile on Maude's features when the contact was reluctantly finished and she forced herself to move aside.

"A tiger," she said dreamily. "Very definitely a tiger."


Packing had been under way for most of the morning. Lizzie, who would be accompanying the Tregallens, had been directed to put in only a few of Clarissa's rig-outs, three hats and a similar number of pairs of shoes. Accessories had barely been mentioned. When Lizzie hesitantly picked up the duke's gift of a fountain ring, Clarissa shook her head firmly.

"There is no room for that."

Lizzie threw her a questioning glance.

At any other time, Clarissa would probably have looked at the ring, recalled her decision, and burst into laughter. At the moment, she didn't feel that she could produce a laugh.

"I'll wear that," she said. "Give it to me, Lizzie."

But she hesitated before putting it on, and wouldn't realize until the carriage ride had begun that the ring had been left behind. Accidentally, to be sure. Entirely by accident.

* * *

Aunt Hetty was one of those women whose first thought at the mention of an excursion was to plan on which foods to bring along. The sole haircloth trunk had been packed with clothes and effects, but she gave all her time to overseeing the filling of hampers with food.

In vain did Clarissa point out that they would be close to various country inns and could buy meals when necessary.

"You forget that hunger pangs may seize any of us when no inn is nearby," Aunt Hetty replied.

She had taken the time to speak with Clarissa while managing the packing. They had encountered each other in the anteroom to the library, and Aunt Hetty had run in to say a few words.

"If someone becomes hungry before we reach an inn," Clarissa said reasonably, "that person can wait a short while."

"One never knows what sort of people may be patronizing a country inn, dear. Can you give me any notion as to whether Aubrey likes cold ham?"

"For his sake, I hope so," Clarissa said wryly.

"It is vexing that you have so little fondness for cheese, Clarissa. I don't know what else can be put in that will be so filling."

"Eggs, perhaps."

"There is already a sufficiency of eggs, and we cannot travel with hot coals to keep them warm."

"True enough."

"Nor can we keep the liquid refreshment cool, though I do think that beer and water and claret should be sufficient for the roadway."

"I concur."

"There is no time for satisfactory desserts to be prepared."

"We will all have to bear up under the loss."

"There is no amusement in knowing that one's stomach will be subjected to torture—oh, Lord!"

"What's wrong?"

"It is time for luncheon and I have not yet finished planning food for the excursion," Aunt Hetty wailed. "Indeed it is true that a woman's work is never done."

Aubrey and Lady Winifred had been riding, and appeared halfway through the luncheon hour. Each was prepared to change outfits as soon as the informal meal was completed.

"My dear," the duke sniffed thinly, taking Clarissa's hand in his, which was as cold as ever. "Are you ready for the trip to London?"

"I look forward to it," she said tonelessly. "Was your morning's ride satisfactory?"

"Mine, yes, but Winifred's animal seems to have sustained some injury and quite put her out, I am afraid."

Maude gave a cry and hurried off, causing the duke to look startled and then shrug.

As Aunt Hetty ran in and out preparing further for dining on the road, Clarissa found herself alone with the duke and his sister. They launched into a conversation about London friends. Names like Bobby Peel and the Earl of Pembroke passed their lips along with those of Priscilla Gwydir and Harriet Raseberry. Clarissa drank lapsang-souchong along with cakes no bigger than a ha'penny, and listened to words that meant nothing to her.

She began to see her future life now. She would listen to much talk of no interest. She would make herself talk just to hear her own voice. She would be unable to fend off her husband's marital demands. She would grow older, with harsh lines across her forehead and discolorations in the hen tracks beneath her eyes. Children

159

would condescend, not aware of their ignorance or lack of compassion. The only gratitude she would ever feel again would be in those minutes just before she passed on, knowing that a hurt-filled life was over.

"I will dress quickly," the duke was saying as he got up from the table. "An hour will suffice for me, Winnie, and I hope for you."

"Certainly," said Lady Winifred.

She smiled vaguely at Clarissa, thanking the hostess. It was hard to avoid the impression that she was trying to recollect Clarissa's name.


One of the footmen had to go out to bring Maude back to the house. Maude reported contentedly that Gingerbread, the horse, had sustained no injury of importance.

"I do hate to leave before she is fully recovered," Maude added.

"Well, you're going to." Aunt Hetty's patience was wearing thin.

The duke appeared next, fully prepared for travel. He wore a buttoned waistcoat over a wide shirt and rainbow-colored cravat, tight trousers, and Hessian boots from Hoby's in London. Over the left arm he carried a dark topcoat.

"At last," he said as Lady Winifred made her descent on the stairs, only five minutes behind the hour.

"I cannot wait to return to civilization," she said, not caring who heard her.

She had already put on a cloak. The disarray of her hair was hidden only in part by a silk turban which had been knotted loosely. Lady Winifred was indifferent to what others might think of her unattractive costume.

Aubrey smiled at his sister. "Soon, my dear."

He was proved wrong. Just as he turned to face the outer door, a knocking came upon it, the sound gentle but persistent.

Maude put a hand to her heart. "Something worse has happened to Gingerbread!"

Aunt Hetty turned to Jamison, the underbutler, who had been hovering nearby to escort the family and guests out to the carriage. It was a duty which Creddon, the butler, chose not to perform these days on account of the rheumatics which acted up during damp weather.

The underbutler approached the outer door uncertainly. It soon turned out that his attitude was very nearly justified.

For the door opened on none other than Bryan Deverell.

*Chapter Seventeen*

During the next minutes, the duke protested vigorously at the delay in leaving. Maude, at the same time, was deeply touched to see that "Cousin Bryan" wasn't looking his usual alert self. Aunt Hetty, as impatient as the duke, muttered under her breath but made no move to leave.

It was Lady Winifred's reaction which caused the duke to keep from marching out to his brougham by himself if need be. She simply ordered the underbutler to set a fire in the drawing room and direct Bryan Deverell to follow her to that place of refuge.

As for Clarissa, she was appalled. Confident that she would never see Deverell again if only for his own security, she had proceeded to make arrangements for her own future. Now, like the traditional bad penny, and at some possible risk to himself, he had returned.

Aunt Hetty had watched regretfully as the food hampers were taken out to the carriage. Possibly she felt that their contents would grow lukewarm and even chill on account of the delay. She found a certain satisfaction in ordering hot tea for Mr. Deverell. It was Clarissa who suggested hot chocolate instead. He did seem to have a preference for the stuff.

Lady Winifred asked almost immediately, "Where have you been?"

She sounded like a governess getting ready to scold

one of her charges. Or a wife, Clarissa thought bitterly.

Bryan Deverell faced everyone in the room except the duke, who was standing with feet wide apart. His dark hair and clothes were rumpled. Mud seemed to have been almost painted across his wide forehead. Only Clarissa noticed his hazel eyes dancing with mischief.

"I have had a difficult experience."

The duke said coarsely, "Set upon by marauders once more?"

"No, but what happened was caused by that episode."

"The aftermath of your injuries would seem to be flexible. One minute you feel at the top of your form, the next minute you are helpless."

"On this occasion, I was entirely helpless," Bryan said, but his quick look at Clarissa made it clear that he was fancying up a story. "I suddenly fell."

"And picked yourself up, I am sure, judging from the evidence of my eyes."

"I was unable to help myself for a long while," Bryan said, indicating that he resented the skeptical questioning. "I fell and slept, unable to rise until a short time ago."

"And you expect us to believe this taradiddle?"

Lady Winifred spared an angry look at her brother. "It is plain that Mr. Deverell been hurt."

"Is it indeed?" the duke snapped. "We will be leaving now. Come, everyone!"

Clarissa suddenly blinked at a fresh realization. Deverell had stayed away to satisfy himself that Taggart's dragoons wouldn't be mounting a search for him.

But in that case, why had he come back?

The thought no sooner entered her mind than she knew the reason. He had seen the carriages prepared for a long trip and he wanted to escape from justice in the greatest possible comfort. He would surely change his plans when he knew that the carriage was leaving for the capital city of his enemy, for London.

163

It was Maude, in the meantime, whose generous nature caused her to play into his hands.

"But we cannot leave Cousin Bryan behind," she protested warmly. "He must be where his family can care for him if he should become ill."

Bryan had the grace to look uncomfortable because Maude was plainly stirred. He must have felt like the hunter who shot sitting ducks in a barrel. Clarissa, noting his regret, couldn't help feeling another twinge of liking for him.

*Damn Bryan Deverell for making me like him! Oh, damn Bryan Deverell!*

Regrets or not, he made himself sound weaker than he felt (Clarissa could tell). "I would not wish to impose."

"Quite," said the duke. "I have no intention of taking him with us to London."

"To L—?" It was impossible to know exactly what was on Deverell's mind. That infernally vexing devil might for some reason have been pleased.

No further protests were forthcoming about the possible wickedness of leaving him behind.

"I will be all right, I am sure," he said, sounding even weaker than before. "I only need a little more rest, and cannot trouble anyone else to be of help."

There was something on his mind (Clarissa knew), some scheme which he was going to put into operation before anyone could leave. When he was done, the feelings of others, except those of the duke, would be strongly in his favor. They would probably beg him to do exactly what he wanted and join them.

"I will take some rest now," he said, getting slowly to his feet. "Thank you all for your kindness."

"There is no need," said Lady Winifred, "to thank my brother."

The duke snorted. Clarissa noticed briefly that the eye of every female in the room followed that forlorn figure as he moved slowly. Every so often he paused as

164

if he couldn't possibly go farther, but he always stayed in motion. His body actually struck part of the frame of the door, but not with vigor.

The Duke of Mainwaring, aware that three pairs of eyes had turned accusingly toward him, insisted firmly, "I will not permit him to ride in my carriage."

Whereupon Maude, on her way to the door to help the hurt one, said spiritedly over a shoulder, "Then we must take our town coach! Aunt Hetty, we must!"

Hetty Tregallen would have been far more sympathetic to the woes of some spinster. She was not without feeling for other humans, however, and allowed herself a nod.

"I will give the order to Jamison." She rang the nearest silver hand bell, summoning the underbutler.

Clarissa had not made any response. She was truly puzzled. There was no way to resolve the problem.

No doubt Deverell was shamming. If he had suffered any injury, it amounted to very little, which meant that he wanted to go off with the family to be in London, that place where he would be least safe, the place inaccessible to the coast. From there, he couldn't reach other spying mischief-makers in Bonaparte's forces. Worse yet, the duke could more easily turn him over to the Bow Street runners or whatever the native thief-takers were called. Bryan had previously expressed a justifiable distaste for a meeting with Jack Ketch, the hangman, yet he seemed willing to ride full tilt into Jack's arms.

Maude and Aunt Hetty were looking to her for a third opinion in the matter.

It was Lady Winifred who spoke instead, her voice raised so that its tones would carry to Bryan at the door.

"You must take Mr. Deverell with you, Miss Hetty. It is, after all, the merciful thing to do."

There was another pause so that the town coach

165

could be prepared for the trip. Deverell made a point of sitting near the fire but facing away from the wall. In that position, as Clarissa realized, he could keep the restless duke under observation. The latter was no longer pretending to be well disposed toward him.

"Come," Aubrey said sternly to Clarissa. "We will wait in the brougham."

She would much rather have been in the same carriage with Bryan Deverell, even if she wasn't able to speak frankly or touch him. Her husband-to-be must be obeyed. She had made her choice.

Lady Winifred accompanied them to the carriage, again at Aubrey's words. The ground was soggy, and that unmistakable smell of moist earth rose toward them with each movement. In Clarissa's sour mood, she was reminded of dirt that had been turned over before receiving a coffin.

Clarissa's maid, Lizzie, was sitting impatiently with Lady Winifred's disapproving maid and the fussy coachman. Four silk-smooth horses pawed the ground restlessly. Indeed it seemed as if restlessness from one and all was the order of the day.

Clarissa found herself sitting next to Lady Winifred. Aubrey was muttering under his breath as he climbed inside, settled himself, and looked with a jaundiced eye as a varicolored lap robe was adjusted over the others. He was in none too serene a mood, either.

Both women looked around Aubrey's profile to see Deverell and the other Tregallen women leaving for the town coach. Deverell walked between them, taking care that his steps were slow.

Maude joined Deverell in the town coach, but Aunt Hetty walked to the brougham. She shouted up for Lizzie to ride with the Tregallen coachman and she herself would join Aubrey, his sister, and Clarissa. Very likely she was determined to keep an eye on the food hampers and make sure that their contents were eaten fresh. If Clarissa's memory served, less than twenty minutes would go by before Aunt Hetty was urging food upon everyone.

Clarissa waited until her plump aunt was settled comfortably. "Do you think that Maude should be permitted to stay alone with a man to whom she isn't married?"

"Bryan Deverell is not himself," Aunt Hetty pointed out severely, "and can do no harm."

"All the same," Clarissa began.


She opened the door of the town coach and looked in. Maude was keeping her distance from Bryan Deverell, but lines of concern were etched on her forehead.

Deverell had his work cut out to keep from helping Clarissa inside. As a man who was supposed to be ill, extending himself this time was impossible. He did see to it that the hamper of food brought over with her was put into a position from which it couldn't be damaged.

Maude, wide-eyed since Clarissa's appearance, finally said, "I am surprised that Lord Main—Aubrey, I should call him—permitted you to come here with us."

Clarissa allowed that remark to go unanswered. She preferred not to say that it had involved persuasion, coquetry, and a great quantity of stubbornness. Lady Winifred had been no more pleased than Aubrey. It was Aunt Hetty's intervention which kept the peace.

"Nevertheless, I am here," was all she said. "It occurs to me, Maude, that you might want to ride with the footman and Lizzie, and make certain that the chestnut horses are taking the ground satisfactorily and remain unhurt."

Maude's eyes lighted up. It was what she preferred to do when she was in one of the carriages being taken out, as Clarissa well knew.

Deverell spoke up as she was starting to the door. "I suggest that you wait until we have been under way for several minutes. Then we will halt very briefly. That will prevent any possible misunderstanding and delay at, ah, Aubrey's request."

"A very fine idea," Maude grinned. "If it is necessary to bring the horses back, there will be time to spare them any greater injury."

"Of course," Deverell smiled.

Clarissa, looking into his eyes, saw that the slightest suggestion of returning to Narborne was likely to bring out the very worst in him.

The change was accordingly made. After her sister was firmly established next to the coachman, Deverell and Clarissa settled back. For the first time after too long a lapse, he was smiling at her and no one else.

"At last," he said easily, "the two of us are alone."

## Chapter Eighteen

"You cannot build any hopes upon such a frail structure." Clarissa wished that her heart wasn't beating so rapidly.

Bryan chose to make his next point in the fewest possible words.

"I formed the impression that Mainwaring's offer for you has been accepted."

"That is correct." Would her heart ever stop beating so quickly?

"If the ceremony hasn't yet taken place, it is still possible to run off. France is very pleasant at this time of year, and Mainwaring isn't there."

"Lord Mainwaring is a credit to the Empire," she said haughtily.

"Yes, I see him in the front lines during the battles against Bonaparte."

"At least he is a loyal Englishman."

"His loyalty to the crown is hardly the subject under discussion."

"It isn't the subject that *you* wish to discuss. Perhaps you are tired because of your recent painful wound while you were a guest at Narborne."

He shrugged. "I had to be slightly less than truthful, Clarissa. I admit as much. There are reasons for it, however."

"I realize there are, and I know them."

"No, you do not!" Loss of temper was rare for Bryan Deverell, but he was teetering on the brink of a memorable explosion. "There are matters which I cannot discuss."

"Oh, I am well aware of that much, 'Cousin.'"

A look of complete earnestness was not suitable for him. It clouded his magnificent hazel eyes, narrowed the scholarly forehead and gave the curious impression that his splendid shoulders were actually quite thin. He was a man born to make serious points with that blessed light touch which had briefly forsaken him.

"I can clear up one matter on the instant." He sounded pompous. "I am not a smuggler."

"Of course your word is to be cherished."

"And I am not a spy for the French."

With her whole heart Clarissa wished she knew that last point to be the truth. She could forgive smuggling, which had engaged the sympathies of every Cornishman from time immemorial. She could forgive the possible bribery of law officials, the threatening of citizens to keep them quiet. Now that she gave it some thought, there was a long list of possible offenses which she could forgive this man.

Murder was not one of them, and she felt just as strongly about the offense she knew he had committed.

He insisted once more, "I am not a French spy."

He had been moving closer, wanting to convince her by his closeness. He seemed certain that she would question his motives only from a distance.

"Stay there," she demanded, and looked out at passing farms and village main streets, each with a rectory and dozens of straw-topped cottages. She had seen them many times, but would rather look out than turn to him.

A long period of silence followed. During that time the coach passed Newton Abbott in Dartmoor. The weather was changing, the wet warmth of Cornwall slowly giving way to traces of December chill.

Not until a stop near Blandford in Dorset, where the horses were watered and food from the hamper was eaten, did he take up the discussion at the point where it had been left.

"You won't be happy married to Mainwaring," Bryan said, speaking slowly and with care.

"A gypsy prophet can always foretell the future."

"Clarissa, don't try me too high," he warned, a most unbecoming flush starting to steal across his forehead. "I am only made of flesh and blood, and cannot always behave like a knight in armor when confronted by a willful failure to see what is plain."

"It should be plain that an offer has been made for my hand in marriage and that I have accepted it."

"Why?"

"Aubrey is a fine man, a credit to the Empire."

"You said something like that before. You were wrong then and you are wrong now. No man can be a credit to Britain if he is malicious and petty. Lord Mainwaring is that and much more."

She had no response.

"You remember the way he treated me after the dragoon captain did not arrest me? First he was contemptuous, then he treated me like an old chum. Now I've fallen out of favor again. Conclusion: Mainwaring is insincere."

Clarissa raised her head farther, as if she felt proud. "You are insulting the man I intend to marry."

"He is capable of duplicity, as I have just proven. He hides his feelings until he can strike back at whomever may have aroused his displeasure. You have seen an illustration of that."

"He is also capable of—" She had been about to say "warmth," but that word refused to leave the sanctuary behind her lips. "He is capable of being an upright man."

"Upright men don't bide their time until they can take vengeance for a real or imagined affront."

171

Again there was nothing she could say that might have been an intelligent response. She had to sniff, indicating that she might have spoken volumes in Aubrey Seldon's defense.

"Worst of all, that tinniness of nature will act upon you," he continued. "You will be exposed to it day after day and he will turn you into a woman who no longer has a sense of pleasure and who fears showing her feelings, a woman whose feelings themselves are locked so deeply inside her that it is as if they never existed."

Clarissa suddenly turned in surprise, her mouth opened. She couldn't tell him that he may well have been right, that his vision of her future was much like her own.

She fell back on sarcasm. "I suppose you expect me to marry a man of substance, a man as reliable and dependable and straightforward as you are?"

He said, "I do have a great feeling for you, Clarissa. Surely you know that."

"A man who makes such a claim ought to speak about himself with less dishonesty."

"I have never been . . ." he started, and came to a stop as the coach did.

Aunt Hetty was walking toward them just as Maude left the coachman's perch and climbed down to the ground without a wasted motion. Nor was she out of breath. She had performed the same action many times in the recent past.

Deverell said swiftly and quietly before anyone else was in earshot, "After we reach London, I cannot tell how soon I'll be able to see you again."

That was understandable. He would be a man on the run.

"I hardly think you need to bother," she said icily.

Aunt Hetty reached them at last. Having opened the door, she inspected the state of the food hamper. Only then did she permit herself to be helped inside.

"Aubrey noticed that Maude was leaving the two of

172

you alone, so we both felt that I should come back here and act as a chaperone."

Clarissa nodded appreciatively. Even though she was seated, her knees had become rubbery and breathing was difficult. A few more minutes of this combined logic and blandishment, and she might well have been in his arms yet again, forming a habit that would be harder and harder to break.

"That was an excellent suggestion," she said approvingly. "My husband-to-be is a man of uncommon wisdom."

She expected awkward silences among three people with nothing to speak of when together. It was a mistake. Bryan set himself to be charming. Conversation proceeded in a lively and animated way, which was delightful.

All the same, Clarissa wanted the trip to end. She would be no happier, but at least Bryan would be on his way to greater safety.

No sooner had she thought that than she became aware of a delay.

The town coach suddenly halted. Looking out at the stationary landscape, Aunt Hetty reported that a coachman of Aubrey's was in the road.

"What is it, my man?"

"Begging your pardon, but His Grace wishes to let you know that his carriage is in need of some repairs."

"We will wait for him, of course."

"His Grace will be proceeding into the nearest village, ma'am."

"I will instruct my coachman to follow Lord Mainwaring's carriage."

"Yes, ma'am."

"You heard?" Aunt Hetty asked, bringing her head back.

"Indeed, yes. I think we are close to Farnsworth in Reading," Bryan said. Clarissa wasn't surprised to learn that he was a much-traveled man of the world.

The trek resumed. Past the only street in the next village was a carriage builder's shop. Deverell, impatient at the delay but hiding it only from Aunt Hetty, stirred himself.

"I shall join Lord Mainwaring to see if this matter can't be hurried along."

Clarissa decided to accompany him. Drawing up her skirts she entered the carriage builder's quarters, which resulted in her getting a look of disapproval from Aubrey. Apparently this was no place for a mere woman.

Clarissa was beginning to think that there was something to be said for the duke's point of view. There was an almost overpowering odor of different types of paint, and another of chopped wood. The sight of the carriage builder was not particularly winning, either. He was a man with big arms and hands, a huge torso, and very few yellowed teeth.

"Josiah Dimbleby at your service, Your Grace," he said when the duke mentioned his rank and indicated the nature of the difficulty and how soon he wanted the carriage fixed. "Let me inspect this carriage of yours."

He had to go outside to do it, and took a couple of workers along. There was a nip in the near-London air, but this change of locale was pleasurable.

"Hurry it up, my man," the duke ordered. "We don't have all day and night."

"Yes, Your Grace."

Dimbleby took his time, suggesting that the horses be released from bondage and led over to the nearest trough. He and his men conferred importantly in whispers. Even Clarissa thought things were taking longer than necessary.

"Well, my man?" the duke prodded. "Is there to be no end to this?"

"In just one more moment, Your Grace."

But the moment lasted. Ordering Josiah Dimbleby to hurry was the one certain way of making sure he wouldn't. Bryan gestured at the duke to control his tem-

174

per, but Aubrey looked away irritably.

"I know how to handle these people," he insisted.

"The French aristocrats made that same error not too long ago," Deverell remarked imperturbably.

Clarissa, who happened to be watching the carriage builder's features, thought she saw a quick look of appreciation cross his red face. She wished that the negotiations could have been entrusted to Bryan, who seemed able to get along with almost everybody.

"Well now, Your Grace," said Dimbleby, pausing to wipe his hands on a filthy apron. "Might I ask how long you've owned this carriage?"

"No," said the duke coldly. "You are to tell me only how quickly the repair will be made."

"I certainly don't want to say bad things about the work of another in my profession," Dimbleby continued, unwilling to lose track of the point on his mind. "What I do see, though, is that the spokes are not made of good English oak, as they should be. They are of hickory, which is fine for the wheels. On the spokes, though, it doesn't give enough freedom to go with the wheels when they are in motion, if you take my meaning, sir. As a result, after a little while, the riding can cause some difficulties. What you need is wheels of hickory and oak for the spokes. I could make that change."

"There is no time for that," the duke said briskly. "I am not going to lay up in this miserable village for a month while someone destroys the family brougham."

Clarissa knew, and so did Bryan Deverell, that the spark in Dimbleby's slate-colored eyes was caused by muffled anger.

"And I may tell you, Your Grace, that while I'm at it I could see that Leslie—the big fellow with nary a hair on his head—gives it a fresh coat of paint which would make it look fresh-bought."

"I will attend to any necessary changes when I return to London and the vicinity of my usual carriage

175

builder," said the duke in an icy tone that would have done credit to Hetty Tregallen at her worst. "My question has not yet been answered, and I am growing impatient."

"Of course, Your Grace," Dimbleby smiled. "Well, sir, my professional opinion about the basic difficulty is that the body of your carriage was not sufficiently tested after being put together. In my shop, I have the men go inside and jump up and down to test it for standing up to everyday riding. I also have them sway from side to side — ah, yes, yes, I see that Your Grace is a little impatient with rural ways. Those of us who don't make it to London are simply not up to the crack, though I do think — "

Clarissa and Bryan exchanged glances, silently sharing the observation that Dimbleby was getting ready to extract every possible ha'penny from the bad-mannered peer.

"I will be brief, now, Your Grace. The underpinnings are your basic trouble. Her steel isn't quite Sheffield as it should be. After a while, she has trouble moving without she makes unseemly sounds."

"I will allow no more than ten minutes for you to make the change, my man."

"Can't be done, Your Grace, beggin' your pardon. But I will see to the job and keep the men at work all night."

"All night?" the duke was startled. "My party and I cannot sleep in the road."

"There is a fine inn not too many steps away, begging Your Grace's pardon, I'm sure. The Pig and Whistle, it's called."

Clarissa had to put a hand up over her mouth because she was so amused by the notion of the Duke of Mainwaring staying overnight at a hostelry with that name.

"My sister's husband runs it, Your Grace, and you can certainly tell him I suggested for you to go there.

176

He's not good for much in the way of carriage building, Junor isn't, but he does provide a comfortable doss and good strong British ale."

"And of course a part of the fee will come to you," the duke said rigidly. "I will take my party to another inn, any other inn."

"None is closer than Farnsworth, Your Grace. Too far to walk."

"I see."

"And one other thing, Your Grace. As a matter of business and because I've had some awkward experiences with strangers, I must ask that you pay the six guineas before I start to work."

The duke made no further protests. He handed the money over and stalked over to his carriage. He could be heard loudly explaining to Lady Winifred what had taken place and what needed to be done.

Alone with Clarissa, Deverell spoke quietly. "If I could've put in a word and made the difference, I'd have said that the carriage could be returned to its proper condition if only briefly with a ha'penny worth of grease."

Clarissa responded with mock pomposity. "One has to speak sternly to these rustics in order to put them in their place."

It wasn't a good impersonation of the duke, but she did have the satisfaction of seeing Deverell suddenly turn away, his shoulders rising up as he laughed soundlessly.


Bryan Deverell wasn't at all surprised to see that Clarissa's Aunt Hetty was taking charge of the room arrangements for all three Tregallens. She put them into one chamber with two beds. Judging by the one in Deverell's chamber, they were the size of sticks and felt the same way.

He didn't know where the duke had been placed, nor

177

was he surprised to hear Lady Winifred demanding a separate chamber. Any evildoer who came up there to strike out at her would have to fend for himself. Lady Winifred would stand for no presumption from the lower classes.

Bryan was in no mood to go to bed. He proceeded into the tavern which was on the lowest floor of the establishment. Over a drink of negus, he found that his skills at getting on with others were being put to a severe test. Strangers squinted and said nothing to him and very little among themselves. Bryan might have been a ghost making an unexpected call.

It took an hour before his fellow drinkers went through a change of attitude. He sat by himself at first, having his drink refilled, speaking to nobody. Mr. Junor, the proprietor, served drinks and offered an occasional observation to the stranger, but it went unanswered.

It occurred to Ned Cowperthwait, a miller, that the stranger didn't want anything from anyone. In that case, no harm could result after a "Good evening."

Bryan soon found himself and his party so many objects of curiosity. He couldn't answer questions truthfully, but he didn't want to insult these strangers with lies. He actually said very little about his own business or anybody else's. The impression was universal that this stranger was telling the truth. As a result, Bryan left with no hard feelings behind him.

At nine-thirty, he decided to go up to his chamber. Because of renovations being made during the day to the passage that led to the inn, he stepped outside. A short walk and a right turn would take him where he wanted to go.

He had time to notice that the evening was turning raw and that the moon was gone from the inky sky. Behind him, a voice spoke.

"Mr. Deverell."

Bryan recognized the voice, but not the tone. There

was a softness in it which he hadn't heard before. Its uncertainty was even more of a surprise.

Not the slightest trace of surprise showed on his features when he turned to the woman who had stepped out of the shadows and called his name. He was smiling, warmly as he always did whenever possible, at Lady Winifred Seldon.

## Chapter Nineteen

Lady Winifred was wearing a dark blue cape which looked as if it had been singed, a fur muff made from some animal no one was likely to identify, and unbecoming arm-length gloves. There was no doubt that her footwear, too, would be expensive but inappropriate. She treated clothes in the way that landowners of old had treated serfs.

Unless he made a mistake, she was unable to start the conversation without hesitating.

"You don't seem ill any longer, I am glad to see."

"Thank you, Lady Winifred." He remembered how she had tried coming to his aid in the argument with her brother back at Narborne. "You know that youth has great recuperative powers."

He could have bit his tongue when he saw Lady Winifred flush in embarrassment.

"Extreme youth, I mean, to be sure." He was making it worse somehow, but couldn't bear to have been unintentionally offensive. "Callow youth, as it's called."

"Thank you, Mr. Deverell." She spoke after a pause. "I realize you are indicating that a difference exists between us in the matter of age. It is perceptive of you to say it so readily at this special time."

The damage, whatever it had been, wasn't likely to be undone.

"I was mostly blethering, Lady Winifred, exercising

my lips."

"No, it matters, and I should have been more keenly aware of it." Lady Winifred could never have spoken apologetically to anyone else. "I realize now that you will only respond warmly to a woman who has youth to offer."

It was Bryan's turn to feel awkward. He could never have anticipated that the crisp and regal Lady Winifred, after seeing him for several days, had developed a *tendre* for him.

"I will tell you of a wish that is shared by many women after twenty summers," Lady Winifred said with a rueful smile. "They dream of meeting a man who can divine their emotions after a touch, a word, a mere look! A man who is finely attuned to their feelings. You, Mr. Deverell, are keenly aware of a woman's feelings."

He had hardly been aware of Lady Winifred Seldon over the past days. Saying so at this time would be pointedly insulting. He racked his brains to find words that would allow her to retire unhurt.

"Lady Winifred, I must tell you that there is another woman in my life." In desperation, he had fallen back upon the truth.

"Miss Clarissa Tregallen, is it? I have noticed that the two of you sometimes exchange glances as if you share a feeling, a thought, a witticism which cannot be spoken when among others."

And she didn't have to add that she had been envious.

He hadn't expected to be truthful, but could respond in no other way to this woman's plain baring of her heart.

"I am aware that she has agreed to marry your brother," he said.

"As someone who is better acquainted with her than I, Mr. Deverell, I take the liberty of putting a question to you: Does she need the money that marriage to

181

Aubrey will bring?"

"I am not aware that she does."

"Is she anxious to gain social position in London? Most women wish to do so, but not all of them."

"I doubt that Clar—Miss Clarissa Tregallen has a serious interest in becoming a distinguished woman in London society."

"Then in heaven's name," asked Lady Winifred, "why does she intend to marry my brother?"

"I am sure she has some feeling for him," Bryan said smoothly. "Lord Mainwaring must impress all who know him."

"Has he impressed you, Mr. Deverell?"

Bryan took the liberty of responding with a smile.

"You must forgive a woman who is growing into a disagreeable, acid-tongued spinster," Lady Winifred said bitterly. "My point was that Mainwaring does not overwhelm all who meet him, and he has certainly not done so with Miss Clarissa Tregallen. That much is clear from her attitude."

"Then why has she agreed to marry him?"

"Exactly the question I posed to you."

And a sound question it was! The only answer that occurred to him was that as the Duchess of Mainwaring, Clarissa could help the other women in her family make successful marriages. Even, in spite of her age, Miss Hetty.

Was that enough of a reason?

In a girl who lived on the tip of the Cornish coast at a time of warfare with Napoleon Bonaparte, was that enough of a reason?

But how in heaven's name could he find out the truth? *How?*

The duke's carriage had been brought to the front of the inn by the middle of the next morning. Clarissa, leaving her shelter with sister and aunt, looked around for Bryan Deverell. He wasn't in sight. At the prospect of losing even a few moments with him, she felt her heart sinking.

Aubrey had stepped down from his carriage to escort Clarissa inside.

"No, thank you. I'll ride with my family in the town coach."

"If you must." He tried to shrug, but it wasn't easy for him to make believe he was indifferent. "Perhaps you are put out because you think that I allowed myself to be gulled by that carriage builder last night."

"I haven't given it the least—"

"I can assure you that I will arrange for a local solicitor to make Master Dimbleby's life a horror over the next months. Should the solicitor fail, I am ready to hire others who will proceed more drastically against the rascal."

"Oh, Aubrey," she said in mock admiration, "truly you are a man among men."


Bryan had found his way into the town coach. He didn't look physically ill, but seemed unhappy. Those striking hazel eyes were clouded, and his hands were folded in his lap.

At first she thought he was disturbed by the weather It happened to be one of those cool days with threatening clouds that might never burst into rain, the sort of climate that she herself liked but which made others restless.

"Did you have a difficult night?" she asked before Aunt Hetty could put the question.

"Only after I went to bed."

"Did your recent illness return?"

"No, it was something else." Now that he was talking, Deverell looked cool. "I had an interesting discussion with Lady Winifred last night and it didn't leave my mind."

"Indeed?" Was Clarissa supposed to be jealous?

"Lady Winifred posed a conundrum to which I cannot confirm an answer, namely, what is it that makes you want to marry Lord Mainwaring?"

"We have already discussed it. The subject makes me weary."

"It is plain to Lady Winifred that you have no feeling toward him, no romantic feeling, and yet you are determined to go through with a ceremony."

For once, he wasn't halted by Aunt Hetty's entering the carriage and sitting down. He knew as well as she did that time would be gone for them as soon as the carriage reached the great gaudy metropolis of London.

Aunt Hetty, having settled herself, took part in the conversation. "I cannot see how my niece's behavior can be a concern of yours."

Clarissa decided not to spend her last minutes with Deverell in argument. She spoke directly.

"The income from Narborne is reasonable at this time, but may not remain at its present level without the help of a man with money."

"Part of the problem is resolved," Deverell said, settling back a little farther. "Is there any other possible reason?"

"Certainly. In case of need—again as a sort of talisman against a bleak future—a fine marriage could be made for my dear sister."

She pointed upward, to where Maude was probably settling herself with the coachman and Lizzie.

"Another part of the problem is resolved." Deverell paused a moment. "Could there be any additional reason, Cousin Clarissa? We won't see each other much longer, so there can be no harm in telling me. It would soothe my bump of curiosity."

"What different reason could there possibly be?"

"A political reason, perhaps?"

"Excuse me?" Aunt Hetty had spoken, clearly bewildered. Clarissa knew that her own features reflected the same feeling.

"I had wondered whether you wanted to establish innocence by marrying an impeccable member of the peerage just before the battles with Napoleon reach their highest pitch of intensity."

Clarissa had gone from bewilderment to sheer astonishment. "Are you saying that I — I — ?"

"You were at the scene of a ship's landing from France, and I cannot know what you might have accomplished before encountering me," Deverell said. "I don't believe it, Clarissa, not of you, but I can't be certain. And that is the hell of it."

Aunt Hetty, deeply offended for her niece, said sternly, "Mr. Deverell, you should apologize immediately or leave this umbrella of Tregallen hospitality."

"I do indeed apologize to Miss Clarissa. I apologize sincerely."

Clarissa believed him, but wasn't mollified. Nothing would have pleased her more than to start a long argument.

It was impossible to do so in this situation. Only a little time remained for them to be together, and that in the company of another. Very soon now, she would almost certainly see him for the last time. If they ever met in the future, she would be married to a man to whom she found herself indifferent.

Aunt Hetty said nervously, "I would not accept his apology, if I were you."

Clarissa glanced at Deverell's pursed lips, his unnaturally serious features. "You are entirely correct, Aunt. The apology is refused."

Her eyes smiled as she looked at him and his eyes twinkled. They didn't look away from each other, Clarissa and Deverell, as they rode on, treasuring the intimate silence, the unspoken laughter which was marking their last moments together.

* * *

185

The duke's coachman approached the Tregallen town coach. Both vehicles, Mainwaring's and the Tregallen's, had halted in a clearing. The horses were taking water.

"Begging your pardon," the coachman started earnestly. A puffy cloud of air released itself from his mouth as he looked up.

"Yes, my man?" Aunt Hetty popped her head out.

"Lord Mainwaring wishes to know if Mr. Deverell is in better health."

Clarissa blinked rapidly. Nothing could have been more unlike Aubrey Seldon than a show of feeling for someone against whom he had formed a grudge. Deverell, as keenly aware of it as she, leaned slightly forward.

"Mr. Deverell seems in fine fettle," Aunt Hetty said a little acidly.

"His Grace asks if Mr. Deverell would care to join him and Lady Winifred in his carriage," the coachman continued. "As the brougham is of better quality and more sturdy, the ride into London may be made easier for him."

Clarissa turned to Deverell, alarmed. It was easy to see what wicked scheme had found its way into Aubrey's thoughts. If Deverell was in the same carriage, it would be easier to hand him over to the Bow Street runners. Deverell would be charged with spying, and in a short time be put down, as Maude might have called it, allowing the duke to consider himself avenged for a slight on the first day that the two had met.

The coachman added, "His Grace would like an answer immediately."

Bryan looked across at her, eyes sharing a fresh humorous notion, lips twitching a little sardonically. Clarissa felt relieved. Leave it to Bryan Deverell to know exactly what was happening and why. Aubrey Seldon would have to work harder if he wanted to make a fool of Bryan.

*My Bryan.*

Aunt Hetty, still smarting over the recent insult to her niece, called out, "The duke offers us an excellent opportunity to rid ourselves of an unwelcome guest. Of course Mr. Deverell will go over to the brougham."

Clarissa was frantically shaking her head, trying urgently to gain her aunt's attention. Hetty Tregallen finally looked around.

"When a man consistently breaches the rules of hospitality," she pronounced, "he has to be sent off about his business."

"No, you mustn't do this!" Clarissa's voice was lowered to a strangled whisper.

"It has been done," Hetty Tregallen said imperiously. "Mr. Deverell, you will leave us now."

Clarissa put out a hand to Deverell's right arm as if to keep him in place. Muscles rippled in that arm and she drew her hand away as though it had been scalded. Her breath came too quickly.

Bryan spoke as if no harm had been done. "All may yet be well, Clarissa."

"You must stay!"

He sounded amused as he turned lazily. "I do thank you for the opportunity to have been a guest at Narborne and I appreciate the privilege of having met my British relations."

Hetty Tregallen said mercilessly, "If you dawdle any longer, Lord Mainwaring's carriage will have left before you are ready."

Was that his plan? Did he intend to take so much time in a flowery farewell that the duke would impatiently give up on that quest for vengeance?

"Give my best wishes to Cousin Maude," Bryan said, then looked directly at her. "And I especially thank you, Cousin Clarissa, for your kindness."

Hetty Tregallen sniffed in disapproval.

Clarissa felt herself close to unshed tears. It did seem that they were destined to make continual farewells.

Their courtship, if it could be called such, was made up of farewells in quantity.

He started to get up.

She couldn't keep herself from calling out, hoping that her distress would make him sit again. He looked down with understanding, but did not return to the seat. Instead he raised a hand in her direction as an acknowledgment. The brittle smile, the raised hand, the reluctance to look away, were taking the place of passionate kisses.

The door was opened, letting in a rush of chill air. Clarissa Tregallen was feeling another sort of chill entirely, feeling it deep in her bones.

Bryan descended to the earth. Not looking behind him, not troubling for one last turn to see Clarissa, he started toward the lair of the enemy.

*Chapter Twenty*

Clarissa was unable to draw a breath. Nor could she keep her eyes from Bryan's figure as he walked slowly. It did seem as if he wouldn't be able to defend himself in case of need, so weak was his health.

"And good riddance," Hetty Tregallen snapped, then, more softly, "Perhaps he will indeed feel better in Aubrey's carriage. I don't think that Aubrey likes the man, but he is capable of great thoughtfulness, which is a good quality in a husband."

The coachman turned to lead the way back to the brougham, no less than two hundred feet off. Bryan's stride suddenly quickened, almost as if he could not wait to find himself eventually in the toils of the law.

A moment passed before she realized that he was not walking toward the duke's carriage. There was a stand of leafless elms to the right, and Deverell was moving at full speed to that refuge.

Clarissa let out a gasp of gratitude, causing her aunt's eyes to follow.

"What in the world is that man doing?"

"He is going toward the elms and will leave by the other way in order to save himself." Clarissa was enthusiastic. "Bravo! And again bravo!"

No sooner was he out of sight than she relapsed into despondency. She could not help thinking that she might have just seen the last of the only man she knew she loved or would ever love, the last of Bryan Deverell.

Clarissa didn't like London. The city's hugeness was enough to make her feel overwhelmed. Instead of one street or two at most, London boasted dozens. Hitching posts appeared in rows, and houses could be observed on a single street cheek by jowl with each other. London boasted as many residents as might be found in the army, but she felt no safety among them. Londoners of even the higher orders seemed to have faces scarred by red and brown spots, like a moorhen's eggs.

Not only were there more than two or three inns, but each catered to a different class of person. Naval officers patronized one place almost exclusively, while army officers infested yet another. Undergraduates clustered at an inn of a certain type and the wealthy at another entirely. It would have been no surprise to find out that there was an inn used only by short people and another for those who were tall.

She was saying as much to Maude on the first full day of their arrival. The duke had wanted them to put up at the Clarenden on Oxford Street, a place which appealed to men and women of position. Clarissa had held out for Limmer's on Bury Street, where she had stayed on her previous visit. Most of the Limmer clients were country squires visiting for a short time, who talked of country matters and nothing else. Maude was certain to like the place as much as she herself did.

"If Roderick was in town, too," Maude said, "I would be happy spending some days here."

Clarissa supposed, come down to it, that she felt the same way about Deverell. She wouldn't let herself think of him for long. Let her do so, and she would burst into tears and never stop crying.

She and Maude were sharing a room with colored drawings of animals on the walls, and bilious paper. The desks and chairs seemed fragile, the bed so sturdy that no human body could ever change its shape. All in all the accommodations were no more comfortable than those at the Pig and Whistle. It was morning of their first full day in the metropolis.

Restless, Maude looked out the window. "There are no animals but dogs and cats, and horses pulling hayracks. There is not a tree in sight. There are no cliffs, certainly."

Clarissa had to agree.

"How soon will we be able to go back to Narborne, Clar?"

"When we have bought beautiful new rig-outs in the latest modes."

A promise of new dresses would have brought docility to the manner of any other young female. Maude, however, sank back on the bed and hammered both fists against it in her vexation.

There were two knocks at the door. Aunt Hetty entered. Her sky blue day dress, which Clarissa had often seen, looked as strange in London as Hetty Tregallen herself. In one hand, a little awkwardly, she was holding a sheet of foolscap.

"A message has arrived from Aubrey," she said sunnily. "He wishes us to visit him and Lady Winifred in Berkeley Square for luncheon at one o'clock."

Maude looked up. "I thought that we were going to examine fabrics for new clothes and then return to Cornwall."

"You will have to cultivate patience," Aunt Hetty said firmly.

"And so will I," Clarissa murmured. "So will I."


The duke's home was a red brick with two fronts, two windows between them, and twin pillars at each end. It did seem appropriate for a man like Aubrey Seldon, who was certainly two-faced.

Coming out to meet them, the duke ignored any

need to wear a lined cape in this chill weather. He was splendidly attired in buckled breeches of satin, a silken waistcoat, rigid white shirt, and impeccable cravat. He seemed to be carrying a reddish wax candle, but it was actually a gentleman's cane.

"What an honor to return hospitality that was so cheerfully given," Aubrey Seldon bubbled. "Winifred is most anxious to see you again."

"How nice," Clarissa said between her teeth.

They walked past an ample hallway with figures in armor and paintings of birds such as could never have existed. There was a parlor with a large once-red rug, Greek revival chairs, a crocodile couch, and shell stools. Amid this splendor, Lady Winifred waited to greet the new arrivals.

"It has been a long while since last we met, has it not?" Her lightness was unexpected, perhaps caused by the knowledge that she was now the hostess. "You have hardly changed."

Clarissa suddenly found herself almost warming to this older woman who had fancied herself a rival for Bryan Deverell's attentions.

"You make a visit seem a pleasure," the young woman said with a slightly greater appearance of sincerity than she was feeling.

Lady Winifred turned away to greet the others just as generously.

Luncheon was served rather than taken from a sideboard in the breakfast room. It was a London custom of which Clarissa naturally failed to approve. The meal consisted of warmed-over soup, cool fish that could well have been gray gudgeon with a side dish of sizzling potatoes, a chill dessert, and a glass of Regent's punch, which was the London name for weak tea.

"An exceptional repast," said Aunt Hetty almost as if she meant it to be a compliment. "You are blessed with a splendid staff."

"It isn't easy to find good servants in these difficult

times," Lady Winifred responded. "By dint of great care and constant supervision, I am able to show some slight results."

The duke waited until the table had been cleared before he spoke again. "You realize that I can hardly remain behind and talk to myself for I am the only male who is present. I suggest, then, that we stay here and indulge ourselves with a certain amount of plain speaking."

"I am sure that we are all in favor of plain speaking," Aunt Hetty said wisely.

"Excellent! I refer, as you may have gathered, to a brief discussion of plans for my wedding to Clarissa."

"That is understood."

"The first step is to obtain a special license directly from the Archbishop of Canterbury."

Clarissa, who felt a chill at discussing plans for marriage to Aubrey, made herself ask lightly, "Isn't a special license a little unusual?"

"All of the polished exclusives of the *ton* have taken to using that procedure."

Discussion on that point was closed. He brought up the quizzing glass which was suitable in London but had been far too grand for the provinces. It made his exterior more forbidding than nature would have allowed.

"I believe, Miss Tregallen, that the cost is no more than twenty-five pounds, give or take a few."

"We will bear that cost, to be sure," Aunt Hetty said.

"And in this case such a license will indeed be necessary," the duke continued. "Not that I am unwilling to be married during the canonical hours of eight a.m. to three p.m., but because Clarissa can then marry in London."

She said instantly, "I have always told Mr. Carteret that he would marry me at my church of Little-Middleton-in-the-Dell."

"You are not marrying some Cornwall fool," the duke

said briskly. "The next step is for announcements to be put into the best papers. 'A marriage is arranged,' they will say, 'and shortly take place between Miss so-and-so, daughter of who-it-is and Aubrey Seldon, Duke of Mainwaring.' "

Aunt Hetty said magisterially, "We will, of course, defray the fees for those announcements."

"As to the matter of the church, Winifred tells me that there are only two fashionable locations. There is St. George's or St. Peter's."

"We will inspect each and make a choice," Aunt Hetty said. "Of course the rental expenses will be borne by the Tregallens."

"There remains only the matter of the settlement," said the Duke.

Clarissa knew what he meant. A friend had once described the procedure. The money of each party to a marriage would be formally placed in the hands of trustees for the benefit of both.

"I shall arrange for my local solicitor to be in touch with the solicitor of your choice and a time set for the signing of necessary documents."

Again that infernal quizzing glass came into play. "A London solicitor for each participant would show more respect for London protocol."

"I will ask Mr. Rossiter to arrange for a colleague in London to represent us, as you feel so strongly about the matter."

"Can I infer that these difficulties will be attended to in a short while?"

"I will write to Mr. Rossiter before the sun sets, and other matters will be attended as soon as may be."

"Splendid." Aubrey's smile, which had been intermittent, now widened. "I have never spoken to a woman about such matters, or any matter that might be construed as business. I could have expected no better sense from a member of my own sex."

"Thank you," said Aunt Hetty drily.

Maude, who had stationed herself at a bay window rather than listen to the chattering at table, suddenly turned.

"Do all Londoners walk on the streets at the same time?"

Clarissa, too unsettled to make any response, shrugged.

"Imagine having strangers passing to and fro before one's home," Maude marveled.

Lady Winifred took it upon herself to say lightly, "Some of those strangers might be men who are handsome and worth looking at."

"Not in London," Maude answered firmly, offending the duke.

Lady Winifred threw him a look of amusement.

Aunt Hetty spoke sternly. "Maude, you will want to apologize to your future brother-in-law."

"Oh, I didn't mean—"

"That is perfectly all right," the duke said, but a metallic smile had thinned his lips. "It is not of any real importance now . . . As I was saying before the interruption, Clarissa, all plans will be complete in a month while Winifred is preparing for our annual ball."

"Pardon?" Clarissa hadn't been listening to every word.

The duke misunderstood. "The ball is a good opportunity to introduce you to any exclusives you haven't met by this time, to people you must know, Clarissa."

"I see." By the time a month had limped past, the marriage plans would be known to all of London, even known to any possible French spy who had sought refuge there.

"You have not much more than thirty days," the duke chortled, "to remain free."


Maude didn't explode into tears until the town coach was well away from Berkeley Square. Then she cried achingly into a section of dark cambric. It was pointless to ask what was wrong.

Clarissa finally waited until her sister paused for breath. "If you do not tell me the reason for this demonstration," she said harshly, "I shall shake you like a child's plaything."

After a burst of fresh tears which lasted only long enough to prove that she wouldn't listen to anybody, Maude said haltingly, "It's London."

Aunt Hetty, who had been watching the sisters from a face of stone, put in, "You have to tell us exactly what you mean."

"I—I cannot stay in London for an entire month!"

"Many a young woman would give every tooth in her head (not that those would be worth much, you understand) for a month's stay in the heart of civilization. There are theatres, shops . . ."

Clarissa, catching the spirit of her aunt's strategy, added, "And the ice-skating parties where you can meet young men without seeming to go out of your way to do so."

Maude responded strongly, "But I *have* a young man, already."

"Oh! I understand why you are in tears," Clarissa said at last. "I fear I was so involved with my own difficulties that I did not appreciate yours."

Maude offered no further sobs, but smiled instead. A weak smile, as was only to be expected.

Aunt Hetty asked grimly, "Would you be referring to that foolish officer of the light dragoons?"

"He isn't," Maude started, and then closed her lips as she suffered for the one she felt certain she loved.

"Has he told you that he loves you?"

"We only met last week."

"So he has said nothing?"

"He will. Roderick may not be as sure of himself as some, perhaps, but I know that he will offer for me."

Clarissa winced, being reminded that Bryan

Deverell was absolutely certain of himself in dealing with the fair sex. Bryan had made his feelings clear within moments. The man she loved was perfection itself in every way but one. That one, however, made every happiness seem a hollow mockery.

Aunt Hetty was pursuing the argument with Maude from the view of practicality. Clarissa could have told the spinster that she was embarked on a hopeless cause.

"He can offer nothing because he has nothing," she said crisply.

"There is money in the estate," Maude persisted. "If necessary, Aubrey must have more than enough to tide us over any bad time."

"Oh, heavens!" Aunt Hetty wailed. "Have you no pride?"

"Not the least."

The conversation promised to go on until the end of Clarissa's youth and Maude's as well. It had to be stopped.

"Maude, we are on our way to look at fabrics for clothing to be run up for us." Clarissa's voice was that of someone who would brook no further nonsense. "We will meet Lady Winifred at the dressmaker's establishment, and she will serve as a guide. Do you recall hearing these facts?"

A sob caught in her sister's throat was the only answer.

"I cannot tell how long it will take for the clothing to be run up, and it should be clear that we all have to be available for fittings at irregular intervals over the next days. Is this also clear to you, Maude?"

"Of course it is."

"We are making progress, then. In the meantime, arrangements must go forth to find the most suitable church, for announcements in the best papers, for invitations to be issued and sent. Furthermore, as you also heard, Lord Mainwaring will be giving a ball at his home and I must be there in full rig. You and Aunt

Hetty are duty bound to do the same, for reasons which I will not dignify with a further explanation."

"You're saying that I will have to remain in this awful town—no, city, for thirty days."

"After which, of course, we should be able to go home until shortly before the wedding."

Aunt Hetty, knowing that tears were beginning to subside, immediately said, "Only thirty more days, dear, until the end of January."

"January?" Maude's face crumpled up again. "But that will be next year!"

Hetty Tregallen threw up her hands at the new wave of tears. More practically, perhaps, Clarissa was shaking her sister as the family arrived at St. James Street to the modiste's place of business.


In spite of the war with France, the clothing firms of London were given French names. Fanchon's was one of the best modistes. Rosette's made and sold fashionable shoes. Olympe's was London's first hatmaker. Undergarments could be discreetly fitted and run up at Clothilde's. There might have been an unspoken understanding between dealers and customers that the war with Bonaparte—a Corsican, after all—was no more than a fleeting inconvenience.

Mlle. Fanchon's establishment took up the second floor of a red brick building. There was so much light in it as almost to hurt the eyes. Mirrors reflected gasoliers. Instead of two windows on each side, there were four bays. Chairs and tables were colored brightly. It was impossible not to see clearly the garments offered or fabrics shown.

Lady Winifred had arrived before the Tregallens. She sat imperiously examining bolts of material, finished products, and a volume of drawings that showed current fashions at their most desirable. She was looking critically at the illustration of a garment that was to be soaked in water, thereby showing a female figure with the clarity of image that might be seen by a physician.

"I would go out of my way to avoid that," she said to the woman who was waiting upon her. Now she looked up. "This is for Miss Maude, perhaps, but not me."

The advantages of the indicated gown were explained to Maude, whose eyes were dry and whose features reflected no sign of interest. Clarissa would have been delighted to wear such a gown, but felt that for a future duchess it would be unsuitable.

"Surely you can suggest something that would be more seemly," Lady Winifred told the clerk cuttingly.

A walking dress of gros de Londres was then inspected. Clarissa felt it would be suitable for her, an opinion which Aunt Hetty confirmed with an eager nod.

But Lady Winifred said, "You will have that garment run up for me."

The clerk made a note on pink foolscap. Clarissa and her aunt exchanged glances in which the previous eagerness had died.

Another walking dress, this one of amber crepe, drew a reluctant nod from Clarissa. Once more the approval was in vain.

"Run that up for me, too," said Lady Winifred, brooking no interruption. "A shade darker, perhaps. Let me see what is available."

By the time the duke's sister was willing to proceed, Clarissa felt as if she herself had aged considerably. Maude, shrugging, walked over to the nearest window to look outside, which seemed like one of her newly developed hobbies for her stay in the city.

An evening gown of rose-colored gauze was next to draw Lady Winifred's admiration, except for the color. A gown of cerulean blue satin, cut low at the bodice and with bugle trimming, won yet another accolade, except for the trimming.

Clarissa found the spectacle less than entertaining, and a source of curiosity as well. Lady Winifred had been dressing as if she hadn't ordered new clothes since she was Clarissa's age. It seemed that after showing some interest in Bryan Deverell, she was ready to make herself more comely. If this kept on, she would buy everything at Mlle. Fanchon's, including tables and chairs.

Lady Winifred suddenly said to the clerk, "Leave us till I call you back." Next she turned toward Aunt Hetty. "I would appreciate—ha! yes, appreciate a minute alone with your niece."

Confronted by an attempt at courtesy, Aunt Hetty obliged. She joined Maude over at the nearest window.

"Miss Tregallen, you are asking yourself if I am buying so many clothes in order to fascinate Mr. Deverell should I ever see him again."

Clarissa appreciated plain speaking, but wasn't used to it from a woman who was more than a decade older.

"I cannot say anything about that."

She hardly knew what words were coming out of her mouth. They seemed disconnected from her. She wished she could keep her lips closed when speech wasn't required. Never had she felt more awkward.

"I may tell you that I had a brief discussion with Mr. Deverell the night before last in front of that tarpit which calls itself an inn at which we stopped."

"A discussion?" Clarissa was taken aback.

"Mr. Deverell reluctantly made it clear that he did not feel a *tendre* for me."

"I am sorry about your disappointment." Clarissa hated herself for the lie, but followed it with another. "I can understand that it is difficult for a woman not to have caught that man for whom she casts a net, as I have caught Aubrey."

"Whether you cast the net or Aubrey tumbled into it headfirst, my dear Clarissa, is quite beyond the scope of this conversation. What I wanted you to know is that

I formed the very clear impression that Mr. Deverell remains interested in you."

Clarissa nodded before realizing that she was supposed to look embarrassed, that she wasn't supposed to care a fig about the yearnings of Bryan Deverell's heart.

She sought for a way to change the subject. "May I ask out of curiosity alone why you purchased so many clothes?"

"For a reason that a girl of your tender years may not understand." Lady Winifred actually hesitated before speaking further, in itself a delicate compliment. "You see, I was taken by Mr. Deverell, and as a result I learned something from the experience."

"Might I ask what it was?"

"Simply that as long as I remain interested in finding a husband, I should keep searching."

It was a maxim which Aunt Hetty, of greater years, would never accept.

"So you see, my dear Clarissa, I am here to order clothes which will be of some use."

It was impossible not to respond warmly, a circumstance which Clarissa would not have anticipated. The aloof and vain Lady Winifred had been replaced by another, not so much warm and compassionate as wholly human. Yes, that was the truth. Lady Winifred Seldon had been transmuted into a human being.

"I wish you a successful hunt," Clarissa said quietly and sincerely.

"Thank you." Lady Winifred raised a hand, autocratically signaling for the clerk to return with the book of drawings.

Clarissa was unable to think about a purchase until it was clear that Lady Winifred felt her needs had been satisfied. When that was done, and Lady Winifred was at the other end of the establishment and behind a screen where she could be measured for fit, Clarissa inspected previously unseen drawings. She and Aunt Hetty agreed about a lavender brocade gown with faint yellow stripes to bring out her eyes. There was some heated discussion about a white muslin frock with russet borders. Eventually Clarissa carried the day and the dress was ordered.

Aunt Hetty finally said, irritated, "I am sure that Maude will be more amenable to reason."

She looked around in vain for her other niece. Maude was not at any of the windows. Nor had she wandered over to the display tables. There was no sign of her.

Aunt and remaining niece exchanged worried glances. Clarissa was on her way to discuss the matter with a clerk, who might have some information. She turned, distracted.

A sound had come to her through the window, the sound of a young woman under great agitation. There was a note of shrillness in that tone, with which Clarissa was familiar from her life west of Devonshire, at home in Cornwall.

She allowed herself one fevered glance out the window. Her greatest fear was confirmed. With a cry to her aunt, she ran for the staircase and down to the street.

## Chapter Twenty-one

She ran out to St. James Street, not far from where the Regent's own Horse Guards were stationed on perpetual display. She had eyes only for the quarrel that was taking place in the middle of the street.

A hayrack had come to a stop in spite of surging traffic, and drivers of carriages and other hayracks cursed fiercely as they passed.

Standing at the right of the vehicle was Maude, who had taken a stick of firewood from in front of a nearby shop and was flailing at the seat normally used by a driver. She could get no closer to the driver himself. Otherwise the driver would've been unable to stand with whip in hand while he swore at his scarred horse and at Maude.

Clarissa had to clear her way through the ongoing traffic. She reached Maude at last and only after taking great care. Then she drew both arms around her sister's middle, causing the club of firewood to fall into the dirt at their feet. Maude flailed away at the constricting hands, wanting to court danger by confronting the driver.

Clarissa pulled her sister back. Maude suddenly stopped screaming. She wasn't anxious for both sisters to be knocked over by a passing carriage. Clarissa wasn't the only one, blessedly, who was keenly aware of danger to them.

"What on earth has happened?" Clarissa demanded as soon as they were safe.

Maude turned to glare back at the hayrack driver. She looked puzzled instead. The driver had moved off and was nearly out of sight. Running to him in this clotted traffic would have presented an even greater risk than before.

"You saw what happened!" Maude was breathing with difficulty, fury at the driver not having left her. "You saw what that vile rascal had done!"

"I saw you holding a piece of firewood and hitting the driver's seat."

"I wish I had hit him over the head with that firewood." She was on the point of reciting a list of tortures she would have liked to have inflicted on the stranger.

"Why? That is a simple question, Maude."

"Didn't you see the horse with whip marks across its flanks?" Maude demanded. "I was looking through the window of that shop and I saw the horse halt out of weariness. Then I saw that—that *vermin* start to whip the animal again. Is it any wonder that I ran out to try and give him some of the treatment he was offering the horse?"

"No, it isn't any wonder at all," Clarissa admitted. "If I had known, I would have felt privileged to join you."

Aunt Hetty appeared, having just run down the stairs from Mlle. Fanchon's shop. The activity, as ever with Hetty Tregallen, hadn't affected her.

"I see," she said when a breathless Clarissa had explained. "I'm afraid that London is filled with men whose behavior is no credit whatever to the human race."

Maude finally stopped quivering with recollected anger, which brought Aunt Hetty's mind back to the business at hand.

"Clarissa, go up and be fitted. Maude, you will join

me. I am taking no sauce from you on that matter."

"No, Aunt," Maude agreed quietly.

"You, too, will choose new rig-outs for yourself, with my indispensable help. You will be fitted. And we can only hope," Aunt Hetty added, "that Lady Winifred was being measured all the while."

"Why?" Clarissa was startled.

"If Lord Mainwaring learns about this episode, this public display by a soon-to-be relative after marriage," Aunt Hetty remarked, "then, Clarissa, I don't know what might happen."


Clarissa's first thought when she awoke was that the London weather was enough to make anyone gloomy. It had become much colder overnight. People on the street couldn't walk without being doubled up against the wind. Clarissa much preferred the good honest Cornwall mist.

With Lizzie's help, she chose a high-waisted long-sleeved day dress in a shade that could be described as off-lavender. It was one of those horrors she had originally wanted to wear as an adventure of sorts. She had come to find it appalling. For her mood of the moment, it matched perfectly.

Her hair was drawn back, but in such an artful way as not to expose the ears to any chill. She insisted on wearing a kashmir shawl, though it made her look older. She told herself that she would have worn lighted sticks of firewood to keep away the cold.

As it happened, the breakfast room at Limmer's was so strongly warmed by twin fireplaces that Clarissa soon found herself feeling overheated. She had to send for Lizzie and have her take the shawl back up to her chamber.

Two other visitors, up from West Sussex, as their talk made plain, were in a spirited discussion about the value of raising sheep during a time of war.

Clarissa spent a few otherwise idle moments distinguishing their speech patterns from those with which she was most familiar. She turned when a sullen Maude entered.

"Didn't you sleep well?" Clarissa asked as her sister approached the table warily.

Breakfast in a London hotel, as Maude had been appalled to find out, was tendered by the staff. In London it was apparently possible to have all one's needs handled and not move a muscle except to turn over so that the other half of one's body could be warmed at a fireplace.

"No, I slept badly," Maude remarked, taking ham slices and lukewarm eggs from the tray that had been brought. "I dreamed that Roderick was ill and that a horse had joined me in attending him."

It was the sort of dream that Clarissa wouldn't have had for worlds. She was on the point of hinting as much when Aunt Hetty hurried in.

"We will eat quickly and proceed to my chambers," she told them.

"Has any difficulty arisen?"

"Indeed it has."

"I feel confident," Clarissa said carefully, not at all surprised, "that if any possible difficulty can arise during a visit to London, it will do so."

"And I am not prepared to say," Aunt Hetty remarked after some consideration, "that your confidence is entirely misplaced."


Aunt Hetty's chamber would have been suitable for an empress of China. Oriental figures were engraved on the fireplace. Chinese ideographs filled the chair backs and upper walls. Two paintings showed Oriental people enduring ordeals with great serenity. Raising one's voice in these quarters would have been shameful.

Aunt Hetty saw to it that her nieces were seated. Only then did she reach over to the bookcase. From there she took a newspaper.

"It was issued this morning," she said. "Lizzie procured a copy at my request. I knew that if yesterday's brouhaha would be reported in print anywhere, it would happen in this paper. I have heard of it before."

"And yesterday's episode had been noted?"

"I will read you the hideous details as they have been perceived by these ragamuffins." Affixing spectacles to ears and nose, she sought out a particular page of *Sport News and Society Revels*.

There, it was gleefully reported that a young woman on St. James Street had berated a hayrack driver before being pulled away by an older woman, joined by a third who was still older, and then all had trekked up the stairs to the shop of a fashionable dressmaker.

"They are being accurate," Clarissa pointed out softly.

"Too much so."

"No name is mentioned."

"Not ours, no, but that of another is given in this account."

The report added that a carriage of no less a peer than the Duke of Mainwaring, a vehicle recognizable because of the seal on its doors, had been close by. After a short wait, Lady Winifred Seldon, sister of the duke, had been observed leaving the shop and hurrying into the carriage. She left the scene immediately.

Maude, spirited as ever, said "They are trying to make trouble by using a name that is well known in society. They have no other facts to offer, no other names."

"Nevertheless, Aubrey will see the account (leave it to a peer to look through the scandal papers for any mention of his name). He will then inquire of the coachman who drove Lady Winifred. The coachman knows us by sight. He will confide in his patron, you may be sure."

Clarissa said firmly, "The only course is to deny everything. The newspaper is mistaken. The coachman's eyes were deceived by sunlight. Tell no part of the truth. Aubrey cannot prove you are doing so."

Aunt Hetty, who had been intensely serious up to this point, suddenly drew back as if to look at her older niece for the first time. On her lips was the start of a smile.

"Your response, Clarissa, brings up an interesting point," she said lightly. "Denying everything is exactly what you have done on numerous occasions when you were guilty of some breach."

"And it can be very effective," Clarissa was unwilling to let herself be distracted. "We make our faces as rigid as those of the people in the drawings on these walls. Aubrey will not have any idea of what the truth is."

Maude was still young enough to laugh in an unseemly way. She drew up a hand to cover that youthful lapse.

Aunt Hetty bit her lower lip in thought. "No better idea suggests itself in case Aubrey does decide to raise a difficulty," she said, having given the matter her most earnest consideration. "In fact, it does seem possible that Aubrey will know nothing about who may have been responsible for that fault. After all, we are in London, where the streets teem with women of all ages. Some other trio may have been in the vicinity of St. James Street and have caused the display."

The door panel moved lightly under a series of deferential knocks.

"Come in!" Aunt Hetty called.

It was Lizzie. The maid looked disconcerted.

"There is a visitor in the hotel morning room."

"A visitor? Who would that be?"

"Lord Mainwaring, ma'am. Lord Mainwaring is downstairs."

* * *

Aubrey Seldon was handsomely dressed, as ever. Those light gray eyes of his, with his blond hair and narrow head, gave him the look of a Greek god who anticipated making some mortal girl his own beloved.

He was, however, in a foul mood.

That disposition changed everything. The clothes seemed to have a fidgeting life of their own. He looked like a Greek god in the throes of some minor ailment.

It was a sight that Clarissa knew indicated trouble to come. Aubrey Seldon was getting ready to be at his most aristocratic, making demands, laying down rules.

"I want to have it clear," he said, before any greetings could be exchanged, "that I am well aware of the demonstration such as took place yesterday on St. James Street."

Aunt Hetty proved that she had absorbed the instruction Clarissa gave.

"I don't understand what you mean," she said, doing her best to seem bewildered.

Aubrey looked like a cannoneer who had fired off a shell which refused to ignite. The look didn't last long.

"It will save time if I tell you that Maude's fit of hysteria on St. James Street—"

"It was *not* a—"

"Quiet, dear!"

"—was seen by one of Mlle. Fanchon's clerks, who was aware that the parties were known to my sister. As a result, Winifred was informed of what had taken place."

Clarissa jumped into the breach. "The clerk was mistaken."

"She was not. And neither was my coachman, who also saw the incident and knows all of you."

Further arguments could have been made: everyone's sight was poor, everyone had a sinful passion for gossip whether or not there was any truth in it, the Tregallens had been at the other end of the shop during the time of any eruptions in the street.

Clarissa kept quiet.

Here, almost at hand, was a solution to her worst difficulty. If Aubrey felt that the family's behavior would not be suitable for a Mainwaring connection, he could call off any idea of a marriage to Clarissa. Once again she would be free.

Wryly she told herself that she would be free to wait long enough to read in some other newspaper that Bryan Deverell, a spy for the French, had finally met the fate he so richly deserved.

And Maude would be free to stay unmarried for life or make a match with some soldier while claiming that she loved him.

As if love could change anything. No love would turn Bryan Deverell from what he was and make him an honorable citizen of Bulldom in the battle line of the current war.

Aubrey was speaking.

"I want to make it clear that no such odious exhibition must ever take place again." He even waggled a forefinger to reinforce the point. "It is unsuitable; it is not done by the family or any connection of a peer of the realm."

So Aubrey had not been incited to abandon the idea of marrying her! Clarissa didn't know how she felt about it. Relieved in a way, she supposed. A young woman had to marry and the man she particularly wanted for herself was not available.

Aunt Hetty had been looking calm, but her serenity didn't last.

Maude, angry and irritable, burst out, "When I am married, I won't have to listen to you."

"Maude, your husband and I will confer between us and decide what it is right for you to do," the duke said imperiously overruling Aunt Hetty's attempt to make herself heard. "Let us hear no more of this prattle."

" 'Prattle,' is it? Let me tell you that Roderick Taggart may listen, but will pay no attention to anything you say if he thinks it will be harmful to me."

"Taggart? Roderick Taggart?" The duke was startled. "That infernal buffoon!"

"He is a *drag*oon, not a *buff*oon."

Clarissa had to turn way and hide her own laughter. The matter was in deadly earnest, affecting the Tregallens and their future. Yet it was impossible at this moment to keep a straight face. Could it be that the most serious of life's encounters was tinged with levity?

In this case, the distraction was brief. Aunt Hetty urgently spoke a few quiet words to her niece. Maude subsided, but remained rebellious.

The duke drew himself up to his full height. "You will not marry without my permission, to be sure. And you certainly will not marry a soldier of no importance."

Maude started to cry turning to her sister for comfort.

"About this I am firm," the duke insisted. "I will not tolerate behavior from the two of you which is unsuitable in any way whatever."

Without adding to that ultimatum, he walked to the door. In front of it he turned around and said formally, "I remain your most obedient servant."

The Tregallen women had been chilled to the marrow by this meeting. But the grimness had been diluted by a wicked infusion of farce. As soon as the door was safely shut behind the duke, Clarissa and Maude burst into wild laughter.

"I had almost forgotten something," Aunt Hetty said when the laughter faded. She reached into her reticule for a sealed envelope.

"This came for you," she said, turning to Clarissa, who barely retained the strength to put out a hand for it. "I suppose a friend is writing from the village. I know that eighty post chaises leave London every day, but it surprises me that the post from Cornwall would be brought here so quickly."

Clarissa held it at a side, still too dazed by laughter to investigate. Maude, holding her middle, left the room. Aunt Hetty started to do the same.

Clarissa promised to be with them in moments. She never knew what caused her to stay behind, but later thought that it might be a realization that the upper right hand corner of the envelope was blank. It did not bear a penny stamp with the words *Postage and Revenue*. This letter had not been sent by post.

More striking was the sudden knowledge that the handwriting was not in a script with which she was instantly familiar.

She already knew what she would be told if she spoke to the hotel clerk about this note. It had been brought to Limmer's and left for her, probably by a messenger from a tall and muscular man with broad shoulders as well as laughing hazel eyes. A man of strong voice and valiant character.

If something like this could happen in London, she assured herself, then the city of London must be a wonderful place after all. Just as she had thought during her first visit.

Knowing who had touched the letter, let alone written inside it, made her want to prolong the anticipation of opening it, to guess what he may have told her. She stared at the gray-white seal. Was there a pledge of eternal love to match her own? Was it a suggestion for a rendezvous. If so, she would return the love and go to the meeting.

Best to open it quickly, though. Otherwise Aunt Hetty might come back to ask what was keeping her and might also want to see the letter.

Clarissa opened it with great care and took out the sheet of foolscap, then unfolded it slowly. It was as if she feared that the words would run off the sheet.

29/12

Dear Clarissa:
  Be patient a little longer.

He hadn't even signed his name.

Clarissa's first impulse was to feel anger as she put away the letter. Be patient and what would happen? No one had ever written a note that was less to the point, that meant so little.

True enough, he knew where she was staying, having taken the trouble to keep track of her. It was more than pleasant to know as much. It was gratifying.

But he wasn't here now when he was needed. He wasn't giving her the slightest help against Aubrey's high-handedness. And in that case, his encouragement wasn't of any use.

## Chapter Twenty-two

It ought to have been a great adventure. Here she was in London, showing Maude the wonders of Almack's, the club where dancing took second place only to gambling. Clarissa had been thrilled by the sight during her London visit last year. In a brief stay, it had offered a memorable interlude.

Her feeling at this visit was different. She could smell the red cru wine that had been spilled on the shiny floor by at least one careless drinker. Women's dresses were a shade too daring. The men were unpleasantly sure of themselves. Clarissa didn't feel that the place was enough to cause any real excitement in Blossom the cow.

Or perhaps (again!) she was jaundiced because one certain man was among those absent.

The procedures followed were the same as on the previous occasion. Tickets had been secured from one of the three patronesses who sat in their boxes and watched the dancers below. During the other visit, she had been introduced to that patroness, the likeable Lady Cowper. On this occasion she spoke briefly with Lady Jersey, who seemed ever so slightly starchy.

Beside her, the Duke of Mainwaring was togged in the knee breeches and white cravat that were crucial to the rig-out of any male visitor. He seemed at ease, as if he spent his every Wednesday night on-season or off at the establishment in King Street.

The duke had previously written a note to Aunt Hetty. In it he said that they would all visit the one place in London where members of the *ton* could be found in their brightest plumage. At least he hadn't instructed the girls when to smile or curtsey.

Aunt Hetty took the proceedings in stride. Maude, however, behaved as if she had ventured into a land of miracles. She stared from one visitor to another, was awed by the shiny floor, and reported her findings to Clarissa.

"It is different from a dance at Truro," she began.

"Is it better, do you think?"

"Only different."

Maude, such an enthusiast when her feelings could be aroused, was in no danger of losing her head over the glitter of London. That much was a blessing. One of the few in this situation.

The duke had noted Clarissa's indifferent manner. "Here are twenty pounds," he said, thrusting the bills at her. "Go into the gambling room and lose it at whist or faro while I renew some friendships. Join me again in thirty minutes."

Another order. Clarissa could hardly avoid the money and waited until the duke was moving forward. She turned to her sister.

"Here is some of the needful, Maude. You can go into the next room and gamble till it's used up, if you wish. Whatever you may do, don't win."

Aunt Hetty took the bills out of Maude's hands and dropped them into the reticule she insisted on carrying. "That money will buy something for you at some time, dear."

An acquaintance from the time of Clarissa's first visit must have overheard that caution. "I would be only too happy to take those few pounds and make your fortune with them. Easier done than said."

"But would you make my sister's fortune, Lord

215

Alvanley?"

"I would try my best," said the round-faced and button-nosed profligate. "It is written that the cards and counters are fickle, but not in the hands of those who master them by force of character."

It was reliably rumored that Will Alvanley owed several fortunes because of his gambling at Almack's as well as White's and Boodle's. Clarissa believed it. Lord Alvanley had the air of a man who cared little for the next hour's difficulties, let alone those of the coming day.

During the minutes that followed, Clarissa found herself renewing brief acquaintances with Mr. Thomas Raikes, who was known, for some reason, as "Apollo," as well as the Baroness Monson, Lady Heathcote, and a woman who looked more like a drawing of William Pitt than anyone else living, Clarissa was sure.

"I hope you lost all the money I gave you," Mainwaring said, cheerfully swaying over at her side. "Gambling is a pleasant hobby, but a dreadful excess."

He had been drinking, to judge from his breath. He could have made the same remark about whiskey.

"A waltz is being played," he remarked, having cocked his head. "Now you will see how it is danced in the very center of world civilization. Better yet, come out and dance with me."

Clarissa held back, kept in place by a strong recollection of the duke's unpleasant behavior when they had danced together last.

"Come, come," Mainwaring said, lowering his voice so as not to be overheard by Miss Harriette Wilson, who was nearby and had looked saucily at him and speculatively at Clarissa. "Don't keep me waiting."

He put a hand to her back, causing her to move in the direction of the dance floor. When she turned to ask him not to touch her unless it was necessary, he was standing in place and swaying.

"I will wait for you to feel better," she told him.

"I am not indisposed," he said insistently, refusing to concede that he didn't have the endurance of a bull.

It seemed foolish not to admit what would have been clear to the smallest intelligence.

"In that case, let us dance," she snapped.

"I told you that as soon as I —" He inhaled deeply, then tried to prove all was well. He didn't move his feet. A middle-aged man was passing, and the duke practically touched him, affording a reason to stand in place at least a little longer.

"I want you to meet," he began, passing off the incident as a normal social matter, "ah, to meet —"

"I am Herbert Rathbone," the man said firmly, irritated by Mainwaring's lapse.

No nickname was added, so he probably hadn't been given any. His posture was rigid. Those brows of his looked as if they'd been singed but remained perfectly straight. In his mid-fifties, he was a man with little tolerance for humor. A possible reason for his sternness was hinted by the shadow in his eyes. This man had suffered. His experiences had wiped away any feeling for what he considered irrelevant.

The duke gestured vaguely at the others in his party. Rathbone glanced at Maude with only the rudiments of courtesy. His gaze rested on Clarissa, but not long enough for him to venture a smile.

That miracle did happen when he saw Hetty Tregallen. It was a cool smile, even a wintry smile, but his lips did thin even though he made a sound that reminded Clarissa of ice cracking.

"Indeed I remember you, Miss Tregallen," Herbert Rathbone said. "We met last year when you were in London."

"Oh, yes." After a brief start, Hetty recovered her equilibrium. "I recall how you told me that your wife was seriously ill. I do hope that the poor lady is herself."

217

The shadow over Herbert Rathbone's eyes was more pronounced. "My dear Dilys passed away in March of this year.

Aunt Hetty didn't give in to facile regrets or sympathy that might be cloying. She showed her true colors, being compassionate without sentiment.

"Better for her, I think, to judge from what you told me of her sufferings. Her welfare was paramount."

"I agree, but to feel that way is most difficult." Herbert Rathbone would have said more if not for the surroundings and the listeners.

Clarissa was moved by a notion that she had never expected would cross her mind: Aunt Hetty, who always lamented her spinsterhood, was still attractive to some suitable man.

Clarissa said to the duke, "If you would like to waltz with me, I am agreeable."

"Yes, yes, a waltz." But he seemed unable to move. The music had got under way.

"Let us take the air," she said to the duke, gesturing at Maude to join them. "It will do you good, and me as well."

"Yes, that's it. We'll help you recover yourself by taking the air." But his feet remained stubborn.

Maude, who had understood her sister's signal, walked to the other side of the duke. She was prepared to join Clarissa in urging the intemperate peer to a point away from Aunt Hetty and her conquest.

Herbert Rathbone had noticed the girls maneuvering. He held up a hand to a shoulder as he reluctantly half-turned, keeping them in place.

"Perhaps we will see each other a third time, Miss Tregallen," he said a little hastily. "I would consider it most fortunate."

No one who hadn't known Aunt Hetty for years would have guessed that she was feeling keenly disappointed.

"You have a meeting to attend, of course," she said

evenly.

"Not the way you mean it, no," Herbert Rathbone told her. "I have come because I felt that all London would be on the premises on a Wednesday night no matter what the season, and it is a suitably busy place to have a few words with your niece."

"With Maude? Clarissa?"

"Miss Clarissa, as it happens."

Aubrey drew himself up as best he could, prepared to help Clarissa by turning regal and imperious.

"What do you wish to speak to Miss Tregallen about, Rathbone?"

Herbert Rathbone returned the duke's stare.

"I will speak to the young lady alone," he snapped, cutting off the argument.

"Now look here—" Aubrey was unable to change Rathbone's mind. He was at his firmest in dealing with females, in giving them orders.

Clarissa remained mystified about the reasons for Rathbone's wanting to talk to her in privacy. Only one answer suggested itself, and it was enough to cause her heart to thump with happiness. He wanted to discuss something connected to Bryan Deverell. Perhaps he was a messenger from Bryan, perhaps he would take her to him. Rathbone looked an unlikely Cupid, but in London he might fit the image to perfection.

If only to get away from the inebriated peer, she nodded and said, "Please excuse me, Aubrey, Aunt, Maude."

The duke called after her, "Be careful, Clarissa. He may be preparing to detain you at Newgate or some other such place."

"What does that mean?"

"You are speaking to the famous Col. Herbert Rathbone," the duke said cheerily. "He is employed by the Foreign Office to track down spies."

\* \* \*

Clarissa was in two minds as she followed Col. Herbert Rathbone out to an alcove which was otherwise unoccupied. It was soothing to know that Deverell was out of the colonel's reach, so he couldn't be harmed.

On the other hand, it was a great irritation that the duke could have previously gone to Rathbone and asked the colonel to question her in such a way as to arouse fear in her. In that case, she indirectly had Deverell to blame. She would never again, in theory, think a good thought about the godlike Deverell.

Certainly it was possible. It would have been typical of Aubrey Seldon's manipulations. He seemed to be on her side, but he encouraged the opposition. He was a friend to all and an enemy to all.

The considering of one possibility after another had been enough to make her head feel bruised. It had to be faced quite simply that she didn't know the reasons for this forthcoming inquisition. Time would give the answer. Perhaps.

"I have been made to understand," Colonel Rathbone began, "that you had an encounter with a stranger during Christmas week at your home in Cornwall."

"I did, yes."

"And that the stranger, a male, said he was a cousin. Further, that you believed him."

"I had no reason to doubt it."

"Did this stranger give the name of Bryan Deverell? In that case, do me the favor of describing him."

"He was about a head taller than you and very strong-looking. His hair was pitch black, his eyes the same hazel color as—"

"Hazel, yes." Rathbone's own eyes were half-closed in thought. "Does he have a wide forehead and a strong voice?"

"He does." She asked hesitantly, "Do you know much about him?"

"My path has crossed his in the past." Was Colonel Rathbone speaking in a voice that hid volumes? "Can you tell me more about him?"

She very much wanted to say that Bryan Deverell was a brave man with humor and a strong intelligence. She would have told another woman that to be held in his arms was a feeling as close to Paradise as anyone would ever know. And she would have added happily that he kissed with great passion.

But she was speaking to a man, to a hunter of men, so she answered with a fact that was trivial.

"All I can think of is that he drinks hot chocolate for breakfast."

"Does he indeed?" Colonel Rathbone's expression was unreadable. "Did you have any suspicion that he might not in fact be the person he said he was?"

"There was no reason to feel like that."

Now she was being inspected carefully. Colonel Rathbone was not a man to whom it was easy to tell a lie.

"A stranger comes to you from the road, or you go out to him, and you believe everything he says. I hope that not everyone in Cornwall is so trusting by nature."

"I believed *him*." Clarissa held up her head, chin thrust out aggressively. She had never known a man like Deverell before that night, so she felt no shame for any weakness.

"Did he make any request of you?" Rathbone went on. "Did he ask you to do anything for him?"

"Nothing. Nor did I do anything at all except to help him stay over the holiday season."

"Have you heard from him since he left?"

Again Clarissa's head was raised, chin thrust out. Somebody had once told her that she should always behave as if no one would doubt her, especially if she happened to be lying through her teeth.

"He has not been in touch with me since that time."

"If he should seek you out or write, will you tell the duke about it? He is sure to notify me."

"Of course I will tell the duke. I am to marry him and would let nothing of that sort happen without informing him."

"I can ask no better than that." Colonel Rathbone inclined his head courteously. "Myself, I had always thought that every young woman relishes an adventure, but it is professionally satisfying to know beyond doubt that for so many years I have been in the wrong."

"I can assure you, Colonel, that dealing with a man who is a spy against my country goes against every fiber of my being as a Briton. I must say to you that having such a man under my family roof was as much of an adventure as I will ever want in my life."

Wasn't that exactly what he and the duke expected to hear from her?

"I gladly accept your assurances, Miss Clarissa," said Colonel Rathbone.

He turned away. Clarissa, following his back out to the dance area, wondered why the last look she had seen him direct at her should have been embellished by the beginnings of a faint smile.


She found Aunt Hetty looking at the place from which she had come, the area that had held Colonel Rathbone. The colonel had passed through the room like a flame and was nowhere to be seen. There was an expectant smile on her face as she turned to look round and only with reluctance turned back to her niece.

"How did you like the colonel?"

"He is well mannered."

"But doesn't he have a thrilling voice and superb presence?"

"Oh, yes. Certainly. A matchless presence."

"Did he by any chance tell you where he was going?"

"No, but I would suppose he wants to question someone else's bona fides, perhaps Lady Jersey's."

"Surely the colonel did not question your identity, let alone your goodwill?"

Clarissa refused to make it clear that she and Rathbone had discussed the honor of the man she loved. All she wanted now was to make her way back to the infernal hotel at which they were staying. She wanted to get between the sheets and stay there.

"Can we possibly scoop up Maude and leave?"

"It's a bit early to make a grand exit from Almack's."

"I'm sure that is true, dear Aunt, but I have been worn down by the incessant conversation and fencing with words. I do not know all the rules of verbal duello, dear Aunt. I cannot play the game of words too well."

She was keenly aware of her aunt's sharp look. Aunt Hetty spoke after some moments of consideration during which the rippling of a girl's laughter could be heard.

"I don't truly believe that you are indisposed, Clarissa. You will pardon me, my dear, for this."

Once again, as in childhood, her aunt's palm was on her forehead and then the back of the neck. Anguished moments passed before the hand was withdrawn.

"You do not suffer from a fever," Aunt Hetty decided, rendering a verdict in the same tones as a judge would regret not having to put on the black cap. Even a minor illness would have made her feel more useful.

Clarissa was on the point of saying that if love is a fever, she was certainly high on any list of those who are afflicted.

"Nevertheless, I am determined to go back to the

hotel, as we are too far from home."

"I must notify Aubrey of this change in our plans, Clarissa."

"That will only take more time."

"Nevertheless, it must be done."

Aunt Hetty walked off to one side, still looking around and especially in back of her in hopes of seeing Colonel Rathbone. Her hope was in vain.

Clarissa turned toward the staircase leading to the cloak room, ready to shake the dust of Almack's. Only a few minutes would pass before she was cloaked and roosting once again in the family carriage.

She was aware that a clot of people had appeared in the hall. Two women moved easily among some twenty men. One of those men in particular stood out. He was dressed better, his jacket fitting more tightly, his waistcoat laying more easily, his black silk breeches catching no shine from the candles, his stockings darker, his cambric-covered wrists adorned with pearl buttons. Even Mr. Brummell would have approved.

Probably the approval would have stopped at the outer garments. The man's midriff was heavy. His cheeks were red-veined unbecomingly, as was the nose up to its bridge. Only the watery eyes were small. This was a man who had partaken of much more food and drink than any one person needed.

"Don't disturb yourselves on our account," said the wheezy voice, breaking the silence. "Proceed as you were, I pray of you."

Clarissa knew that she was looking at the Prince Regent himself. Prinny, as he was disrespectfully called. This overweight fop would be the next King of England, but now he had to make do with being the Prince Regent of all he surveyed.

Clarissa's eyes were caught by motion in the nearest gambling room, where a door had been flung open. Players were setting down rouleaus of coins worth fifty pounds. Many were on their feet and taking off frieze greatcoats. Those who had turned their coats inside out for luck were hastily removing them and turning them right side front before putting them on again. One man was swiftly removing the leather appendages which were supposed to preserve his lace ruffles. Another, who wore a high-crowned straw hat to keep him from touching his hair in the frenzy of play, had taken it off. The flowers and ribbons on many other hats were hurriedly pushed off. A number of men wearing masks, which were intended to keep them from showing feelings as cards were dispensed and played, knocked off the masks swiftly. When the gamblers finally turned to face their Regent, every one of them was smiling deferentially.

"Please carry on," said Prinny again.

Only with the greatest difficulty was it possible to make out what he said. The Prince Regent sounded as if he spoke while swallowing a cheese.

Aunt Hetty returned swiftly, Maude in tow. At sight of the Prince Regent, both curtseyed, but it was long after every other woman in the room had done so.

For the third time, Prinny instructed everybody to proceed as if he were another patron.

Clarissa said briskly, "Let us resume our plans and leave."

"What are you saying, girl?"

"We have been instructed to proceed with our concerns, and I feel strongly that we should do so."

"It is forbidden."

"What do you mean, Aunt?"

"I have done much reading about the protocol that involves royalty," Aunt Hetty said. "No matter what may be said, there is a code of usage to be followed. No one leaves any place before royalty does."

"But the Regent could decide to stay here all night long, Aunt."

"That is the risk we have to take in a freedom-loving country," said Aunt Hetty serenely.

"And if I had been indisposed I would have to stay and be miserable?"

"I fear so. It occurs to me that there is more than one good reason to be grateful that you are physically well."

Aunt Hetty wanted more of a chance to see and speak with Colonel Rathbone. Maude, who was now glassy-eyed, had lost her interest in the revelers. As for the duke, he would probably be indifferent. Unlike Maude, the Duke of Mainwaring could be bored in one place as easily as in another.

"I don't think the Regent will be here long," Aunt Hetty said with regret. "He shows signs of restlessness even now."

"Good."

"One has to take these matters calmly," Aunt Hetty said, hiding the glee she certainly felt at even the slightest delay.

"Dear Aunt, how I envy your serene disposition."

Hetty Tregallen had the grace to blush.

## Chapter Twenty-three

Aunt Hetty was inspecting the gowns which her nieces would be wearing to the opera at Covent Garden. She approved instantly of Clarissa's polonaise, with the vivid skirt drawn up at a side. Her only complaint was that Clarissa had worn it very recently, on New Year's Eve, in fact.

Maude had insisted on a gown with a falling front, and it would have been wicked to disapprove because Maude didn't yet have the weight at her breasts to justify wearing such a garment. Aunt Hetty spoke pacifically, while Clarissa nodded as if in silent agreement.

"Colonel Rathbone will be joining us tonight," Aunt Hetty said finally. Her cheeks were flushed by anticipation of pleasure rather than by gloss or any other mechanical means.

"Oh, Aunt, it is so good to see you with a gentleman."

"Thank you, Clarissa." Aunt Hetty ruminated out loud. "Of course the situation is not an ideal one. Herbert has been previously married, as you know. If nuptials were to take place between us, he would be making comparisons with his late wife, who was far younger, and not always favorable comparisons."

"Not too unfavorable, either, I am sure."

Maude, just as loyal, added, "If he did anything

like that, I would set him straight immediately."

Her tone indicated that she wouldn't have flinched from the use of violence in a cause so worthwhile.

"Aunt, I am curious about something," Clarissa said. "Surely you could have garnered marital interest from a number of local men. Even as I speak, I can think of three admirers. Yet you never chose to do so. You have often spoken about the sadnesses of spinsterhood, but have not for years tried to obliterate them for yourself. I want to know why you have taken so warmly to Colonel Rathbone and none of the others."

"Oh, Clarissa, dear, we are visiting the greatest city that the world has ever known. Visits stir the blood."

"In this case, I would expect some other reason, too."

Aunt Hetty spoke carefully by way of answer. "I have been your guardian for a number of years now, yours and Maude's. I think I have fulfilled my obligation quite well as of this date. My brother, your father, would not be disappointed by all I have done. But now the prospect of a suitable marriage is clear for you, and Maude will undoubtedly find a man worthy of her. I believe, too, that such an event will happen in a short while, now that her interest has been stirred. My obligation is nearly at an end."

Clarissa waited. Surely there was something more to be said.

"And so you must realize that I have decided to arrange my own future as best I am able," Hetty Tregallen added flatly, dotting the last *i* and crossing the last *t*. "I made the decision when we came here that I would do my best to ensure a suitable husband for myself. I believe I am doing so."

"Indeed you are, dear Aunt."

"Herbert's first union was blessed with seven children, all in their majority and living far from London, so I expect no difficulty from that quarter."

All of which was enough to leave but one question: What would Aunt Hetty do if Clarissa's own prospective marriage didn't take place?

Maude, who had never seen an opera, did not like that mode of theatre. She made her feelings clear after the first act of the night's presentation at Covent Garden.

"No matter what happens to the characters in the story, they sing," she said as she raised herself from a plush chair. "If the heroine needs a glass of water, she doesn't say, 'Bring me a glass of water,' but she sings, 'Burr-ring me a glass of wa-ater.' I cannot believe any part of it."

Her criticisms might have annoyed Signor Rossini, who had composed *La Cambiale di Matrimonio*. As for Clarissa, they made her smile.

The duke, who had been at least half-asleep during the presentation, stood slowly. Aunt Hetty and Colonel Rathbone, deep in conversation, paused to chuckle together on their way out of the duke's box.

Clarissa could hardly wait to leave it. The box was painted in gilt with white, but an odious green laurel pattern appeared on every panel. She found it showy as well as distasteful. Covent Garden wasn't a place in which a girl from Cornwall could ever feel at ease.

She became even further unsettled when she looked away from the stage apron and its ring of coal-oil lamps in glass containers. Her eyes had rested on the pit benches. She started to glance idly at the men and women who were leaving for intermission. They used the wide center aisle, which was known as Fop's Alley. Her glance suddenly sharpened and she nearly called out.

One of the men was Bryan Deverell.

There could be no mistaking him. To her mind,

Bryan couldn't have been taken for anyone else despite the evening rig-out of black tailcoat, white waistcoat, black silk breeches with diamond buckles, and black stockings. Dressed no differently than most of the men, nevertheless he stood out.

Clarissa's first happy notion was that the opera was after all a place of excitement and that it stirred the blood. There could be no opera as good, especially when it was being given in a city like none other in the world.

Her next thought was much more unhappy. Even if she said no word to him, Deverell's presence must at all costs be kept from the duke.

She turned around and spoke fervently to Aubrey. It turned out that his opinion of the opera was very much like Maude's. Clarissa felt no astonishment at hearing it.

She didn't see Bryan when the performance resumed. She looked around at the pit benches as well as at Fop's Alley. She didn't feel that London was so marvelous when there was no sight of Bryan. Suddenly convinced that the duke's eyes were following hers, Clarissa looked only at the performance.

She did not see him during any of the numerous pauses which followed. Signor Rossini had apparently been determined to write a large number of musical notes to earn his commission, and no one could complain about the quantity of his work. With Bryan at her side, she would have felt more tolerant, she was sure.

The duke walked by her side as they left the box at the conclusion. He, and Maude only a few paces behind, couldn't wait to put Covent Garden behind them.

In Fop's Alley, she saw Bryan Deverell once again. He seemed to have been waiting, for his eyes met hers.

Clarissa could do nothing. There was pleasure and

delight in her response, but it was going to be dangerous if his eyes continued to hold hers. She turned to face the duke, hoping that she would once again catch his attention.

"I think you are right, Aubrey. The opera could be improved," she began.

She had waited a fraction too long. The Duke of Mainwaring's jaw was falling in dismay. He started forward, not aware till then that he had taken on too much alcohol to make him effective. He nearly lost his balance and fell against a regal-looking woman who was walking away with a grandson in tow. He smiled briefly, but apologized with one word only.

With more presence of mind than Clarissa would have expected from him, the duke turned toward Colonel Rathbone.

"I say, there—you!"

Rathbone didn't recognize that form of address. Happily, he continued chatting with Aunt Hetty.

The duke leaned forward and gripped Colonel Rathbone by a wrist ruffle.

"He's there—he's there! The spy is over there!"

Rathbone adjusted his mind slowly to the intrusion. He wasted time blinking slowly as his eyes followed the duke's white-gloved hand.

"The spy is over there, I tell you!"

Clarissa had already whirled around to give Deverell a silent warning. It wasn't necessary. He was no longer in view. Clarissa felt that her heart had gone with him, but her body could not.

"I don't see him," she said, intending to halt any possible pursuit. There must be no attempt by the colonel to seek out Bryan. "Perhaps you've had a little too much to drink, Aubrey, so you imagined seeing that man."

"I—I imagined nothing! Demme, he was there!"

Rathbone looked the duke up and down, taking in the swaying, the bleary eyes, the moisture-drenched

231

lower lip.

He had no need to make any remark. The duke drew back, abashed but still convinced he was right.

"Perhaps it is time for us to all go to the dinner party at the Blakeney home," Clarissa said, changing the subject.

"Oh yes," Maude agreed, eagerly helping. "Do you think that Lady Blakeney's husband will be present? He seems to be at home very infrequently, from the little that even I have seen."

"Bah!" Just as irritably, the duke added, "Another spy for the Frenchies, Sir Percy Blakeney is. Mark my words on it!"

## Chapter Twenty-four

On Sunday morning, the Duke of Mainwaring ordered his carriage to halt at the north side of Rotten Row. As soon as he was sure that no carriages in the Sunday church parade were going to do him any harm, he stepped out and turned back.

"Let us enjoy the air," he boomed.

Clarissa was helped out, then Lady Winifred. Colonel Rathbone, who was with Miss Hetty Tregallen, helped his lady to her feet. Maude insisted on jumping down unaided, a habit of hers from childhood. It was pleasant enough day for January, with only a touch of rawness. To a tried and true Londoner, this weather was suitable for strolling.

The duke hurried to Rathbone's side, keeping the colonel from communing with Miss Hetty.

"And how soon do you think you will find him?" the duke asked, as if resuming a conversation.

"Who?" Colonel Rathbone was occupied elsewhere, looking behind him to where Hetty Tregallen walked with one niece and Lady Winifred. He allowed himself a sigh of heartfelt regret.

"The spy!"

"Oh yes, of course, Your Grace, you have reference to Bryan Deverell."

"Well?"

"Ah, that is difficult to say."

"What on earth do you mean? I don't expect to hear 'ah' and sighs when I ask a question about business that involves the state. What I want to know is how soon you expect to find Deverell. It won't be long after that until he is strung up."

"Even as we speak, Your Grace, I would hazard the guess that Bryan Devrell is not to be found far from London."

"Blast it, he was *in* London and I saw him! Why did you let him have the time to get away, if that is what he has done?"

"If Your Grace saw him not long ago, then I think it is safe to assume he is still here."

"Why do you have to 'assume' anything? Why don't you run out and find the devil and string him up?"

"That is not as easy as Your Grace might be inclined to think it should be! London is the apex of civilization, as we all know, and many people are to be found here. One cannot inquire of each grown male if he is Bryan Deverell."

"What *can* 'one' do, then, this mythical 'one' that you speak of? What I know is that I pay rates to have such devils disposed of, and if it is not being done I can reasonably say that somebody is not performing his task."

"Let me say this much, Your Grace: I am quite certain that before your wedding to Miss Tregallen can take place, Deverell will be—"

"Under restraint? Is that what you mean?"

"Bryan Deverell will make himself and his whereabouts known."

"And in that case, you will detain him at His Maj esty's pleasure and see that he disappears from the face of the earth."

"I will do my duty."

"I ask nothing more." The duke rubbed his hand in satisfaction.

Colonel Rathbone smiled and managed to take another look behind him. Miss Hetty Tregallen was a damned attractive woman!

The object of his affections walked carefully, avoiding mud and trying not to crumple the grass underfoot. It was as great an effort as she had ever made. The grass seemed everywhere despite universal recognition of this area as a path. She had learned from Maude that a person did not trouble living structures.

In truth, she had never taken such a thought into her head until she met Colonel Rathbone and felt stirrings for him as well as for the security and companionship he could provide. Now she found herself brooding about trees as well as grass and animals. She occasionally even found herself considering the working condition of servants, which was proof beyond doubt that she was becoming lightheaded. Everyone knew that servants were gifted with extraordinary strength and that the conditions of labor didn't affect them at all.

She walked next to Lady Winifred, and couldn't refrain from speaking, from not telling the nearest person that life was exciting and beautiful.

"London is lovely at this time of year," Hetty Tregallen said.

Lady Winifred was pettish, now. "If you have nothing of substance to say, Miss Tregallen, favor me by not saying anything."

Aunt Hetty would have liked to say that Napoleon Bonaparte had given birth to twins and then let Lady Winifred claim that she made no communication of consequence!

"I meant no discourtesy, Lady Winifred, to be sure."

Maude, who had been proceeding in front of the two ladies, suddenly stopped and turned, her features

235

suffused by a look of admiration close to awe.

"Did you see that?" She had thrown her head back and was looking up to the sky. "That was a speckled wall."

Lady Winifred was moved to ask, "What is the girl talking about?"

"I had never seen a speckled wall before! It's also called a gatekeeper."

"Some sort of animal?"

"A butterfly, Lady Winifred." Maude lowered her head now that the creature was out of sight. *Hipparchia Megara,* the speckled wall."

"There are many butterflies and birds and animals in the length and breadth of The City, young lady. What difference could one or more make to anyone?"

Aunt Hetty surprised herself by saying militantly, "Maude and I are happy to know that a butterfly is alive and enjoying the London day. I am sorry that you don't appreciate it."

Lady Winifred briefly rolled her eyes to heaven, but said no more about it.

Clarissa, in a somber mood, was wondering if it were possible to jump into the Serpentine and stay under. She imagined no cheer anywhere.

One of the neighboring strollers drew up at her side and said in quiet but deep and memorable voice, "Don't shout, Cousin Clarissa."

Bryan Deverell was disguised to a certain extent. A coat, upturned, covered the lower part of his face. A tricorne hat fit perfectly.

Clarissa's heart gave a great leap of joy followed by palpitations of fear.

"Why have you come? Don't you realize what may happen?"

"I want to know something, and no one but you is likely to tell me."

Although he was walking at a level with her, he

kept some five feet apart. To the casual eye they might have been strangers sharing the same sandy path. He was looking straight ahead rather than at her. Clarissa, regretting it keenly, saw the good sense of doing so and followed.

"Ask your infernal question and leave!"

"Are you to be wed to Mainwaring?"

Now her heart was hammering, but she spoke mulishly. "I don't know of any reason for not marrying him. No one else has offered for me. Certainly no one else might be interested who is not in danger of losing his life. I would have no intention of marrying on the scaffold."

"Nor I, Clarissa, and I am glad to say that I am now convinced you have never been a spy for the French."

She nearly whirled around and called out with fury. "How dare you! You, of all people!"

"One has to be certain of these things, Clarissa, if he wishes to—but never mind! There is much remaining time for that."

"There is no remaining time for you if the duke turns around."

"He will neglect you here, too, Clarissa, you may be quite sure," Bryan Deverell said easily. "I take it that you are not happy. Your cup does not runneth over, Clarissa. Isn't that true?"

"I am as happy as might be expected."

"Then I think I do know the answer to the question that Lady Winifred asked me on a memorable occasion. You expect to marry him because he will be of aid to your sister's matrimonial future."

Clarissa was silent.

"But your sister has fixed her eyes upon a dragoon officer, and Maude is not someone to set a goal for herself and settle for anything less. As for your aunt, a loyal woman who inspires loyalty in return, she appears to be contented with Colonel Rathbone. When he asks her to marry, and I feel reasonably certain that he will, she can no longer cause you worry at her being left alone."

"How do you know all thi—?"

But his eyes had been on the duke's back and when Aubrey turned to adjust his cloak more firmly, Deverell walked behind her. He would soon leave the path. She knew she didn't dare look around. It was very possible that she would never see him again.

Hetty saw that Colonel Rathbone had pulled back from the duke in order to approach. She drew away from Lady Winifred, leaving her with Maude. A suitable pairing. While one of them marveled about the wonders of nature, the other would proceed in gloom.

She was grateful that she had brought her best walking dress for the expedition to London. Jaconet muslin over the pale peach-colored sarcenet slip was becoming to her. The high body of the gown, trimmed with a triple fall of lace at the throat, hinted at a full bosom. The bottom of the skirt, flounced with rich French work surmounted by a rouleau of muslin and beaded with fancy trimming, gave the impression that her limbs were exquisite. The spencer that came with this dress was of white striped lutestring, the front conveying that her figure was superb. The large-brimmed leghorn hat, turned up behind in a soft roll, gave the impression of a becomingly small head, just as straw-colored gloves offered the promise of tiny hands. Like many dresses, it promised much but fulfilled less.

Not that Hetty Tregallen was a bad-looking woman. Her face was lined, but only lightly. If she was plump, she remained graceful. It was surprising that a spinster in the fifties, a woman who should long ago have accepted her status and resigned herself to waiting for old age and inevitable dissolution, cared about how she looked and was regarded by men. Perhaps she had always known that someday she would meet Colonel Rathbone.

The colonel, his sad eyes blinking on account of the sun, hesitated before he spoke.

"I thought you had forgotten me."

"Quite to the contrary."

He could be heavily humorous if that was what he wanted, but it seemed foolish at her age to sound like a coquette. She changed her tone immediately.

"I saw that you were busy with the duke, and I had no reason to interrupt."

"The duke, I find, can be rather peremptory, Miss Tregallen."

It was an indirect apology for having to be diverted from what he considered the true business of this Sunday morning, which was to further his acquaintance with Hetty Tregallen.

The apology was gracefully accepted in the spirit with which it had been offered. "I looked in your direction every so often, Colonel, but the conversation between you and the duke was continuing. I felt regretful."

"Thank you. Rather peremptory in his demands, as I said. Things must proceed as he would like them to and at the time he insists upon. There is a certain (you will pardon me, perhaps) spirit of childhood in such a temper."

"Indeed there is, Colonel, but far be it from me to say so in public."

"There is an aura in a man who is chronologically grown, of someone who has not had to deal with another, to make compromises. Would you agree?"

"With all my heart, Colonel. But you must realize that somewhat the same situation exists for me. True, I had a brother, but I was always able to ignore him and get what I wanted. Then, too, he was away from home and married at an early age."

"But you did have parents to teach you that dancing can best be done with another, so to speak."

"Both died in a plague year, leaving me alone and with a small holding. My brother died not long afterwards, and I began living a life alone with no one to whom I must answer. I was in charge of the upbringing of two girls, my brother's children. I had to take note of them, but from a position of authority. The same applies to servants."

"Perhaps you have been fortunate in some ways."

"I do not know what a woman of my disposition would be like if she were put into a situation in which she had to respond to others who were equals."

There! She had made a fool of herself. She was as bereft of reason as George the Third. She had railed against the condition of spinsterhood for many years, but when a man came along who showed that he might be interested in changing her status, she patiently explained to him why he would regret doing so.

Rathbone was not silent for long. "And yet you have an air of common sense about you, Miss Tregallen. You have a capacity for kindness, as I can see in the way you behave to your nieces. You are aware of the needs of others."

"Colonel, you are very kind."

She would have liked to say that he was besotted, if one could imagine those feelings in anyone of the colonel's age. And she would have pointed out afterwards that she herself was at a point where she was unable to think clearly.

"You must be well aware of what is on my mind, Miss Hetty. I am not so blinded that I fail to realize that you are sympathetic to my wishes and desires."

"I — yes, Colonel, I am."

240

"It is understood, then, that we will discuss these matters when the problem of Bryan Deverell has been resolved and I am able to work without so much urgency." He nodded as the duke called his name, preparing to rejoin the thwarted peer. "I am grateful to you, Hetty, for your consideration."

"And I for yours." Should she add "dear Herbert"? Not so soon. But before she could speak to him any further, he was gone.

## *Chapter Twenty-five*

The duke's home was looking festive for the ball at which his engagement to Clarissa would be announced. Chinese lanterns were seen almost everywhere. The odors of food being prepared couldn't be missed. Even servants moved more rigidly than usual, convinced that they, like the home, were on display.

Clarissa, after making so many purchases, had settled on a lilac bombazine gown with puffed and banded sleeves. She found herself less interested in her own appearance than in the differences between a ball in the country and this occasion, which seemed glorious for everyone but the betrothed.

She had arrived with her family at a little past nine, an hour which was considered in the country to be suitable. Lady Winifred came down to greet them. She had climbed into a high-waisted long-sleeved and gleaming dark gray which was the best rig-out she had worn in many years. It was she, with no one else in sight, who told the Tregallens about the error of their ways.

"We shall not begin until at least eleven. That hour has long been fashionable. There is no opera or theatre tonight. I believe that Lord Denegan is offering a ball, too, but as he is not an admired man the bulk of his guests will be here afterwards."

"Is the second ball the one that is favored?"

"In London absolutely. Guests go to one and then arrive to spend most of their time at the better function of two."

Another difference she soon found was that no dressing room was put aside for the female guests to primp at the last minute before making their appearance in the ballroom. There was, as a result, no room for outer garments. The Tregallens had to brave the increasingly chill weather in order to leave their capes in the carriage which had brought them. Clarissa returned inside covered with goose pimples.

The ballroom itself was on the first floor, which was unheard-of at home. Oddest of all, the tables behind a ballroom double door, those tables at which guests would dine after midnight, were exposed to view. Clarissa didn't even feel certain that the double door would be closed when the main body of guests started to arrive.

Nonetheless, she liked the surroundings. She imagined herself delightedly entertaining here, if the owner of the house were somebody else. She had actually filled her ideal husband's features out before recognizing them.

She sighed. Surely her whole future was not going to be scarred by one persistent regret.

No, surely it was.

One brief advantage to the evening, so far, was clear. Aubrey was out of sight. Lady Winifred said that he was behind closed doors with a few friends. Her future husband wasn't going to cause difficulties for a while.

The first guests, a baronet and his lady, arrived at a little after ten-thirty. Lady Winifred, who was receiving, spent time with them and introduced them to the Tregallens. Only Maude was able to find common ground, as she and the baronet's wife shared a revulsion for fox hunting. The baronet, who wore a tricolored decoration on his crest, looked disappointed because no one asked how it had been earned.

Lady Winifred waited until a few minutes past eleven before telling Clarissa sadly that she had heard from an unimpeachable source that the Regent would not be attending this function. Neither, perhaps as a direct result, would Mr. George Brummell.

"I will learn to accept that infamy," Clarissa said drily.

The duke appeared at last, gesturing Clarissa over to him. "Stand on the welcoming line with Winifred," he ordered.

"I hardly think that would be appropriate." To do so would make it clear she was practically part of the duke's family.

"I *do* think it would be appropriate." The duke settled the matter.

Guests began arriving in some force at twenty minutes past the hour. Aubrey strolled his ballroom, talking to only a few men.

No one asked why Clarissa was on the receiving line. She was instantly accepted by the likes of Lord Robert Manners, Mr. Arthur Paget, and a Mrs. Searle, who behaved as if Clarissa had been greeting them for years. To them, in particular, she was grateful.

A name was called out by the second footman and then the first. The name was unrecognizable, as ever in those circumstances. The man who walked in could be identified immediately. He was Bryan Deverell.

Bryan seemed totally unaware that he was anything but another of the duke's guests. He strode to the reception area like a man who anticipated being greeted accordingly.

Only someone who looked at him closely would have seen that he turned his head very slightly to find out whether or not Aubrey had noticed his arrival. He had done the same back at Hyde Park, but the danger to him here must be infinitely greater.

Clarissa watched him as closely as he might have wished. There had been a moment when she'd have sworn her heart was bursting out of her body in happiness. She moved back and forth without willing it, and for a moment seemed to be observing two Bryan Deverells.

Lady Winifred spoke first as he came in earshot. She kept her voice low, but her tone and words reflected disapproval and keen regret. "I must inform my brother that you are here."

"I see no need for that," Bryan said in the voice that would live forever in Clarissa's dreams. "He will find out soon enough."

Clarissa had to take a deep breath before she could speak normally. "Why have you come here?"

"I want to be among the revelers who celebrate your good fortune, Clarissa."

He had been looking in the direction of the duke. His eyes suddenly narrowed. The duke must have suddenly made a move. Deverell turned around and walked into the growing crowd.

Lady Winifred left the reception area, probably to tell her brother what was taking place. Otherwise, Aubrey would know she had been negligent and be nastier than ever. She was only showing foresight. Would that Bryan had behaved so sensibly!

Clarissa dealt with six fresh guests. Just as the seventh appeared on the horizon, Lady Winifred returned.

"Aubrey is hoping that you will join him in the library."

"Of course."

She started to the door as the musicians struck up the first chords of a dance. A pause gave her enough time for one more look around. It was what she'd been doing at every possible moment since Bryan Deverell disappeared into this awesomely large group. This time, too, she looked in vain.

The library didn't display many books, but there was more furniture than anybody could have wanted in a room this size. A fireplace with cherubs on the mantel, satinwood chairs, and a Sheraton cabinet caught Clarissa's eyes before she saw the Chippendale desk with a sturdy chair which currently contained Aubrey Seldon, the Duke of Mainwaring.

"Come in, Clarissa, and close the door behind you. Tightly."

Some sounds had filtered into the room, such as greetings that arriving guests made to others. She heard parts of the garbled names being called out by three footmen. Clarissa didn't find the sounds at all bothersome. Aubrey, who looked as if he'd had a shade more drink than was best for him, probably didn't find anything bothersome.

All the same, she shut the door. Tightly.

"That spy is in the ballroom," he said, exactly as if they had been talking for a while about it. "Better for you to stay here and out of his way."

It took all of Clarissa's will to force herself to remain, as her future husband was directing. She gripped a satinwood chair by its sturdy back, pressing her fingers against it till they were taut.

"I have ordered three footmen to observe him till I want him subdued."

"Yes. Of course."

"Perhaps that fool who is fond of your aunt (Colonel Boneless, ha-ha!) will arrive and make a formal arrest when I tell him to do so."

"I hope so, Aubrey."

"You won't be surprised to hear that one of my footmen told me that he was close enough to the rascal to hear him speaking in French, which he does like a native."

Clarissa didn't know whether or not to believe him. It was true, though, that many a loyal citizen of Bulldom spoke Napoleon's second language with at least as much facility as the Corsican-born leader of the French.

"Why didn't you order your footmen to ease him away from the ballroom now?"

"Because I want Deverell to hear my announcement that I plan to wed you," Aubrey said, dropping both elbows to the desk before rubbing his palms gleefully. "I formed the impression that he was developing an interest in your direction. What I will insist on is for him to know that in every way he has been beaten."

"Then you will want to make the announcement as soon as Colonel Rathbone appears," she said. "In that case, we should return to the ballroom and look out for him."

She had no particular interest in the colonel, but warmly hoped that she might be spared one more look at Bryan Deverell, one last look.

Aubrey got to his feet easily and came around the desk till he was close to her. It was possible to smell the whiskey on his breath as well as the unguents with which he had soothed himself. His hand extended toward her.

"We can allow ourselves a few minutes to pleasure me," he said huskily. "The door is closed, the room warmed, and the carpet is thick."

She understood that he was suggesting they do something she didn't want to do, that she would regret doing with him.

"I will enjoy taking you for the first time," Aubrey said, reaching a hand around her waist, "when that traitor is under the same roof."

He was trying to put his other arm around her

when Clarissa broke free.

The duke seemed amused. "Oh, so you want to be caught, eh, dearie? If that's your game, I'll play it."

He started after her.

Clarissa made for the door, hoping she could reach it first. The duke had taken on enough drink to slow him, yes, but his body could compensate as he was anxious to gain the elusive goal.

"Demme!" he whispered, breathing hard. "Demme!"

There was a series of knocks at the door.

In mid-motion, the duke halted. Clarissa, grateful, let out several deep breaths. The knocking was repeated insistently.

She walked slowly to the door, and opened it on Colonel Rathbone.

The Foreign Office man walked in briskly, closed the door on them all, and looked directly at the Duke of Mainwaring.

"Lady Winifred has informed me that Bryan Deverell is in the ballroom," he said. "I have taken the liberty of instructing one of your footmen to tell him he is wanted elsewhere."

"No! He is to be left alone until I give the word." The duke's face was redder than whiskey could have made it. "You're to go out there and tell that footman to pay no attention to your previous ranting."

"It is too late for that," Rathbone said. Automatically he added, "My apologies."

"Your apologies be damned and you be damned with them! I have never heard of such arrogance. Coming into a peer's home and overruling his orders to the menials. Why, I shall raise a question in the Lords about his, see if I don't!"

Clarissa asked quietly, "Mr. Deverell is detained now, is that correct?"

It meant she had no hope of so much as seeing Bryan again. Her last opportunity had come and gone.

"I have given instructions," said the colonel, "that Mr. Deverell be directed to come here."

"To my library?" The duke was freshly outraged. "Isn't it enough that he has befouled one room of my home? Must you see to it that he infests any of the others?"

"I am afraid that is the situation we face, sir, I must ask him in here."

"I will have no part of it!"

"Sit!" Colonel Rathbone ordered.

Aubrey's jaw fell. "Do you dare to tell me what to do?"

"I strongly suggest that Your Grace be seated," Colonel Rathbone said, recovering himself. "A few more moments of your time, sir, and I can assure you that Mr. Deverell will no longer play any part whatever in your life."

The duke hesitated briefly, but went back to his desk and sat. "Clarissa, come here with me. I want you on my side of the desk. Let Deverell see that you are with me."

She shook her head firmly.

Colonel Rathbone avoided further discussion between her and the duke. "There is not time enough for that, I fear, sir."

Clarissa stayed in place, where she could be that much closer to Deverell during his last minutes in civilized surroundings.

A series of surprisingly peremptory knocks sounded on the door.

The colonel opened it. He was facing none other than Capt. Roderick Taggart of the light dragoons. Captain Taggart was in uniform.

"Mr. Deverell will be with us in moments," said Captain Taggart to the colonel, leaving the door partly open. "He wished to make his farewell to Lady Winifred."

249

"What is happening in my home?" The duke half-rose from his chair, eyes wide in anger. "Why are you here?"

"I am on leave, Your Grace, and came to London to surprise Miss Maude Tregallen," said Captain Taggart. "The colonel suggested that I join him and Miss Maude on this occasion. He added that my career could be aided substantially after the capture of a traitor on this night."

"Your career will be hindered by *me*, of that much I assure you. What *is* all this?"

At that moment the door opened on Bryan Deverell. He looked at Clarissa, whose face was aflame. Only when he had looked his fill did he spare a glance for others, and lastly for the duke.

"You and Miss Clarissa, Your Grace, are entitled to a full explanation," Bryan Deverell smiled.

## Chapter Twenty-six

"Explanation, is it?" the duke snarled. "You are a spy, and you will be hanged. I will arrange to spring the trap myself."

Bryan had not lost the smile. He settled into one of the satinwood chairs, crossed his legs, and looked from Rathbone to Taggart to the duke.

"Half of what you say is correct," Bryan admitted. "I have acted as a spy."

"You concede it!" The duke said triumphantly, while Clarissa's heart dropped to her shoes. In no way would he be able to successfully deny what he had just told four witnesses.

"However, I spied for England," said Bryan Deverell, looking directly at the duke. "That is enough to make me a hero. I have spied, which is contemptible, but for the correct side, which is admirable."

Aubrey's closed fist pounded his desk. "What is this traitor talking about?"

"I am clarifying what took place," Deverell said. "I was sent to France to gain information about an attempt to overthrow Bonaparte. We wanted to support the conspiracy in secret and recognize the chief conspirator—I will not mention names—as Louis the Eighteenth. You understand, of course, that the unfortunate son of Louis Sixteen and Marie Antoinette, the Dauphin, is considered the Seventeenth Louis of France."

"Who are these people? One cannot believe this story without names."

"I have explained that much."

"If this story is true, which I doubt, and a liaison is to be established, as a peer of the realm I could be of help where you failed."

Deverell turned to Clarissa. "I was instructed to bring back a timetable for the attempted overthrow. (Frankly, I am not hopeful of its success, but that is beside the point, now.) I obtained a letter from the chief conspirator giving the information that I had been required to bring back."

Light burst upon Clarissa at long last. "And it was that information in the oilskin packet you buried on the shore."

She wanted to say that she should have known he was innocent and never questioned it. She didn't believe it would be the truth. Certain possibilities had been suggested by others and apparently confirmed by the evidence of her senses. She had to listen to the demands of common sense, to forego blind trust, which was not an easy position to take. She had to question, she had to judge. Only a fool would expect that love conquered all.

Bryan said carefully, "I had bribed smugglers to get passage from Calais, but on arrival I was wounded and left for dead. No valuables were found on my clothes, but the search was only rough. That pouch was next to my skin."

"Why couldn't you have told me as much some three weeks ago?" Clarissa demanded.

"I had to keep silent till the papers were safe at the Foreign Office. They are safe now."

"There was some other time at which you could have told me, in the last days."

"Clarissa, I could not be sure but that you might

252

tell someone else what you know."

"Tell? Tell whom?"

"I will have to explain in a roundabout manner," Bryan began. "Not long ago, Lady Winifred posed a question. Why, she asked, did you want to marry the duke? I understood the possible reasons later on, but my first thoughts led to another consideration. Lady Winifred had put her question the wrong way around, you see."

"The wrong—? I do not understand."

"What she should have asked is this: Why does the duke want to marry Clarissa? Can it be for love? No. He couldn't love a girl who makes it clear by word and deed that she scorns him, who follows his instructions hardly at all. Is it for money? The duke can raise what he needs in case of any difficulties. Is it for property? The duke owns land which is more profitable than Narborne."

"Why, then?" Clarissa whispered. "Why?"

"Because you have something that he wants. What do you have? Only an estate which is moderately profitable. But that estate is in Cornwall and near the shore. A house, to be even more blunt, from which spies for the French who land secretly by ship could be received and freshly supplied before going to do their foul work against Great Britain."

"This is actionable by law!" Aubrey's face was turning green.

"There is no other possible answer, Your Grace. Further, it clears the way to resolving a number of other riddles. Somebody paid for the attack on me, somebody who had been secretly informed of the means by which I would be returning to Britain. It ties in with the fact that someone called the dragoons in the hope of having me hanged as a spy before I could give my information to the government."

Clarissa asked weakly, "Why would Aub—Lord Mainwaring, do that?"

253

"It has been confirmed that he has acquired debts at Almack's and other gambling hells," Bryan said carefully. "He chose to meet his debts with the aid of the French. For this he had one particular reason. Like some other well-placed Britons, he is certain that Boney will win this war, and wants to gain favorable consideration from the French conquerors. The duke would be fulfilling two goals at once."

Aubrey said hoarsely, "You can prove none of this, Deverell. None at all."

"Until tonight we couldn't, but now we will soon be in a different position. The colonel, who had expected this when he first spoke to me, found out that His Grace had invited three other people who are suspected spies for the French. Anthony Fullarton is here, as is Jean Pierre Domremy, and the woman Bridget Stovall. I spoke to Domremy in French just before his capture, which scandalized a footman. One of those three will speak against Seldon."

The duke suddenly got to his feet and started to run around his desk. He must have wanted to reach the door and run to freedom. Too much liquor stopped him. Just as he rounded the desk, he tripped over the blood red carpet and fell. He lay on his face, striking the carpet over and again while he cried bitterly.

Clarissa covered her ears, turned, and stumbled out to the hallway. She felt a hand fall gently on hers.

## Chapter Twenty-seven

"You could have told me the truth when we spoke in Hyde Park," Clarissa protested. "Those papers must have been safe by then."

"I wasn't sure that a girl like you, a girl who hungers for adventure, might not scorn me and admire Mainwaring, instead, for doing something so dangerous."

"Admire Aubrey?" Those words and a wince were all the answer that Bryan needed. "I suppose you asked Colonel Rathbone to quiz me and learn my true attitudes toward Mainwaring."

"Herbert was helpful, and I think he is being helped in turn."

"Because of my aunt? Yes, I suppose she will marry, and that Maude will bless Captain Taggart. I feel badly for Lady Winifred after this news becomes public."

"No need for that," Bryan said comfortably. "Just before coming into the library, I spoke to her and made it clear that trouble was close by. She was not entirely surprised. She is a woman of sturdy fiber, and will overcome the stigma by addressing herself to good works that come to hand. My opinion is that some older peer will be so intrigued by her notoriety as to ask her hand in marriage."

"I will gladly offer her any assistance but money,

which I truly cannot spare."

"*I* can," Bryan said almost casually. "I have land in Shropshire along with a rent roll of eight hundred pounds. Furthermore, I will be able to address myself to its improvement as I have been promised that if I completed my recent mission I would never be sent on another. I may add, too, that I expect to receive a title as a further reward. It was strongly hinted to me as a possibility by no less a dignitary than Mr. Spencer Percival."

"The First Minister? Oh, Bryan, it *will* come to pass."

"Something else should come to pass first, Clarissa. I have loved you since you risked your own future for me. I want to be with you always, and have it understood that your feelings agree with mine."

"Oh, Bryan!"

"As proof of it, and since your engagement was to be announced on this night, I suggest that the announcement be made by me. I also feel that there should be a change in the wording."

"Oh Bryan, dearest Bryan!"

Disregarding passersby, he bent his head to hers and kissed her soundly

With that done, Bryan and Clarissa proceeded hand in hand to the ballroom.